After Death

The After Death Series

Evan Bond

Published by Evan Bond, 2022.

AFTER DEATH

First edition. October 10, 2022.

Written by Evan Bond.

Also by Evan Bond

Ethan McCormick Series
To the Wolves
Sins of the Mother

The After Death Series
After Death

Standalone
Death Can Wait
Getaway
Echoes of the Past
Charred Remains

Watch for more at https://www.evanbondauthor.com/.

For the survivors. Roxie P. and Mark C.

Chapter 1

The darkness that shrouded young Cara Brown's bedroom was like any other. At bedtime, it was always the same. Her parents would tell her to go upstairs and put on her pajamas. After that, she was to brush her teeth and come back downstairs. There would always be five or ten minutes more of television she could get away with before her parents remembered it was bedtime. After hugs and kisses, Cara would scurry off to bed.

She didn't have a television in her room. Her parents told her she wasn't old enough yet. Cara didn't quite understand how having a television in her room required an age limit. The only channel she watched was Cartoon Network. Her favorite shows were *Courage the Cowardly Dog* and *The Powerpuff Girls*. If she could watch that downstairs, why couldn't she watch them in her room? Maybe when she was ten, she would get one for her room. It seemed silly for a two-year gap to make the difference, but that was the rule.

Once she was tucked in bed, it didn't take Cara long to fall asleep. Her little Buttercup nightlight cast a thin light on the far side of her bedroom. Buttercup had always been her favorite Powerpuff Girl. She was the tough one of the trio. Buttercup could fight. Cara wanted to be like her when she grew up.

Sleep wasn't coming as easy to her tonight for reasons she couldn't explain. She thought about sneaking over to her bookshelf and grabbing a book to read. Whenever she had trouble sleeping, reading did the trick. Tonight, she didn't feel like getting up from her bed. There was no logical reason for her feeling. Something in the back of her mind had convinced her to be worried. Like an invisible hand would shoot out from under the bed and drag her into the pits of darkness if she got up. Everything looked as it always did in her room. Still, the feeling persisted.

Her nightlight flickered for a moment like the power had threatened to go out. But it stayed on. The air in her room grew colder like the air conditioner had kicked on at full blast. It wasn't enough to see her breath, but it was cold enough to make her shiver. Or was that her nerves? She couldn't tell. People would often tremble when they were scared. That much she knew.

She had never experienced it in her life. There wasn't much for a little girl of eight to fear.

A noise came from her closet that sounded like hangars sliding across one of the garment rods. She pictured a big, scary man hiding in her closet and she pulled the covers up to her chin. The logical side of her brain kicked in and told her it was simply a draft pushing her clothes around. The closet door was open a few inches which would allow for the air vent to pump a stream straight in.

She let the covers slide back down from her chin. There were no monsters in her closet. Even though she was a young child, she didn't believe in such things. Monsters and ghosts weren't real. They didn't hide under your bed, and they never lurked in your closet. It was silly to think they did.

As these thoughts ran through her mind, she heard another noise come from the closet. This one was harder to explain away. It sounded like a sharp breath or a quick inhale. She pulled the covers back up to her chin and tried to think of what would cause such a sound. Cara continued to tell herself monsters weren't real. Though, she was starting to believe it was a lie.

The closet door slowly creaked open farther. Sounds of heavy breathing echoed from inside and Cara let out a scream. It only took a few seconds before her father burst into her room with a worried look plastered on his face.

"Baby, what's wrong?" He asked through short breaths caused by his vault up the stairs.

Cara couldn't speak. She could only point towards the closet. Her little hands shook with fear. Her father turned towards the closet and stepped forward. His arm reached inside the darkness and pulled the chain which activated the single light bulb. Cara jumped when the light came on, expecting to see someone or *something* standing there. But it was empty.

"Cara, honey, what is it? What happened? Did you have a bad dream?"

"I-I don't know. I t-thought I heard someone in there." She stammered.

"There's nobody in your closet, sweetheart."

Her father bent down and looked under her bed as well. He stood back up and smiled.

"Nothing under there either." He said.

This made Cara feel better, but not by much. She had heard something in the closet. And the door had creaked open. There was no possible way she had imagined it all. The darkness was good at playing tricks by casting shadows, but shadows couldn't make you hear things.

Cara's father approached her bed and pulled the covers up to her neck. He sat down on the bed and stroked Cara's hair. Leaning forward, he planted a kiss on his daughter's forehead. Cara loved her dad. He always knew how to make her feel better. She always felt safe when he was around.

"Thank you, daddy," she said with a smile.

"You're welcome, sweetheart. Remember, nothing is going to hurt you while I'm around. I won't let it. Your daddy isn't afraid of anything."

"Boo!" Cara said and her dad faked a scream, recoiling in overdramatic horror. It was a game they often played. He would prattle on about being the bravest man in the galaxy. When Cara said boo, he would let out a mock scream and pretend to tremble. It never failed to make her laugh. Now, she giggled at her father.

"I love you, Cara. Good night." He kissed her again and walked out of the room.

She felt better now. Whatever had happened before had drifted from her mind. Sleep was now drawing in. In the morning daylight, she would look at her closet and feel foolish for believing something could lurk inside.

Sleep had almost overtaken her when something jolted her awake. Another sharp exhale echoed through her room. This time it did not come from the closet. Instead, it came from under her bed. Cara's eyes flew open and glued themselves to the ceiling, afraid to shift her gaze sideways.

The room had grown unnaturally cold again. Cara was afraid to let out a breath for fear she would see the vapor. If the temperature had dropped that low, something was wrong. She could no longer blame it on the air conditioner. Her hand rose to her mouth, and she held it there so she wouldn't make a noise.

Another sound came from beneath the bed. A bump like something had shifted around. Cara wasn't certain, but she swore she felt the bump. There was something under there for sure. She wasn't about to put her head down there to be grabbed by whatever evil demon dwelled there. Instead, Cara eyed the door. She wondered if she could leap from her bed and make it to the door before whatever lurked underneath caught her.

Her Powerpuff Girls night light started to flicker again. The light pulsated faster than before until it cut out altogether. Cara was left alone in the total darkness that was her bedroom. Noises broke out all around the room. Books on her bookshelf fell to the floor. A desk by her window rattled and shook. The lamp that sat on top started to strobe on and off.

Cara lay frozen in fear as the strobing light revealed the outline of something rising from under her bed. It was a dark and blurry shape. But it was tall. Taller than her father who stood over six feet. It was massive. The body resembled the trunk of a tree more than a person. Cara's hand fell from her mouth, and she tried to scream but no sound would come out. Her throat felt swollen shut.

Air was no longer reaching her lungs and she started to choke. Her eyes grew wide as she watched the dark outline of a humanoid creature approach the bed. There were no facial details she could make out. Yet, somehow, she knew the thing was watching her. Long, shadowy arms reached out from the darkness and snaked their way across the bed towards Cara. She kicked at them with whatever little strength she had left. Fighting to breathe had tapped all her power. Despite her best efforts, the gangly appendages advanced. They were like shadows draped across the bed. She couldn't feel them, but she knew they were there.

Something cold wrapped around her ankle. They felt like ice-covered bones. Whatever it was would finally drag her into the closet and she would never see her family again. This monster would take her and do whatever it did to little children in the dark. She imagined rows of razor-sharp teeth gnawing on pearly white bones.

The invisible arm let go of her leg and the shadowy figure disappeared. It happened so suddenly that Cara jumped. The choking sensation vanished. Cara was still frozen in fear, not sure what to expect next. Except, nothing happened next. She sat for almost five minutes, and nothing happened. The noises had stopped. The ice-cold feeling had gone away. The Powerpuff Girls nightlight had even come back on. She could only hope it meant her monster had left.

When Cara thought it was safe, something appeared in the corner of her room. Unlike the monster before, she could see the full features of it. It looked like a man, though she could see through parts of him like he was a projected image of some kind. He wore a brown, leather jacket and blue jeans. If not for the fact that Cara could see through him, she would have thought a person had climbed in through her window. But she knew that wasn't right. Something about him was off.

There was a mist circling him. It looked like the fog that sometimes rolled through in the early morning. The ghost-man flashed a strange-looking knife unlike one Cara had ever seen. The blade was long and bent. The mist was attracted to the blade. It began to disappear into it.

The ghost-man looked around the room like he didn't notice Cara at all. He waved his knife through the cloud of mist. It swirled around the hilt like a small tornado and vanished into the blade. Cara continued to tremble in fear, not sure what was happening. There was still a lump in her throat preventing her from screaming. Even without it, Cara wasn't sure she would have been able to make a noise. The fear had immobilized her.

The man looked down and started picking at his nails with the knife. Then he looked up with a quick movement and stared directly at Cara like he had just noticed her. He gave her a smile from beneath his well-kept beard. Then the man disappeared like smoke blown by a fan.

Cara sat for a moment in stunned silence. She had no clue what had happened to her. Was the ghost-man she had just seen the monster that had attacked her earlier? If so, why had he left her alone? There were too many questions for her to fathom. Before she could think of any more, she felt a hot breath on her ear and a whisper of the words, "Boo" before she let out a blood-curdling scream for the second time that night. She ran screaming from the room, leaving behind a soft echo of laughter from something unseen.

Chapter 2

There were much older cities across the ocean better suited for his afterlife. Nicer ones, too. But Jeffrey Raines was a southern boy, through and through. Though, he had to admit his current place of residence didn't feel as southern as some places a bit farther north. St. Augustine, from what he had heard, was the oldest city in the United States. And where there was history, his kind could be found.

He walked the courtyard of the beautiful Flagler College. Standing in the center by a running fountain, Jeffrey took a moment to stare at the building towering over him. From his current position, it wrapped around three sides of the courtyard, ending with an elaborate gate made of archways. In the fading sun, the tan and red building almost seemed to glow. But Jeffrey hardly paid any attention to its beauty.

All sorts of people walked past him. Each looked more like a shadowy blur than a person. Which made sense since they all walked in the realm of the living and not on the astral plane. However, one face did stand out to Jeffrey. A man wandered around, looking astonished. He acted like he was experiencing the world around him for the first time. Streaks of shadowy blurs moved past him, and he hardly noticed. Jeffrey was more in tune with the world of the living but chose to ignore them.

"This is crazy," the man said looking over at Jeffrey. "Can you believe this? Who would have thought that this was the afterlife?" He looked like a lost tourist in a new city.

Jeffrey rolled his eyes. "Son, you're in for quite a shock when ya walk through those doors," he said through his country drawl and nodded his head towards the entrance to the college.

"What's it like in there? Hogwarts or something?"

"Not sure what a Hogwarts is, but ya better buckle up."

Jeffrey started for the entrance of the college. He didn't much care if the young spirit followed him in or not. Jeffrey wasn't there to guide the recently deceased in their journey through the afterlife. He had much more important things to do with his time.

Jeffrey walked through the solid doors like they weren't there. He now found himself standing in a circular room which was ornately decorated. Large, wooden pillars circled the room, each with the carving of four women standing back-to-back. Several hallways branched off this main room, all decorated with the same grey mosaic tiling. At this hour, the tour groups had ceased to run, and things would start to quiet down. At least, for the living. For Jeffrey and his kind, there was no sleep. For reasons Jeffrey never cared to ponder, spirits were more active at night. Some said the night brought a thinness to the veil which separated the living realm from the spiritual. They had more power and freedom in the late hours of the night. Jeffrey didn't care much about these rumors. Mostly because he knew them to be false.

A spirit had as much power during the day as it did at night. The fact was spirits didn't possess much power at all. Most spirits could interact with the world around them in subtle ways. Like knocking a glass off a counter or making curtains blow. All spirits who concentrated hard enough, and practiced the ability for years, could pass through the veil and be seen by the living. Jeffrey, being stronger than the average spirit, had found this ability to come easier to him. It was something he used to his advantage or whenever he felt like scaring those among the living, which he quite enjoyed doing.

A wonderstruck voice broke the silence behind Jeffrey, and he rolled his eyes again. It seemed the new spirit had followed him into the college after all. Questions lingered in the air like smog. Instead of answering, Jeffrey pretended he hadn't heard a single word.

Jeffrey walked across the room and headed for a hall opposite the door. Walking to the end, he passed through another set of doors that led to a large hall the residents of the college used for a cafeteria. The space was large and beautiful. It looked more like a grand hall from a castle than a college cafeteria, though the man-made structures barely registered to Jeffrey. He focused more on the hundreds of other spirits gathered in the area. Unseen to the spirits occupying the space was the cleaning crew going about their usual business. Neither party noticed each other. Though, Jeffrey could see the shadowy shapes of the living if he looked for them.

"I've heard about places like this," the familiar, curiosity-filled voice broke out behind him. "Large groups of spirits, I mean us, gathered in places like this. Unbelievable."

As the newbie gawked, Jeffrey made his way across the room toward a table filled with other spirits chatting away and playing a game of poker.

"Deal me in y'all." He said as he sat down at the table.

"Woah, how can we play cards if we're dead?" the newbie asked, causing an eruption of laughter at the table.

"Is *this* re-ceased with you, Jeff?" one of the spirits at the table asked.

"Jeffrey, if you please, Carl," Jeffrey said. "And no, the re-ceased is not with me. Shall we-"

"What's a re-ceased?" the young spirit asked to more laughter.

"Well, go on, Jeffrey. Tell your student what he is." Carl said and there was another roar of laughter.

"Fine. Recently deceased. Re-ceased. Get it? Now, you're stopping me from playin'. So, if you wouldn't mind."

Jeffrey reached forward to grab the deck of cards from the middle of the table. His jacket lifted and revealed the hilt of a knife on his belt. The young spirit gasped and stared at it like some sort of lost holy relic. The table grew quiet, knowing what the spirit had spotted.

"I see ya spotted the Shard. That's my spirit huntin' knife." Jeffrey said as he dealt cards across the table.

"Spirit hunting knife?" the re-ceased took half a step back, looking uneasy.

"Don'tcha worry, kid. I use it on the lost. Wandering spirits that harm the livin'."

"How did you get it?"

Jeffrey rolled his eyes.

"Death."

"Where did it come from?"

Before Jeffrey could respond, all the other spirits at the table chanted in unison.

"The blade is molded from the metal of Death's scythe."

Jeffrey let out a little chuckle through gritted teeth.

"You ain't the first to ask me these questions, kid."

"Oh. So, does that mean Death broke her scythe into pieces? Why?"

"Kid, I can't play cards and give ya a history lesson."

The re-ceased hung his head and apologized.

"Don't take it personally, kid. He's a hellhound. They're all as cold as when they died," Carl spoke up.

The re-ceased lifted his head and stared at Carl.

"Hellhound?"

"Ya know I hate that, Carl," Jeffrey said. "I prefer hunter."

"Hellhound sounds cooler," Carl laughed.

The other spirits at the table picked up their cards and ignored the conversation between Jeffrey and the re-ceased. To them, the story was an old one. It had long lost its luster. But for the re-ceased, the idea was foreign.

"Listen here, son," Jeffrey started. "Death doesn't like spirits stepping out of line. Make sure your time in eternity is a peaceful one. Otherwise, ya get a real nice look at my knife."

The other players smiled and suppressed laughter as the re-ceased gave an audible gulp and inched away from the table. Jeffrey smiled and brushed the bangs out of his face. "Let's play some cards, fellas," he said in his country drawl.

"Having fun?" A monotone voice called out from behind. The players at the table stopped at once. Jeffrey slapped his cards down on the table in frustration. He recognized the cold, matter-of-fact tone. But he knew better by now that when Death came calling, it was time to work.

Before Jeffrey could answer, a hand touched his shoulder, and they were no longer in the mess hall. Instead, they found themselves in the library several wings away. At this hour, the staff had gone home, and the living were nowhere to be seen. Only a handful of spirits browsed the shelves or read books at the table.

"Hey there, ma'am," Jeffrey said with a slight bow of his head. "How might I be of service to y'all?"

"There is a spirit that requires reaping."

"Ah, then you've came to the right hunter. What we dealin' with? Drifter, leech, or maybe a beast? Haven't hunted one of them in a long time."

Death looked at him with her unblinking stare. No matter how many times Jeffrey saw her, he never got used to the strange effect she had. Death looked human enough, but she lacked the emotion of any real living person or spirit. Her skin was pale and her hair dark black. Jeffrey had always wondered if the hair combined with the tight black dress she wore had been the basis for the mythology of the grim reaper. Though a black hooded cloak and skeleton features were far from the truth, it was surprisingly close.

"There's an augur that needs to be reaped," she said in a monotone voice. Her thin red lips barely parted as she spoke.

"Augur, huh? Always the boring ones. Though, I guess since they're usually beautiful women, I won't get too mad," Jeffrey laughed.

"Hold out your knife, Jeffrey," Death commanded, ignoring his comment.

He pulled the Shard from its sheath as instructed. The smooth, curved blade looked as sharp as ever. Jeffrey loved his knife. The unique shape resembled the scythe Death carried in popular culture. Jeffrey had never seen her with it, though.

"Ya know, I don't think I've ever asked," Jeffrey started. "Why don'tcha carry one of them big scythe things. Ain't that what Death is supposed to have?"

Death did not answer. Like so many times before, she gripped the handle over his hands. It began to vibrate and grow warm. When she finished, Death pulled her hand back and stared at Jeffrey. She didn't have to say another word. Jeffrey would be able to use the knife to find his target. He had a special bond with the knife. All Hellhounds did. Their knives could only be used by the designated hunter. In the hands of anyone else, it was nothing more than a regular Bowie knife and could not harm other spirits. Death bonded each hunter with their knives. Jeffrey often wondered what would happen if a hunter went rogue. Since she didn't seem to be in a talkative mood, as always, he kept the question to himself.

"Take care of the augur, Jeffrey. Return the balance." Death vanished before his eyes. She wasn't one to stick around for small talk. Jeffrey had a job to do and he would see it through. There was nothing left to say.

Jeffrey slipped the knife back into its sheath and headed for the library door. He stepped through it and back into the hallway only to find the receased spirit standing there.

"How the hell did you find us?"

"Everyone at the table said she'd probably take you here."

Jeffrey smiled. Obviously, they wanted to shake this kid as bad as he did.

"So, ya thought you'd come eavesdrop, huh?"

The re-ceased stammered as if he didn't know what to say. Jeffrey continued to laugh.

"Look, son. I'm just messin' with ya. There's nothing to eavesdrop on. I ain't a spy or anythin'. Ask around. Everyone knows about a hunter and his job."

"I-I don't know about it."

Jeffrey stared at him for a moment.

"What's your name, kid?"

"Carter." The re-ceased stammered.

"Well, Carter. I hunt lost spirits. They attack the livin' and Death sends me after them. I reap them with my knife here."

"Why doesn't Death do it?"

"Death can't reap a soul that isn't willin'. She doesn't have free will like you n' me. She's a cosmic entity or the universe incarnate. Some shit like that. I don't know. Bottom line, Death loves her balance. She ushers souls from the living to the afterlife. That's all. For everything else, there's me."

"Are there other Hellhounds?"

"If that's what they want to be called, sure."

"What did she do before she had hunters?"

Jeffrey started to answer but stopped short. It was a question he had never thought about before. The kid was on to something. Before she employed the help of her hunters, how did she ever manage the wandering spirits? He pictured a time much like the old west in America. A lawless land with spirits running amuck with no one to keep them in check.

"Ya know, I ain't sure about that. Maybe I'll ask her someday."

Carter stared at him wide-eyed. Jeffrey had seen that look before. Another interested spirit wanting a job as a hunter. He understood the appeal. It seemed like a safe and exciting job. Spirits couldn't be killed except by a hunter's knife. So where was the risk? It was the ones whose lives had been boring and empty who wanted adventure in the afterlife. But Jeffrey knew what Death knew. It was killers who made the best hunters. Though, Jeffrey knew nothing about his time alive. For all he knew, he had been a killer in life. He couldn't remember. That was unusual for the spirit world. Most remembered their lives.

"Sorry, son. Death usually chooses her hunters on their death day. Nothin' personal."

Jeffrey side-stepped around Carter and headed off down the hallway. Carter stood there with his head hung low. Jeffrey didn't feel bad for the re-ceased. He would bounce back soon enough. Once he realized he could travel the world uninhibited, he would forget all about becoming a hunter. As Jeffrey knew all too well, being a hunter wasn't as glamorous as it sounded. For him, it was enough.

Now, he headed outside into the night and walked back across the courtyard. This was always the fun part. Gearing up for the fight. Though, he was still disappointed with the prey. An augur was one of the weaker spirits he could fight. Most of them were disguised as lost women looking for a ride home or wandering in the woods looking for their babies. Those who offered help would become their prey. A simple and easy target for Jeffrey.

The knife directed him towards his target like a new sense. Instinct was the best way Jeffrey could explain it. Like a sea turtle towards the ocean. Somehow, he just knew where to go. He could feel the long walk ahead of him. His target was far. Instead, he chose to drive. A car materialized from thin air in front of Jeffrey. There were several stories about ghost cars all over the world. Jeffrey would have been proud to know he and his car made up several of them.

Jeffrey melted through the door of the ghost-version of a 1963 Corvette Stingray complete with split rear window. Ghost cars were rare in the afterlife. Jeffrey had to beg Death for his special girl. There was something about the car he felt a connection with. He didn't know what it was. There had always been a shred of a memory surrounding his car, though he never understood why. He had named her after a name that floated somewhere in the deep recesses of his mind.

"Time to hunt, Mia," Jeffrey said to his car and shifted into gear. Much like his spiritual form, the car glided through objects present in the realm of the living without issue. Humans couldn't see him or the car if he didn't want them to. Driving down the road, Jeffrey felt the familiar excitement of the hunt.

Chapter 3

He had driven the car as far as it could go. A river separated him from the domain of his target. Even though the car did not have to obey the laws of the physical world, there were some it just couldn't overcome. Luckily, for Jeffrey, he could. Most re-ceased believed they could fly, but that couldn't be farther from the truth. A spirit could float above the ground or descend tall structures without stepping foot on them, but they could not fly. Jeffrey would be able to float over the wide gap of the Matanzas River.

Once upon a time, this skill had not been one which came easy. The first time he had held a foot above the water, he had been certain he would fall in. Of course, he hadn't. He had floated over the river like he was walking on some invisible platform. No longer was there a fear of failure. Jeffrey glided over the river with ease.

He could see a small fortress on the opposite bank. It looked to be several hundred years old. Old places like these tended to attract spirits. Whether it was powerful energy or purely aesthetic, Jeffrey did not know. Spirits loved old places. Most of the time. When it came to dangerous spirits, they almost always loved the old and abandoned.

This fort was not abandoned. Tour groups traveled across the river by boat all day long. From what Jeffrey could remember, the fort was named Fort Matanzas, after the river it was built on. It was a small fortress, built in the shape of an L on its side. It sat by itself on a large body of land in the middle of the river. The perfect hiding place for an augur, though how it was feasting on humans Jeffrey didn't know. His best guess was the occasional park ranger making his way to the island during the night.

As he approached the bank on the east side, he spotted the augur standing atop the fort. She seemed to be staring off to the north in the direction of the full moon. The pale moonlight radiated across the ghostly image giving her an eerie glow.

When Jeffrey approached the fort, he looked up at it from the ground. The main level was elevated above him. There was a wooden staircase leading up for the tourists to use. But Jeffrey didn't need a staircase. He could walk through the wall and emerge on the upper deck. Before he could move, he heard the familiar cry of the augur. Up on top of the fort, she wailed.

"Somebody help," she cried. "My baby is missing."

Jeffrey passed through the brick wall and emerged on the first level of the fort like he was coming out of a lake. He stood still for a moment, listening to the augur's call. She had not heard Jeffrey's approach. He would still have the element of surprise. But Jeffrey did wonder who she was calling out to. No one could have been around for miles.

He passed through another brick wall. Now, he stood in the center of a small room that was once the soldiers' quarters. He paid it no mind and ascended the small ladder in the center of the room. At the top, he found the augur facing away from him. She stood on the ledge and stared out over the empty island. Far off down the trail, a boat sat at the dock. It rose and fell with the gentle rocking motion of the river. A lone park ranger sat at the helm. He seemed ready to take off but stared off in the direction of the fort like he had heard a voice on the wind.

"Ma'am," Jeffrey said as he stood behind the augur. "If you lost your baby out here, I'm afraid to tell you it might be dead."

The woman slowly turned and stared at Jeffrey. She was a beautiful woman with long flowing hair and soft features. Her beauty was her lure. Lucky for Jeffrey, he knew what she really was. She stared at him for several seconds as she tried to hypnotize him with her fluttering eyelids and swaying hips.

Without wasting another moment, Jeffrey removed the knife from its sheath and stared back at the augur. The two stared at each other like cowboys about to duel. Lost spirits gave little thought to anything but their prey. Most were unaware of the spirit world around them. That meant many had no idea about hunters or their knives. Jeffrey had been laughed at by many lost spirits after pulling his knife. Though, he always got the last laugh.

"Oh," she said in a whisper. "Hellhound."

"Come on," Jeffrey sneered. "I guess I don't have to explain it to ya then."

Jeffrey smiled. The augur didn't smile back.

If she knew what a Hellhound was, then she knew she couldn't hurt him. Not in a lethal sense. Spirits could still feel pain. If two spirits exchanged blows, they could still feel it. But one spirit could not kill another. Only the special knife gifted from Death could reap a spirit. Even the powerful and dangerous spirits like the augur standing before Jeffrey couldn't kill a spirit. The only one that could come close was a beast. A terrible lost spirit known in the world of the living as a poltergeist. It tortured its prey and dragged them to a realm that only beasts could access. If there was a spirit that could kill another, Jeffrey had not heard of it before.

The augur knew she could be reaped. It was plastered all over her face. Any second now, she would try to flee. Jeffrey had been through this enough times to know how it worked. He glanced past the augur and saw the lone park ranger scanning the sky, no doubt looking for the source of the wailing woman. The augur took advantage of the distraction and pounced on Jeffrey.

In a split second, she had changed from a beautiful young woman into a hideous monster. Her skin turned grey and rotten. Her pearly white teeth fell from her bleeding gums. The ones that remained were black. Her fingernails turned to razor-sharp daggers. A mass of hair whipped around her head like tentacles searching for prey. Now black eyes sunken deep into her skull glared at Jeffrey as she grabbed hold of him. He made a stab with the knife, but the augur was too quick. She delivered a powerful punch with both hands, hitting him square in the chest. Jeffrey was knocked back several feet.

After regaining balance, Jeffrey turned to face the augur. She had vanished. Jeffrey dropped down through the roof, passing through like it wasn't there, and entered the soldier's quarters again. In the center of the small room stood a wooden bed frame that was made to look over a century old. It was doubtful it was an original. The bed was large enough to fit several men. No doubt soldiers slept in one bed together over a hundred years ago. Jeffrey smiled at the thought. Then he pictured the augur cowering under the frame. Drawing it out, Jeffrey let his boots click on the solid surface beneath his feet. His flair for the dramatic always kept his hunts interesting.

"Come out, come out wherever ya are," he said.

He heard a scream in the distance and remembered the park ranger. The augur must have fled towards him, hoping for a quick victim before disappearing. The human's life wasn't important to Jeffrey. Only his hunt. His target. And now that he knew where she was, it would be easier. He passed through the fort wall and into the night.

Up ahead, he saw the augur advancing on the park ranger. He cried out in terror before the woman lunged at him with her talons. Within seconds, his chest was ripped open in gashes of blood and torn flesh. Her basic instinct to attack the living would be her downfall. It gave Jeffrey the time to close the distance between him and his target.

Before she could turn away from her victim, Jeffrey had closed the gap. She dug her claws into Jeffrey's arm—drawing no blood—as he tackled her to the ground. He tried to plunge the knife into the augur's body, but she landed a well-placed kick that kept him at bay. As the augur tried to flee, Jeffrey grabbed her tangled hair and yanked her back. Her screech echoed into the darkness. Any living person around would have trembled with fear at the sound. Jeffrey remained unphased.

He went in for another strike, but the augur was fast. She dodged his blow and pulled free of his grip. The augur stared at Jeffrey now, teeth bared. "Shit," he said as she pounced on him like a wild animal. Her talons scraped and shredded his arm, leaving behind ghostly shreds of skin that healed instantly. Each scrape was excruciating for Jeffrey but at least he knew there would be no permanent damage.

Jeffrey swiped at the creature with his knife. Her right hand cut free from her body and vanished into mist. The cloud hung in the air for a moment, sparkling in the moonlight. Then, it was absorbed by Jeffrey's knife in a swirling spiral. He could feel the knife grow warmer in his hand as it absorbed the little amount of energy from the spirit's life force. A Hellhound's power was directly connected to their knife. The more souls they reaped, the more power the knife held.

The augur let out a scream of terror as she looked down at her missing hand. There was no chance of her winning this fight. It was either give Jeffrey the slip or knock his knife away from him. But since she couldn't kill Jeffrey, both results would end the same. She would not survive.

As she attempted to flee, Jeffrey grabbed her by the left wrist and pulled her back. She screeched again and tried to swipe at Jeffrey. This time, he didn't try to dodge her talons. Instead, he pulled her in close. Before she could struggle to free herself, Jeffrey rammed the blade into her gut. She cried out in pain before dissipating into a fine mist. A strange coolness hung in the air for several minutes before the vapor flew into the blade of the knife.

Jeffrey stuck the knife back in the sheath and turned to face the dying park ranger.

"Welcome to the other side," he said as he watched the man take his last few breaths. Death would be there soon to either reap his soul or let him wander like so many others. Jeffrey didn't want to be there for that. One re-ceased pestering him with questions was enough for one day.

Jeffrey headed back to the fort and sat down on the ledge. Putting his feet up, he reclined back in mid-air and watched the moon rise into the night sky. He knew Death would be with him soon, so there was no need to run off.

And like that, she appeared before him. She stared at him with the familiar cold gaze he was used to.

"He stay or go?" Jeffrey asked with a smile.

"His life could have been saved." She said matter-of-factly.

"Eh, I tried. She was a quick one."

"I have another target for you."

"A bit quick, don't ya think?"

"It's something I've never seen before."

Something Death had never seen before? It seemed impossible for a being that was at least as old as time. How could there be anything she had never seen before? He would gladly take this mission. Hunting augurs and lost spirits was fine but over the decades had become a little stale. He was ready for a challenge.

"Well, you have piqued my curiosity. Do continue." He said as he stood to face her.

"There's a man who cannot die and I want you to kill him for me."

If Jeffrey were human, he would have lost his balance. He stared at her for several seconds without a word to say. Death was asking the impossible. There was no use asking her if this was a joke. Death was notorious for having no sense of humor.

"Uh, darlin', I think that's impossible. I mean, right? Aren't those *the rules*?" He said, with air quotes around the last two words.

"Someone has figured out a way to cheat me and I do not like it." There was a hint of anger in her voice unlike Jeffrey had ever heard before. In the decades that he had known her, he had not seen a hint of emotions.

"Alright, so how do I reap a living person? Can you grant me that power or somethin'?"

Death shook her head. "That is impossible."

"Darlin', nothing's impossible."

"Then stopping this man should be simple for you."

"I feel like you set me up for that."

"I need you to seek this man out. Find out how he is cheating staying alive. Then find a way to end his life. He is past due."

Jeffrey thought about making a joke about the man being like a library book but refrained. Death seemed unusually unpleasant tonight. There was a look in her eye he had never seen. He assumed the living finding ways to cheat death screwed up her internal workings. How had something like this never happened before? The living had been around for thousands of centuries. Had none ever figured out a way to stay alive longer? Surely one must have been able to cheat death before.

"Ma'am, is there something else going on here that you're not telling me? I mean, the livin' have been around for what, 70,000 years or whatever? None have ever gone past their expiration date?"

Death stared at him for a moment. Jeffrey could almost see thoughts whirling in her mind.

"There is a time frame for when a living person is ready to expire. It is not preordained. There is no fate. Accidents or other events can end a living person's life before their expiration. Time does not work the same for the universe as it does for the living. There is no specific time, date, or second a person should die. It is like a river. If a large tree were to fall over and block the flow, the riverbed would dry up. The river ends in a waterfall. The end of a human life in this case."

Jeffrey stared at her in awe. She had never explained so much before. Usually, when he asked questions, the answers were brief. Hardly answers at all. Whatever was going on now must have been big.

"And yes, many of the living have gone over that waterfall and survived. Most are just lucky. An accident kept them alive longer than expected. Others find ways to prolong life. But that borrowed time shows in their spirit and they never last long."

Death looked out over the island. It seemed she was no longer talking to Jeffrey but to herself.

"This man, however, shows no signs of expiring. In fact, it is the opposite. It seems like his spirit is getting farther from crossing over. It is almost as if he found a way to reverse the flow of the river."

"Uh, hold on a sec. What does that mean?"

"It means his spirit is becoming stronger inside of his living body. He is reversing the process."

"Like he's getting younger?"

"No. Powerful."

Death turned to face Jeffrey again. He could see a look of worry on her usually expressionless face.

"This upsets the balance, Jeffrey. More than you could understand. He must be stopped. If he transcends death..."

She trailed off, but Jeffrey didn't need her to finish the sentence. It was bad news and he knew it. A man who cheated death was one thing. A man who could harness the power of his spirit inside his mortal shell was another. There was no telling what dark fate would befall mankind. Jeffrey pulled the knife from his sheath and held it out for Death. He knew what was coming next. He needed to find this man and figure out a way to stop him. Death couldn't interfere. Especially not with the living. Jeffrey couldn't outright reap a living person, but he could find other ways to kill the mortal so he could reap the spirit.

Death grabbed the knife and embedded the information Jeffrey needed. She didn't wish Jeffrey luck or tell him to be careful. Instead, she vanished. It left Jeffrey wondering where she went in times like this. Did she cease to exist? Or was there some sort of council she reported to? Was it God? It didn't matter. He now had a job to do, and he would stop at nothing until it was done. Even if the task required was impossible. His own words echoed through his mind. "Darlin', nothing's impossible." He shook his head and smiled.

Chapter 4

Eileen gazed out at the ocean from her hotel suite. The Atlantic Ocean never ceased to amaze her. On the eastern coast of Florida, she was used to the Gulf of Mexico. It had its own charms. But it didn't compare to the crisp, blue waters of the Atlantic. Standing on the balcony, she took in the sights and the smells of the ocean.

The sun had slipped behind the horizon only a few minutes ago. This place was almost paradise. Eileen had never stayed at the Hard Rock in Daytona Beach before. It was a mild disappointment to learn that there was no casino attached to this Hard Rock. Where she was from, the closest Hard Rock was a luxurious hotel and casino combo. But it didn't matter. This resort was gorgeous enough without it.

She turned around and walked back into the room. Eileen placed her glass on the small desk and sat down on the bed. She looked at the television and then back to the balcony. Instead of sitting inside tonight and watching some random show, she thought she would take an evening stroll on the beach. There was no point letting the beautiful scenery go to waste. And when she was done with her walk, she could relax at the poolside lounge and enjoy the live band and drinks. Exactly what she needed.

Eileen changed into shorts and a Hard Rock Daytona tee shirt. She had picked it up at the gift shop that very afternoon. Her collection of tees had grown with every visit to a different Hard Rock. Her sneakers waited for her by the hotel room door. She slipped them on and brushed her hair to the side. Ready for her walk on the beach, Eileen slipped out of the hotel room.

Though the sun had slipped past the horizon, it was still light enough to see. A brilliant orange glow hung in the sky. The light was fading fast. Eileen didn't mind. She strolled along the beach, taking in the sights and the sounds. The ocean waves lapped at the shore in a rhythmic beat. Her feet slapped against the damp, compacted sand. Dodging small ocean waves to keep her sneakers dry, Eileen carried on down the beach. Barefoot was the only way to enjoy the sand, but she hated the idea of carrying her shoes. Practicality won out over comfort.

Darkness engulfed the beach with a quickening pace. The orange glow melted away to a soft pink and then to black. Eileen didn't bother worrying about the darkness. A brisk walk on the beach at night was something she did quite often back home.

The scenery around her grew darker. This part of the beach was not lit up by condos for a few blocks. Less people wandered here and barely any lights polluted the sky. It was the first patch of darkness along her walk. As the sky grew darker, the stars grew brighter. Eileen looked up and caught a glimpse of the twinkling lights. She had the overwhelming urge to lay in the sand and stare up at them. So, she did exactly that.

Her eyes had adjusted to the darkness now, but it was still difficult to see very far. She heard the soft crunching of footsteps in soft sand before she saw the figure approach. A man was walking in her direction, though he didn't seem to notice Eileen. She decided to remain still and let the man pass. Hopefully, he wouldn't trip over her.

"Hey, look out!" She cried as the man almost stepped on her. He tripped over his own feet and went tumbling towards the ground. Eileen jumped to her feet and helped the man keep his balance. He was a heavy man. Tall and wide, he towered over her like a building.

"You okay-" She asked but a hand shot out of the darkness and wrapped around her throat before she could finish. Eileen tried to scream. No sound left her lips. She could feel his grip tightening as she struggled for air. Her arms flailed in a wild attempt to free herself. His grip held firm.

Fear burst through her body. Both hands shot out and latched the man's face. She tried to dig her nails into his eyes. His grip tightened and Eileen thought her esophagus would collapse at any second. One good swipe drew blood over the man's right eye. He let go and cupped his hand to the hurt area. Eileen turned and ran without hesitation.

Her throat was raw and sore. She tried to scream for help, but no sound would come. Eileen coughed and gagged as she ran. In her chest, her lungs burned for oxygen. Somewhere above the thundering noise of her pulse blasting in her ears, she could hear the man's heavy footsteps on the sand behind her. He had already given chase. There was a small area of illuminated beach up ahead. The condos. Someone was bound to see her if she could just get in sight of them.

Her attacker was too fast. For such a large man, he moved with incredible speed. Eileen felt a hand grip the back of her neck and thrust her forward. The sand rose to her face at a dizzying speed. She felt her nose crush under the tremendous force. But there was little time to worry about it. The hand pushed her head harder into the sand making it impossible to breathe. For the second time that night, Eileen flailed and kicked to no avail. She had no leverage or line of sight. Her nails dug into the sand and flung it wildly into the air in the attempt to blind her attacker. When she instinctively inhaled a lung full of sand, she knew it was all over. She coughed and choked on sand as she tried to take a breath. Her attacker's hand held firm.

"I'm sorry this has to happen," she heard a muffled voice say. Eileen could barely hear him over the amount of sand now lodged in her ears. "It'll be over soon."

She convulsed now as her lungs fought for air and choked back sand. Her limbs slowed and her thrashing ceased. Only her fingers wriggled through the sand as her body began to shut down. Eileen could feel herself slipping away into the darkness.

As quick as everything had happened, it all stopped. The pain, the suffocation. It was all gone. She was no longer face down in the sand but instead standing upright, looking into the darkness of the beach once again. If not for the behemoth of a man crouched down before her, Eileen would have thought the whole incident had been a nightmare. He was slumped over what looked like a lifeless body. It took a moment for the scene to register. It was her lifeless body half-buried in the sand. She had heard of out of body experiences before but had never believed in them. Instead of fear and panic, a calm washed over her. Everything felt lighter. There was no more pain or danger.

Something in the corner of her eye caught her attention. She turned to see a haggard old man standing a few feet away. His eyes were fixed on Eileen. It was the strangest sight she had ever seen. His skin sagged on his face like a baggy suit on a thin man. He was wrapped in some sort of brown leather-like coat. If this was the face of God, Eileen didn't much care for it. Fear slowly trickled into the back of her mind. The feeling of calm washed away. Something about this person told her to run.

The humanoid shape didn't last long. The man before her threw off the coat which became a set of large wings. The skin shifted into a black, smooth skin and the being took on the shape of a twisted looking bird. It pounced before Eileen could even shriek. Razor sharp talons sank into her spirit, and she watched in horror as she slowly dissolved into mist. The strange bird creature opened its deformed beak and drank in her essence. Soon, Eileen had dissolved into nothing and saw nothing more.

Chapter 5

For the first time since Jeffrey could remember, pinpointing the location of his new target was difficult. It was tough to get a read on exactly where the man was. He seemed to be on the move. Most of the spirits Jeffrey hunted tended to stay stationary for long periods of time. They hunted on the same roads, in the same woods, or in the same homes for years before moving on. Wandering spirits hunted like animals, relying on instinct. The living was a whole new scale for Jeffrey. A full conscious being. This would be no easy task.

One thing was clear. The target was not in St. Augustine. He was a good distance away and traveling fast. Jeffrey decided it would be best to wait for the man to come to a stop before he raced off after him. The last thing he wanted to do was race across the state, following some guy when he could wait for him to stop. While he waited, Jeffrey decided he would waste a little time in one of his favorite haunts.

Jeffrey roamed the top of the Castillo de San Marcos which overlooked the Matanzas River. He had spent enough time there to learn the Castillo was a fortress built by the Spanish in the late sixteen-hundreds. He didn't really care to learn much more than that. Though he didn't much care for the history behind the fort, he did admire the construction. The fortress had two levels. The bottom consisted of a large courtyard with several rooms lining the edge. A large, stone staircase bent into an L shape led to the second level. It was a large open space with small outlook towers on each of the four corners. Once upon a time, cannons would have rested along the walls. Now, it was mostly tourists with cameras and a few replica cannons. Of course, Jeffrey hardly noticed the living people. He did notice the other spirits that walked the second level or sat on the wall admiring the view of the river.

"Hey, Jeffrey. How's the hunt going?" A friendly voice called out from one of the towers. Jeffrey turned to see his friend Alex wandering up the stairs. He didn't have a lot of friends in the afterlife, but Alex was the exception.

"Takin' a little r&r for the time bein'." Jeffrey responded as he approached Alex.

"You know, I'll never understand you Hellhounds. We find out this whole afterlife business is real and we can basically do whatever we want until the universe ends and you decide to work. Not me. I get to kick my feet up and go where I please. Ever think of retiring."

Jeffrey laughed.

"Maybe it's different for y'all. You remember your time as one of the livin'. Maybe I just needed something to keep my mind off it."

"Wow. We're getting deep today. Never seen this side of you, Jeffrey. Can't say I like it."

The two friends shared a good laugh.

"Got a question for ya." Jeffrey said as the two walked the Castillo together.

"Shoot."

"Have ya ever heard of the living finding a way to cheat death? Forever, I mean."

Alex stared at Jeffrey for a moment.

"I've heard of people overstaying their welcome. But I didn't know immortality was possible. Is that what we're talking about?"

Jeffrey shrugged. "Honestly, I don't really know. But Death's got me hunting a livin' person because he isn't dying."

Alex arched an eyebrow. "Why would Death care if a living person hasn't died yet? Something will take him out eventually. People live past their so-called expiration dates all the time."

"This one's different, Alex." Jeffrey said in a low tone. "This one's getting' stronger."

Alex stared out at the Matanzas River for a moment. Jeffrey could only assume Alex was collecting his thoughts. Any spirit who had been around as much time as Alex was bound to know a lot. He knew more than Jeffrey about the rules of the spirit realm.

"I've heard rumors something like this was possible. Not likely, mind you, but possible."

"What?"

"It takes centuries for angry spirits to develop their skills enough to harm the living, right?" Alex said, directing his question at Jeffrey. Jeffrey nodded, knowing that both he and Alex knew the answer. "Well, it takes an impossible amount of time for spirits to develop enough power to harm other spirits. More time than any spirit has spent here."

"Hold on, Alex. What are you saying?"

"I'm saying, I've heard rumors that spirits can become more powerful by killing other spirits. But not just killing them, absorbing them. Sort of how your knife works. But it's impossible. No spirit is powerful enough or old enough to pull something like this off. So, it's not possible. But it's the only way I've ever heard to explain what you're describing."

Jeffrey shook his head.

"So, let me get this straight. You're tellin' me, this man may have found a way to harness sprits to charge him up?"

"Like a battery."

"How the hell's that possible?"

"It isn't. I'm telling you. No spirit, much less the living, could ever pull that off."

Jeffrey leaned against the Castillo wall and stared for a moment. He barely saw his own friend standing next to him anymore. His mind was completely centered on the impossibility before him.

Somehow, this living person was harvesting spirits. It seemed like the only explanation and yet it couldn't be possible. Jeffrey wondered why Death hadn't mentioned he was harvesting souls. She would have known better than anyone else. She must have noticed souls missing, right? There were too many questions for Jeffrey to answer himself. The only thing left to do was find this man and investigate for himself.

Death must have known the man was harvesting spirits and kept the information from Jeffrey on purpose. Though, he couldn't understand why. He supposed it was possible she didn't know if he was or not. As Alex had said, it was impossible. He had always assumed Death was all knowing. She knew when every living mortal died. Would she not have noticed missing spirits? Jeffrey wanted to summon Death and get some answers. Before he could, he felt the presence of the man finally come to a stop. It was time to hunt him down.

"Thanks for the chat, Alex." Jeffrey said as he turned to leave. "I'll let ya know how it went when I get back." Without saying goodbye, Jeffrey turned and left.

Jeffrey stepped down through the floor and made his way to the outside of the Castillo. His target had finally come to a stop. Jeffrey was ready. He would need to get there fast before the man decided to move again. Lucky for Jeffrey, he had a car that wasn't bound by the rules of the mortal world.

His car appeared before him in a cloud of mist and the engine roared to life. Jeffrey couldn't help but smile. The afterlife turned out to be much more fun than he ever thought possible. Though, he couldn't remember what he had thought would be waiting for him on the other side. His days as one of the living was hazy at best. But there was no time to think about that now. Jeffrey climbed behind the wheel and pulled the gear into drive. The wheels spun on the ground for a second- kicking up nothing- and then the vehicle lurched forward.

Just as Jeffrey was getting bored with the silence, Death appeared in the passenger seat beside him. Jeffrey barely reacted. He was used to her coming and going at this point. He looked over at her and wondered how strange it was to see Death sitting in the passenger seat of a car. She looked like an ordinary woman, but Jeffrey knew she was truly the keeper of souls. And then a question struck him that he never thought before. Did she use that human-like form to walk among the living? Being a spirit, Jeffrey could summon enough strength to be seen by the living if he so wished. Not all spirits could do it. Mostly it was a trick used by hunters and their prey. Even then, he didn't look like a full flesh and blood human. More like a person shrouded in mist and somewhat transparent.

"I see you are headed towards the target's location." Death said matter-of-factly.

"Yes, I am. Question for ya. Is he harvesting souls to stay alive?"

Death was silent for a moment. Finally, she looked over at Jeffrey.

"Honestly, I do not know. I can only assume and I do not like to deal in uncertainties."

"Right, but seeing as how y'all need me to hunt this guy, maybe ya could share a guess?"

Death took in a deep breath and looked out the window. She seemed to be acting almost human as she watched the trees go by.

"He may be consuming spirits to keep himself alive. But I do not know and I certainly do not know how."

"Shouldn't somethin' like that be impossible?"

"You told me nothing was impossible."

"Did I just get sass from Death? That'd be a first."

"This is truly troubling, Jeffrey. If this man has found a way to consume spirits and hide it from me, it will not be good news. I should not have to tell you what could be at stake here. The spirits you hunt throw off the balance to a degree, but this tips the scale entirely."

For the first time since Jeffrey had met Death, he saw worry in her eyes. The image was troubling. She looked almost human. The former human inside Jeffrey urged him to brush her hair back and tell her it would be alright. But he remembered who and what she was and the moment past. Now, there was a genuine worry rising in Jeffrey. Whatever this man was doing was serious enough to make Death nervous. He wanted to know what the implications would be, but he was afraid to ask.

"There are spirits missing, Jeffrey."

"What's that mean?"

"There are some living people who have passed on, but their souls are missing. I was never summoned because their spirit never had a chance to call out to me."

"Wait, we call out to ya when we die?"

"Your energy does. It is like a ripple in the river of life that I can detect. It draws me to the spirit, and I offer it peace."

"Ya mean the choice to move on to whatever the hell is after this or stay here?"

"Yes. There have been a handful of souls in the past couple days where that ripple never went out. So, I could not reach out to them. The balance is severely broken. Whatever this man is doing, it must be stopped at all costs, Jeffrey."

"Rest your pretty lil' head, Death. I'm on my way there now. I'll be puttin' a stop to his soul stealin'."

"You cannot fail."

"I never do, sweetheart. The plan is, lead him into a trap that gets him killed. Simple but effective. Haven't figured out the trap yet, but there's time. No need to worry."

Death did not seem comforted by Jeffrey's plan. Jeffrey couldn't tell if she disliked his plan or not. In the end, it wouldn't matter. There wasn't much he could do to the living. Jeffrey would have to lead this man to his death. He could lead him to a balcony somewhere and give a little shove and hope the man lost his footing. Or maybe he could lead him into the road and into oncoming traffic. Winging it was all Jeffrey could do. An opportunity would present itself once he was there.

"Hey, unless ya can give me some sort of ancient weapon that can kill this guy." Jeffrey laughed.

"No such thing exists."

"Is it possible that ya just don't know of one?"

"No."

"Alright then. Maybe I find a spirit in the area like an augur and have it kill this man? Would that work better for you?"

"You can try. Lost spirits are difficult to convince of anything. Perhaps, you could lead this man to a location inhabited by a wandering spirit?"

"Ya know, that's not a half bad idea."

"Let me have your knife. I can locate a second target for you."

"That's possible? I can hunt two things at once?"

"Your knife is made from the blade of my scythe. It is capable of locating every single spirit on the astral plane."

"Woah." Jeffrey said as he pulled the knife free from his belt holster and handed it over. Death did what she always did. It glowed for a moment before returning to its former, dull look. Jeffrey had no idea what it would be like to hold the dagger now. With two targets, how would he differentiate between the two?

When Death handed over the blade, he could sense the location of both targets now. It was an odd sensation. It was like an instinct rather than an actual knowing. All he needed to do was focus on which target he wanted and he would know which way to go.

"Alright, well, that was cool." Jeffrey said, sliding the knife back into his holster. "I'll find this guy first. Scope him out a lil'. Then, I'll find this spirit and see if I can't introduce the two. Sounds like a solid plan to me. How 'bout it?"

Death looked at him with an expressionless face. Jeffrey found himself admiring her beauty. It was odd. She was Death, after all. The Grim Reaper. And yet, she was stunning. He still couldn't decide if that was a clever design or cosmic joke. After all, who would he prefer to see on his death bed? A creepy skeleton in a black cloak carrying a large weapon? Or a beautiful, pale woman in a skintight black dress? He was certain it was the latter.

"Whatever you do, make sure your target expires before he consumes more spirits. The more he consumes, the stronger he becomes. Eventually, he will be too strong to stop." In the blink of an eye, she was gone.

Jeffrey shook his head, trying to make sense of it all. A being had found a way to cheat Death quite literally. He was anxious to find out how. More importantly, he was anxious for a good hunt. It had been ages since a good challenge. He couldn't know how much of a challenge there was before him.

Chapter 6

Jeffrey pulled his car into the alley behind a fancy resort. He knew enough to know he was in the city of Orlando but didn't care to know much else. It was too modern and too much city for his liking. Not the kind of place he liked to spend much of his time in the afterlife. Some spirits liked to be near the cities and close to people. It reminded them of a time when they were alive. At least, that's what Jeffrey guessed. He couldn't understand why some couldn't let go of the past life.

He melted through the car door and stared up at the resort above him. Somewhere in one of the rooms was his target. The man who had been claiming spirits for his own. And across the street, he spotted the cemetery where the drifter was located. For now, at least.

Drifters liked to move from place to place. Unlike the augur, who would often choose abandoned locations to prey on the living, the drifter would seek out its prey. There were all sorts of stories about drifters from the living world. Shadow people, as some liked to call them, were a prime example. As they lurk through areas, sometimes the living would get a small glimpse of the drifter. Between the void of the living and the spirits, the drifter would look more like a shadow than anything else. But Jeffrey knew better. Drifters were horrible looking spirits. Many with deformed bodies and grotesque figures. He had asked Death about it once and she had told him that the power a drifter was able to harness came with a terrible price.

"Alright, here's the plan," Jeffrey said to himself. "I go upstairs, find this bastard, an' lead him to the cemetery. The drifter does the dirty work an' then I kill the drifter. Problem solved. Oh yeah, and reap the man's spirit after. Can't forget that part." He smiled at his genius.

It was going to be a strange one for sure. Not only was this Jeffrey's first time hunting a living person, but it was unusual to conduct a hunt in the middle of a populated city. Most wandering spirits he encountered took up refuge in abandoned places or remote areas. This was done on purpose. Most dangerous spirits knew they would find themselves hunted if they caused too much commotion. So, they took up refuge in remote places and killed as few of the living as they could. It was best to fly under Death's radar. Unlucky for them, Death's radar was nearly inescapable. The moment a person died, she knew about the presence of a dangerous spirit.

The sun had yet to set which meant the drifter would be less active. Spirits like that tended to hunt at night. Which meant, Jeffrey had plenty of time to find his target and learn everything he could about him. Above all, Jeffrey was curious about how this man could harness souls for his own gain. And he was certain Death would appreciate a heads up as well.

Jeffrey approached the front lobby and walked straight through the doors. Inside, he could see the ornate furniture and decorations. Against the far wall, a waterfall cascaded down into a large pool of water. Coins sparkled beneath the surface from tourists desperate for a little extra luck. Of course, Jeffrey didn't believe in such things. Perhaps when he had been alive, but not in death.

Someone stood behind the front desk, but Jeffrey hardly noticed him. Jeffrey cared little for the living people around him. There was only one human in this building Jeffrey cared to notice.

He didn't need to search through records or any sort of manifest to find the man he was looking for. In fact, it would do him no good to do so. He didn't know the man's name. But he didn't need it. He could tell what floor the man was on by instinct. Jeffrey decided he wasn't in any sort of hurry and made his way towards the elevator. He phased through the doors. Once inside, he was able to focus his energy and press floor fourteen.

The elevator rose a few floors before stopping. When the doors slid open, a couple stepped inside. Jeffrey grinned and focused on the couple. They materialized before him, and he saw they were a young couple. He imagined they were on a romantic vacation and decided he wanted to give them something they would remember.

Jeffrey reached out and pulled a thin strand of wavy hair. The woman flicked her head to the side and looked behind her. No doubt, she was trying to find the source of what touched her. Grinning to himself, Jeffrey pulled a strand from the opposite side. He watched as the woman rummaged through her hair, now convinced there was something in it.

"What the hell are you doing?" the man asked.

"I think there's a bug in my hair or something," she said. "I felt something moving."

While the man checked her hair for the invisible bug, Jeffrey passed through them both and looked down at the control panel. He pressed every single button up to floor fourteen. He could hear the air get sucked from the elevator as the couple gasped. When the elevator made its first stop, he watched in amusement as the couple ran screaming from the elevator. Jeffrey laughed as he stepped into the hallway. Messing with the living was always such fun.

Jeffrey looked at the ceiling above him and started to ascend. It was faster than using the elevator, especially now that it would be stopping at every floor thanks to his childish prank. If Death had been there, she would have given him some sort of lecture about avoiding alerting the living to the presence of an afterlife. Something about keeping the balance, of course. Everything with that woman was about balance.

When he arrived at floor fourteen, Jeffrey planted his feet back on solid ground and stood still for a moment. He needed to focus on his target to find the proper room. Of course, not being bound by physical laws on the living, he could walk through every door until he found the right one. But that was for amateurs.

He could feel the knife pulling him down the hallway. The constant flow of energy from the knife to his spirit guided him. There would be no need for guessing games. Jeffrey calmly walked down the hallway in the direction of the invisible force. He sauntered, knowing there was no rush. His prey would never see him coming. He would go unnoticed until Jeffrey wanted to be seen. Then, the trap would be set.

Jeffrey passed through the door to room two thirty-seven and looked around. It was a decent room with a nice view overlooking the city. But most of it was lost on Jeffrey. He spotted his target on the opposite side of the room sitting in front of a desk. The man seemed to be writing something down. Curious as to what he could be up to, Jeffrey walked over and peered over the man's shoulder.

He had a smartphone out on his desk with a list of people pulled up. The man's large finger scrolled over the list, stopping every few seconds to click on a profile. Of course, Jeffrey had no clue what social media was or a smartphone for that matter. The world had moved on quick after his death.

Though, he couldn't remember when he died, he knew enough to know these things didn't exist then.

Next to the phone was a sheet of paper. There were a few names written on the list. Several were crossed off. Jeffrey could only assume this list of names was his victim list. The people he had killed in order to cheat death. But it didn't explain how. It wouldn't be enough to kill this man, Jeffrey knew that. Death would want to know how he had done it. She would *need* to know. Otherwise, someone else could do it again. She would want to put an end to the loophole.

The man's finger stopped moving on the screen and clicked on a woman's face. Her name and location pulled up on her profile. Jeffrey shook his head. He couldn't believe people were willingly sharing that information with everyone. What strange times these were. He didn't see an address, but it didn't matter.

Her name was Cara Brown, and she was a good-looking woman. Jeffrey, who had no interest in the living, even thought so. Dirty blonde hair flowed from under a cap and framed the woman's rounded jaw line. She wore a bright, white smile as she looked past the camera. The woman looked to be in incredible shape. This was someone who worked out in her spare time. Perhaps even more than her spare time. Jeffrey could tell from her tight-fitting shirt that her muscles were toned. If he had to guess, she was a fighter of some kind.

The location below her photo said Miami, Florida. Lucky for her, an address wasn't listed. But Jeffrey had a feeling that wouldn't stop this man. He watched as the large, ogre of a man wrote the name Cara Brown on his sheet of paper. When he was finished, he backed out of the screen and Jeffrey caught the glimpse of the man's picture with a name underneath. Dominic Stone.

"Well, well. Mr. Dominic Stone," Jeffrey said. "Nice to finally catch your name."

He stepped back from the desk, not caring to watch any more. There was nothing to indicate how he was using his victims to stay alive. But he had a job to do. Death's curiosity would have to take a back seat to his main job.

Jeffrey passed through the hotel room door. He wasn't sure quite how he would lure Dominic Stone to his doom, but that didn't matter. He would wing it. Jeffrey wasn't big on making elaborate plans. He preferred the freedom to improvise. If something didn't work out later, he would find another way.

He had to concentrate to interact with the world of the living. Most spirits couldn't do it even if they tried as hard as they could. Some could harness a lot of energy to only move something small across the room like a pencil. However, Jeffrey had the ability to interact on a higher level. He could be seen if he wanted to. He could interact with the world of the living with relative ease. It still took a good amount of concentration, but he had perfected it over the years.

He raised his fist and gave a light rap on the door. But Jeffrey remained unseen. There was no need to spring the trap yet. The idea was to lure Dominic away from his room. Jeffrey waited for the door to open. The man stepped out of his room and looked down the hallway. Jeffrey allowed himself to be seen at the edge of a corner. He gave a quick look at Dominic from over his shoulder before walking out of the line of sight.

"Hey!" Dominic called out in his deep and gruff voice. Jeffrey imagined it was what a rhinoceros would sound like if it could talk. "Who the hell are you?" Heavy footfalls sounded through the hallway until they reached where Jeffrey stood, unseen. He watched as the ogre of a man turned the corner and stood, dumbfounded.

Jeffrey had to stifle a laugh. Not that his target could hear him had he done so. Like leading a mouse through a maze, Jeffrey appeared outside of the stairwell and coaxed Dominic further.

He seemed to be baited by the trap and advanced towards Jeffrey. Dominic called something out, but Jeffrey didn't hear. He stepped into the stairwell and vanished again. Then, he moved straight down the stairwell to the very bottom. As he heard the man enter the stairwell, he slammed the first-floor door.

"What?" Dominic panted as he descended the stairs. "That's not possible."

"Oh, but it is my dead friend," Jeffrey said to himself as he waited at the bottom of the stairs for his prey to arrive.

Dominic was large. Hefty was the proper term. He wasn't a fat man by any means, but nor was he in shape. He was built like a truck. If Jeffrey tried to stand eye to eye with the man, he would feel short. Both of his legs looked like tree trunks and his arms were like thick oak branches. This was not a man Jeffrey would have tangled with had he still been alive. There couldn't have been many people alive that could stand toe to toe with him and win.

Finally, Dominic made it to the bottom level and exited through the door. Jeffrey stayed one step ahead, appearing in front of the back-exit door which led to the alley. Once outside, he would be home free. It would be right across the road and into the cemetery. And if Jeffrey had timed it right, dusk would be falling.

He stepped through the door and saw that he was right. "Piece of cake," he muttered and vanished once again. Close behind him, the target burst through the door and looked for him. There seemed to be serious determination in the man's face. Jeffrey couldn't imagine why. He may have been aware of some sort of spirit world, but he didn't know anything about it. There was no way he knew about Death's hunters or what Jeffrey could even do. Still, he couldn't help wonder what the man was thinking.

Jeffrey appeared close to the road, but this time he decided to speak. He couldn't help himself. He needed to know what was going through his guy's mind.

"Ya must be wondering who I am?" Jeffrey said as he backed up towards the road.

"As a matter of fact," Dominic growled when he spoke. "I am. Who are you and what do you want with me? Why are you spying on me?"

"Spyin'? Well, I'm offended. I wasn't spyin' on ya. I was simply gathering information in a secretive manner." He paused and shrugged. "Okay, spyin'." Jeffrey let out a laugh and crossed the road towards the cemetery. He could hear the man give chase behind him. Exactly as planned.

The presence of the lost spirit was close. Jeffrey could feel it. The drifter would find them, no doubt. And when it did, the rhino-man would be done for. This job had turned out much easier than he thought it would be. Death had been worried over something so trivial.

"When I catch you, I'm going to choke the life from your body," the man grunted as he ran.

Jeffrey stopped and smiled. He turned to face his prey and stared at him. This was it. The drifter was close. They didn't need to run anymore. It had found them.

"Would y'all like to meet a friend of mine?" Jeffrey said. "Okay, well, it's not really a friend, but it will be a lot less friendly to you than me. I know that much."

A dark figure emerged from behind a nearby mausoleum and watched them for a moment. Jeffrey could tell Dominic was struggling to understand. To him, there was nothing there. Perhaps a wisp of shadow in the corner of his eye. Nothing more.

To Jeffrey, the spirit was the shape of a human but with contorted features. An elongated body, drooped mouth and eyes, and long spiny fingers. Not the sight you wanted to see before dying. And now, the drifter had its sights set on Jeffrey's target. There was nothing left to do but sit back and watch the show.

The drifter advanced towards Dominic with slow, but deliberate intentions. Jeffrey admired the creature. It looked like a lion stalking its prey. Any moment, the drifter would kill Dominic and then Jeffrey would reap the drifter. Then, he would reap Dominic's spirit. All in a day's work.

From the darkness, another figured emerged and watched the scene unfold. Jeffrey turned to look at the old man who was standing only a few feet from Dominic and the advancing drifter. Jeffrey felt bad for the old man. He was in the wrong place at the wrong time. The drifter would tear him apart once it was done with Dominic.

The man looked older than the dirt they were standing on. His cheeks sagged on either side of his face like grocery bags filled to their limit. He carried a small, brown cane to support his slender frame. Jeffrey was certain the man would fall apart in a light breeze.

Jeffrey noticed something strange about the man. There was something off about his eyes. They were completely black like the pupils had grown larger. Even more troubling than the blackened eyes was what they appeared to look at. The old man seemed to stare directly at the drifter, which should have been impossible.

"This is interesting," Jeffrey said, waiting to see what would happen. The old man's eyes flicked towards Jeffrey and stared for a moment. The old man could see him. Somehow, he had heard him, too. None of it was possible.

The old man's eyes darted back towards the drifter, and something started to happen. His features began to change before Jeffrey's eyes. The sagging skin around his mouth stretched out to form a beak-like mouth. The long, brown trench coat the man had been wearing flew up and became wide, leathery wings. His wrinkled skin turned smooth and black. The new creature stood there, towering over the drifter and Dominic.

Dominic reacted to the change like he could see the winged creature. Though, Jeffrey was sure he couldn't. The living couldn't see through the veil unless the spirit wanted to be seen. Even then, they had to possess a good amount of strength. But this winged beast was something Jeffrey had never seen before. There was no telling what it could do.

Before Jeffrey could react, the winged creature pounced on the drifter. Its claws clamped down and kept the drifter from escaping. The beak of the monster swung up and opened wide. Two talons from the end of the wings pierced the drifter and it began to turn into a fine mist. Not unlike when Jeffrey reaped a spirit with his knife.

Jeffrey stood frozen in shock. He had never seen anything like this before. Nor had he heard of such a creature. As far as he knew, only Death and her hunters could reap spirits. What he was seeing now was impossible. And yet, it was happening before his eyes. Jeffrey looked over at Dominic who stood watching the scene. Somehow, he could see the creature feast on the essence that was once the drifter and yet he remained still. Any living person who could see this would have run by now. It made Jeffrey wonder if Dominic wasn't a man at all.

"If you're still out there, whoever you are. I suggest you run. Once it's done, it will come for you." Jeffrey stumbled backwards, feeling fear for the first time in decades. The man stepped forward and the creature exhaled a large cloud of mist into Dominic's mouth. For a brief moment, there was a glow to Dominic's body. He was becoming more visible on the other side of the veil. Most of the living looked like shadowy blurs unless the spirit concentrated to view them normal. But Jeffrey could see Dominic clearer with less effort. It was like he was stepping on the other side of the veil. When the creature stopped feeding Dominic, the glow dissipated.

"I don't...that doesn't make any..." Jeffrey stammered as he watched the scene before him. But there wasn't time to finish his sentence. The crow-like creature had turned its sights on Jeffrey, letting out an ear-piercing screech that would have deafened the living. He wasn't about to let some freakish bird absorb his soul and steal his eternity away from him. Jeffrey turned and started to run.

Chapter 7

The beauty of having a car in the afterlife was the lack of laws of physics. It didn't need gas, nor did it need oil. Best of all, it didn't require a key to start. And right now, that was the most important thing of all. There was no time for Jeffrey to whip open the car door and shove a key in the ignition. The creature was close on his tail. If he didn't get behind the wheel and drive like a madman, he would surely be dead. Well, even more dead than he already was.

As Jeffrey ran from the cemetery and towards the back alley where his car awaited, he dared a glance back. The raven-like creature had taken flight. It screamed through the air like a heat seeking missile, Jeffrey being the target.

He continued to run and drew the knife from his belt. If he couldn't make it to the car, he would have to stand and fight. He felt the wings beating a few feet behind him. The creature was coming in for the strike. Jeffrey ducked and rolled, causing the creature to fly past. Jeffrey wasted no time leaping back up and lunging at the winged beast. He drove the knife straight into the creatures back. It only flung Jeffrey away like a person swatting at a fly.

Jeffrey landed on the ground and his knife fell only inches away from him. He stared at it as though it had betrayed him. Somehow, the blade had not reaped the creature. If it existed beyond the veil of the spirit world, his knife should have reaped it. Only Death was impervious to the blade. Nothing else. The only explanation he could think in the moment was that it wasn't a spirit at all but some sort of mythical creature. Though, most of those believed to exist by the living were merely misidentified spirits like vampires or the Chupacabra.

The creature turned and swooped towards Jeffrey once again. He dove out of the way and scooped up his knife. It was as useless as his fists against the monster, so he stashed it back in the sheath. His only option was to run. If he could escape the clutches of this odd bird, he might survive.

"What the devil are you?" Jeffrey yelled as he made a mad dash for his car. The creature screeched in return.

"Right, not sure what that means," Jeffrey yelled as he flung himself into the car. It accelerated instantly. Jeffrey wasted no time putting as much distance between him and the creature as he could. The bird-like creature seemed to have other plans. It continued the chase. Two large talons scraped across Jeffrey's hood as it made a pass.

"Oh, come on, now. Not the paint!" Jeffrey exclaimed with a nervous laugh.

He pressed the accelerator down to the floor and drove in any direction that took him away from the bird. Since he could pass through objects, people, buildings, and cars, he felt confident he would get away. Like his car, the creature could pass through solid objects too. Which meant it had to be a spirit of some kind.

"Of course, it can," Jeffrey said aloud and rolled his eyes.

Large talons scraped along the top of Jeffrey's car. He expected them to claw through any second. A giant wing smashed against the driver side, causing the car to slide out of control. There was no use trying to correct the slide. He wouldn't crash into anything. Though, Jeffrey was worried about giving the creature the opportunity it needed to bust in and grab him. He wasn't about to let that happen.

When the car finished sliding, Jeffrey jerked the shifter into gear and slammed on the gas pedal. The car tore down the street at an abnormal speed. The flying beast struggled to keep up. It managed to slam its body against the car before flying away with a screech of defeat. There was no chance Jeffrey would stop for another several miles. The more distance he put between himself and that monster, the better.

The encounter with the creature had left him afraid. The emotion was a foreign one for Jeffrey. Ever since becoming a hunter, he had never felt fear. None of the spirits he hunted could hurt him. And now one stood a good chance of reaping his spirit forever, leaving him in nothing but eternal darkness much like Jeffrey's shard did. His hands shook against the wheel.

When he was certain the creature would not pop up again, Jeffrey pulled his car over and parked. He stared out the windshield for several minutes. The whole scene played out in his head like a bad dream. None of it could have been possible. Somehow Dominic had seen through the veil and saw the creature. But since Dominic didn't seem to be aware of the drifter advancing towards him, Jeffrey knew that couldn't be right. Somehow, Dominic could see the beast. What was worse, they were working together. He needed to summon Death. If anyone would have answers, it would be her. A small part of him wanted to wait until he knew more.

The idea of going up against that *thing* without knowing anything about it filled Jeffrey with dread. In order to kill it, he needed to be informed. Jeffrey floated out of his car, stopping to see the damage. Where the creature's talons had clawed, marks could still be seen. Three large scratches crossed the hood and peeled metal frayed the roof. Like Jeffrey, any spiritual damage caused could be repaired within seconds. But it seemed this creature could cause permanent damage. Something he had never seen before.

"Death," Jeffrey said out loud, staring at his poor car. "If ya ain't too busy..." He let his words trail off. That would be enough to bring her to him.

Sure enough, she appeared behind him, ready to hear what he had to say. She didn't say hello or any sort of greeting. That was typical for her. Straight to the point. Jeffrey turned around to face her.

"I may have some questions for ya," Jeffrey said and pointed to his car. "What in the hell could do that to my car?"

Death stared at it for a moment. Jeffrey could almost see her mind calculating.

"No average spirit could do anything like this. Tell me everything."

Jeffrey did. He told her about the trap he set. He explained how the old man had shifted into a large bird-like creature. Jeffrey made sure not to gloss over the fact that his target could see the creature too. Of course, he couldn't forget the drifter the beast had reaped as well.

"Call me crazy, ma'am, but the only thing on this side of eternity that can reap souls is my knife and you. That right?"

Death stared at him for a moment without blinking. She looked like she had fallen into some sort of trance. If Jeffrey hadn't been used to her oddities by now, he would have thought something was wrong. Death didn't show emotion like the living or even the spirits who inhabited this realm. She could imitate facial expressions to be more inviting for new spirits. But true emotion was lost on her face. Especially with one of her hunters.

"A winged creature, was it?"

"Yes ma'am. Looked like this elderly gent, skin hanging off his face. He morphed into that thing, killed the drifter, then came after me. If it caught me, pretty sure I wouldn't be standing with y'all right now."

"This creature you speak of is dangerous. And it explains how this man has been able to harness spirits."

"Dominic Stone."

"What?"

"The man's name. Dominic Stone."

Death remained silent.

"Sorry, just sayin'."

"This spirit you came across today is an ancient being. I have not seen one in-"

"Hang on, miss," Jeffrey interrupted. "That thing was not a spirit. There's no way. I've never seen a spirit do the things it did. It killed a drifter without a knife. What kind of spirit can kill others? I thought that was impossible?"

"It is Jeffrey. For an average spirit. But this is no average spirit. What you described in an ancient spirit. I have not seen one in centuries. There are ancient stories from the living which call them Sluaghs. They are soul eaters."

"Soul eaters? Now that sounds bad."

"They prey on the sick and dying. Once the spirit exits the living body, the Sluagh consume it."

"Wait, so you're saying that this man might have one of these *slouch* things working for him? He kills the living, and it eats the soul? But how does that keep him alive?"

"It may be able to share the essence with another to grant them longer life."

Jeffrey leaned against his car. The logistics of it all made sense, but something felt off. Why would one of these ancient creatures help Dominic Stone? Who was he? What was in it for the Sluagh? Dominic had to have an angle. Jeffrey couldn't think of one plausible enough.

"Why does this thing share with Dominic? And how could he have discovered it in the first place?"

"As I said before, I have not seen one in centuries. It is possible this is the last of its kind left. Maybe they fed on each other when food supply was low. Maybe they went into hiding. My guess is Dominic met one the night he was supposed to die. As he slipped into this realm, the Sluagh was there waiting for him."

"Okay, so why not eat his spirit then and be done with it?"

"He must have made a deal with it. Spirits in exchange for his life back. A stronger life, in fact."

Jeffrey pushed off the car and looked at death like a light had just gone off in his head.

"Yes, that would make perfect sense. He's been killin' people and letting the bat-thing eat their spirit. Then it gives him a little essence to keep him alive. He's providin' an unlimited supply of food for the thing."

"I should not have to tell you, Jeffrey, that this upsets the balance. This is out of order and it needs to be put right."

"Can't you reap the damn thing?" Jeffrey asked, trying to keep from sounding worried. He did not want to go up against that thing again. But he didn't want Death to know that.

"Same rules apply here, I am afraid. I cannot reap an unwilling spirit. Even if it is a twisted demonic one. My hands are tied, Jeffrey. But yours are not."

"Yeah, alright, but how do I kill the damn thing? I stabbed it with my knife and nothin' happened."

"Only while it feeds and for a few seconds after can the Sluagh be reaped. The knife does not work because the Sluagh is so ancient and powerful. But with a fresh spirit inside of it, they themselves become fresher. Essentially, you are reaping the spirit trapped inside the Sluagh's body which sets off a chain reaction, killing the creature."

Jeffrey smiled.

"Lucky for me, he's got his next meal lined up."

Jeffrey made his way around the car and climbed into the driver seat. Death stood by the side of the road, watching him as he moved.

"Jeffrey," Death said as she leaned forward towards the passenger window. "He has to be stopped. The more the Sluagh shares with him, the stronger he will become. Soon, even I could not reap him if he asked me to."

If Jeffrey had still been among the living, this would have sent a shiver down his spine. The notion that someone could become stronger than Death worried him. He had no idea what that meant, and he was sure he didn't want to find out. Dominic Stone would die. Jeffrey would make sure of it. This Cara Brown was one of his next victims. And as the Sluagh fed on her, he would kill it. Then there would be nothing stopping him from killing Dominic.

Chapter 8

He was behind schedule now. Falling behind meant missing opportunities he couldn't afford to miss. It was an exhausting job. Hunting down as many loners as he could on social media took time. There could be no mistakes. If he picked too many sacrifices from the same area or someone with too many friends, he ran the risk of getting caught. Dominic had to be careful who he chose.

Social media had made it a lot easier to find his sacrifices. If more people had valued the cyber security, they would still be alive. Several didn't even have the common sense to block their home address. Not that it mattered much to Dominic. He tried to avoid making sacrifices in their own homes at all costs. A nosey neighbor would be all it took to get him caught.

Dominic did his best to make his sacrifices while they were out of town. Somewhere they weren't recognized. People were all too happy to share their exact location on social media. Even those smart enough to keep their home address off the site would still share their location. Like shooting fish in a barrel, if the fish had jumped out of the water and told the hunter exactly which barrel they were in.

It was easier killing someone on vacation. Like a mantis, Dominic would use his surroundings to blend in. With so many people coming and going in the large hotels, it was easier to go unnoticed. Though, not completely impossible given his size. He tended to turn a few heads. Sacrificing his target in the hotel was risky. If he was careful, it could be done. He rarely stayed in the same hotel. When he did, he used a fake name. Cameras were the real bane of his existence and much harder to avoid.

Right now, he had no choice but to find his sacrifice in the hotel. Because of the meddling from whoever it was that tried to lure him away, he was behind schedule. His target was already back at the hotel. No matter. He would make do.

Dominic returned to his room and prepared. He needed gloves to keep from leaving fingerprints. They were stuffed in his pocket along with a cloth to clean surfaces. If he put the gloves on before he entered the room, it was likely to get noticed. In the Florida heat, gloves were an oddity.

The man he was looking for was traveling alone. He thanked the power of social media for the information. There was so much someone could learn by browsing a stranger's profile. And with so many different accounts out there, it was easy to find everything. Dominic had almost turned it into an art.

He would browse Facebook to get their name. Anyone with a private profile would be skipped. Too difficult to learn anything from a secure page. Instead, he would find the unprotected pages and he would sift through the content. Photos, posts, hangout places, likes. Everything. He wanted to learn as much about them as he could. It would help narrow down who would miss them when they were gone, potential ambush places, and even how long it would take for someone to notice they were missing. He could even gauge people's habits by studying their social media feed.

Once he was confident he had learned everything there was to know, he would move to the others. Instagram was the second best. People shared their private lives with the world there. It was a cache cow of information. And Dominic took it all in.

Right now, his target was settling in for the night. He was probably surfing through the channels, trying to find something to watch. Little did he know, Dominic was exiting his room and heading for the elevator at that very moment. Within the hour, his target Mark would be dead. And all because he posted about his Orlando trip on social media. It was a funny world, though Dominic wasn't laughing.

He rode the elevator up a few floors and went over the plan in his mind. The last thing he wanted to do was draw a lot of attention to the room. So, he had to be quiet. Busting down the door and choking Mark to death would be a sure way to get caught.

Instead, Dominic approached the door and placed his palm flat against it. His newfound ability took much concentration. He had felt some sort of power growing in him since his first sacrifice. Each spirit the creature devoured and transferred to him, that power grew. His monstrous companion didn't talk, but it was able to convey message with pictures and symbols into Dominic's mind. It was like some form of telepathy.

Dominic had learned that the creature was something called a Sluagh. They were an ancient demonic-like spirits which preyed on the sick and dying. As they died, a Sluagh would appear to absorb the spirit and become stronger. Somehow, this creature was able to pass that power to Dominic. It's what kept Dominic alive, though his time had already past. A deal had been struck with the creature. In exchange for fresh souls for the Sluagh to feast on, it would keep him alive. Somehow, it was giving Dominic the ability to access his own spirit.

But it wasn't easy. He was still very weak. Only a handful of absorbed spirits gave him enough power to just barely breach through the veil. A hand or a finger, that was all. He knew he would be able to walk in the spirit world over time. For now, he could only do small things. Dominic was fine with this, however. Those small tricks allowed him to do things previously impossible.

His hand pressed against the door and the palm began to sweat. He focused all his energy on the task. Eventually, he could feel what he could only describe as a phantom limb reach out from his palm and pass through the door. With that phantom limb, he could pull the door handle and let himself in.

As the door swung open, Dominic stared at his hand like it might bite him. It was the first time he had successfully breached the veil. The power was intoxicating. There were so many applications for this ability. His imagination ran wild with possibilities.

To his surprise, the hotel room was empty. Dominic could smell the faint smell of cigarette smoke and knew just where he would find his sacrifice. A curtain was drawn across the balcony door, but the gentle rustling of a summer breeze gave it away. Mark was enjoying a late-night cigarette outside. When he came back inside, Dominic would ambush him.

He tucked himself into the corner obscured by the curtain and waited. Only a few minutes past before Mark decided to come back inside. This was it. This would be his last few moments alive.

Mark stepped inside the hotel room and closed the sliding glass door behind him. Without looking, he made his way towards the bed. Dominic lunged from behind the curtain and slapped his large hand around the man's mouth. Mark started to struggle for freedom, but Dominic was quick to subdue him. He wrapped his free arm tight around the man's upper body, locking his arms in place.

"Mark, I want you to know," Dominic said in a whisper. The man whimpered beneath his grasp. "I am sorry for what is about to happen. But it must happen."

Tears rolled down the man's cheeks as he mumbled something muffled by Dominic's hand. Begging for his life, no doubt. Dominic had heard it before. With each sacrifice, it became easier to ignore.

Dominic kept his hand gripped over Mark's mouth and shoved him on to the bed. Mark lay on his back with a look of terrified confusion in his eyes. Mark would never understand what was happening even if Dominic explained it to him. Dominic grabbed Mark's belt buckle and unfastened it. Mark began to kick and flail wildly.

"Shh, calm down. It's not what you think. I'm not going to rape you," Dominic said. "You will die with some dignity."

Mark kicked harder at this. Hearing he was about to die must have scared him. Dominic knew the feeling well. The idea of death was a frightening one. Knowing there was an afterlife did nothing to ease his mind. Not when things like the creature that enslaved him existed.

Dominic pulled the belt free and proceeded to wrap it around Mark's neck. The man kicked and punched and slapped, but it was no use against the brute on top of him. Dominic was built more like a grizzly bear than a human. He had yet to find an opponent that could give him a run for his money.

He pulled the belt tight around Mark's neck. It took only seconds for the man's face to turn bright red. His arms flailed around in search of some sort of rescue. One hand pressed against Dominic's face, trying to push him away. When that didn't work, Mark dug his nails into the man's cheek. But Dominic was unphased. Dominic kept the belt tight around Mark's neck with his right hand. With the left, he pressed down on Mark's chest to keep him from moving.

"I'm sorry I have to do this," Dominic said. The man's face was turning blue, and his eyes bulged like they would burst at any moment. Mark was seconds away from unconsciousness when his hand shot out and rammed a thumb into Dominic's eye socket. He yelped in pain, his grip loosening for just a moment. It was all the moment Mark needed to pull free. The belt around his neck loosened and he rolled over onto the floor. He coughed and sputtered as his body fought to suck in as much air as it could.

His victory was short lived. From behind, Dominic wrapped the belt around the man's neck again. This time, he pulled back with one arm and pushed Mark down with his foot. There would be no escaping again. Below, Mark gagged and scratched at the carpet. It took less than a minute for Mark's body to fall limp. Dominic held on for a little longer, ensuring his sacrifice was complete.

Dominic took a step back and rested on the bed. He knew there was another gruesome scene happening around him at this very moment. The man's sprit would have finally left the body and the Sluagh would have swooped in to feast on its essence. Within a few minutes, the Sluagh would appear before him and offer up his portion of the life-giving mist.

He was grateful for the extension on his life. Still, he could not stop the empathy rising up inside after every sacrifice. It wasn't his intention to force others to their doom. Dominic wanted what most people wanted. A long life. This was the only way to get it.

Just when his mind started to wander to the day he had met the Sluagh, it appeared before him. It still held the revolting bird-like appearance. Dominic couldn't help but feel uncomfortable around it. Though the creature was providing him long life and power beyond his comprehension, he still feared the creature. Its grotesque wings wrapped around Dominic and the beak opened wide. Dominic hated this part.

A mist poured from the creatures gaping maw and Dominic pushed his head forward to inhale as much as he could. He was always aware that his head was inside the Sluagh's beak. If it wanted, it could crush his neck like a toothpick. But it hadn't so far. The truth was, the Sluagh didn't *need* Dominic. It could continue to hunt and feast on the sick and the dying. But with Dominic's help, it no longer needed to hunt. Better still, it got to eat fresh and healthy spirits. But Dominic wasn't stupid. The creature wouldn't need him forever. There would come a day when it would turn on him.

The more essence he absorbed, the more powerful he felt. Eventually, the Sluagh would be unable to harm him. At least, that's what Dominic assumed. The power growing in him felt strange and strong. Somehow, he could tell it meant great things for himself.

When the Sluagh was finished, it vanished into a plume of black smoke. Dominic looked down at the body by his feet. The poor man had suffered. Twice as a matter of fact. Dominic couldn't imagine the terror of dying, only to have something kill you again. And the second death was permanent, from what he understood. There was no afterlife for those eaten by the Sluagh. Fear coursed through his veins at the thought of this.

Dominic leaned down and looked at the bloated face of his victim. "I'm sorry I had to do this to you," he said as he went to work staging the scene to look like a suicide.

"You just don't understand," Dominic continued as he hoisted the lifeless body up on the bed. "Ever since I was little, I've had this fear of dying. The concept would hit me out of nowhere. I would die one day. There was no telling when and no telling how." Dominic sat on the bed next to the body.

"Everyone dies. I get that. But not knowing what was on the other side would drive me crazy. Were these religions right? Was there a heaven and a hell? Do our souls continue on after we die? And let's just say I were to die of old age. I make it to the age of ninety-seven. Will I spend every waking moment of my life worried that today would be the final day of my life? You see, it isn't the concept of death that scares me. It's the action. The dying part scares me."

Dominic took one end of the belt and tied it to the headboard, making sure to keep it around the body's neck. With a slight shove, the body slipped off the bed and down to the floor. It completed the illusion that the man had strangled himself to death.

"I know what you're thinking. I'm obviously aware of an afterlife now that I've seen a ghost or two. And you're right. I am aware it exists, but that doesn't answer the question of what that afterlife is. If creatures like this Sluagh thing exist there, do I really want to walk this Earth for eternity? And what's worse, what if there really is a heaven and a hell and I'm due eternal damnation. Or what if the afterlife is simply a purgatory. Nothing but darkness forever. Alone. I don't think I can handle that."

He stared down at the bulged face of his victim. In the face of so much death, he would have thought he'd be used to it by now. Each kill still left him feeling strange. There was no more regret. He was well past that. But he felt something he couldn't quite explain.

"I'll leave you with this final thought, Mark, but then I have to go," he said to the corpse like it was listening. "I know this world. I know this life. I want to stay in it for as long as I can. I want to see the accomplishments of man. See where we go in the next fifty years. Do we make it to Mars? Do we colonize the moon? Is a cure for cancer ever found? There's so much I don't know about this world and a lot of it I haven't seen. I just want time, Mark. Don't you see? There's not enough time in this life and that isn't fair. I just want more time."

Dominic made sure to wipe down anything he touched before leaving the room. He had come this far and he wasn't about to make a mistake now. Everything was coming together and there wasn't a single person that could get in his way. Time was always ticking away. In order to beat the clock, he had to keep moving. With a last push from his phantom hand, Dominic locked the door from in the hotel hallway. The final touch needed to sell the man's suicide within.

Chapter 9

Her pulse pounded and her breathing had become labored, but she had to carry on. Sweat dripped down her face. Her legs felt like jelly. She had been running for what seemed like hours, but she couldn't stop now. She picked a spot on the horizon and focused on it. The early morning sun had yet to peak above the horizon, but she could still make out the bobbing buoy in the water. If she kept her gazed fixed on it, she knew she could keep running.

Cara finally had enough. She pressed the off button on the treadmill and coasted to a stop. Her legs burned from the exercise. It was a good sort of burn. A good after workout burn always made her feel good. She took great pride in her physical appearance and strength. That was why she had a fitness room in her high-rise, Miami apartment. The view was incredible. Nothing like getting an early morning job on the treadmill and watching the sun rise over the ocean.

She grabbed the towel from the treadmill and wiped the sweat from her face. The nice part about exercising inside was beating the Florida heat. Even though the sun had yet to rise, the humidity and temperature were already rising. Cara was thankful for air conditioning.

Cara tossed the towel in the hamper by the door and grabbed her water bottle. Plopping down on the couch, she settled down with some Netflix before work. Relaxing in front of the TV always felt better after a good workout. She knew she deserved it. Keeping fit was no easy task and she worked hard at it.

She thought about getting back up to change out of her exercise shorts and running shirt. In a couple hours, she would need to get ready to leave anyway. But the couch had already started to feel too comfortable, so she decided against it. Besides, she didn't care what she looked like. Her hair was probably a mess from being pulled back while she ran. Her shirt had a sweat stain across the chest. And her running shorts, well that she liked. She had always thought she had nice legs. Showing them off was something she enjoyed. Still, there was time to get ready before she had to go.

A documentary about unsolved murders played on the television and she didn't bother to stop it. If Netflix wanted to start playing something, she would let it. Besides, she was a sucker for the unexplained mystery stuff. Most people she met figured she was into sports given her toned physique. Though she was athletic, sports weren't her thing. A good true crime documentary was better any day of the week.

The show was captivating. After a while, Cara felt herself sucked in by the story. She had become so transfixed on the program that the world around her seemed to disappear. It was obvious how the episode would end. These were unsolved mysteries after all. There would be no answers and that would drive her crazy. She did enjoy coming up with her own theories as to what happened afterwards.

A noise broke her from the television's hypnotic grasp. Something had fallen to the floor in her bedroom. Without breaking her line of sight with the bedroom door, Cara paused the show. Most people would begin to panic when strange noises startled them at home alone. Cara kept her cool. Panic did nothing but cause mistakes. Those she couldn't afford to make.

She rose from the couch and stood for a moment. Cara listened for any little noise coming from the bedroom. Anything. The slight creaking of floorboards would be enough. But she heard nothing else. Still, she had to be sure. Cara crept silently across the floor and approached the bedroom door. She listened for a moment before pushing it open.

Her bedroom was as it always was. An unmade, queen-sized bed sat in the center of the room. A small writing desk sat on the opposite wall under a window overlooking the ocean. The curtains were drawn back, offering a great view. Her dresser sat across from the bed with a small, LED television on top. Nothing seemed out of the ordinary. Of course, an intruder could be hiding in her walk-in closet, so she decided to check.

The closet was clear. No one in the room at all. She could only wonder at what had made the noise. When she turned to leave, she noticed the remote on the bedroom floor next to the bed. Its place was on the nightstand. Somehow, it had fallen off.

"Well, that doesn't make a lot of sense," she said to herself as she walked over to pick it back up. The fall had caused the battery compartment to pop open. One of the batteries was missing, no doubt having rolled under the bed. Cara got on her knees and bent down to look. There it sat a few feet away. She reached for the battery and scooped it up. As she did, another sound made her jump. She hit her head on the bed frame and cursed.

The show had continued playing on its own. She stood up and stared through the bedroom door, expecting someone to walk in on her. Nothing happened. The show continued to play. Cara put the battery back in the remote and tossed it on her bed.

"Okay, first a remote jumps off my nightstand and now Netflix is unpausing itself," she laughed.

Cara walked into the living room and pressed pause on the remote. "At least everything is malfunctioning at the same time. Oh, so wonderful." She rolled her eyes.

The sound of a light wind caught her ears and she turned to face it. The sound came from the hallway towards the laundry room. She couldn't think of a reasonable explanation for the sound. Her brain tried to come up with any sort of logic that wasn't an intruder. Whoever had entered her home would soon regret it.

Cara made her way back into her room and pulled open the nightstand drawer. A small safe was tucked away inside. She pressed her thumb to the screen and the lid unlocked. Seconds later, Cara had racked the slide of her forty caliber Smith and Wesson handgun. It was aptly named the Shield and Cara swore by the brand. If there was an intruder in her house, she would not be a victim. Her training wouldn't allow that.

With the handgun tucked close to her body just below her right breast, Cara stepped back into the living room. Keeping the gun closer to her body meant less chances for an intruder to disarm her. It drove her nuts seeing people in movies walk through dark buildings with the gun stretched out in front of them. Not at all how a trained professional used a firearm.

There was no sound coming from the laundry room now, but that didn't stop Cara from checking it first. If someone was hiding in there, she would give them the scare of their life. She stepped forward into the hallway and approached the door with caution. Her left hand gripped the doorknob and gave it a quick twist. The latch pulled free from the frame and Cara let go of the knob. She kicked the door open with her foot and peered in from the hallway. It seemed empty, but she flicked on the light to make sure.

No one was there. Her laundry room was the smallest place in her condo. Not much space for a person to hide. It was a plain white room with a washer and dryer in the corner. There were a few cabinets above. None were big enough for a person to hide inside of. The water heater stood in the opposite corner. If someone was here, she would see them.

The sound she had heard could have been the water heater. It was possible it had let off a hiss of some sort. She made a mental note to get it inspected before something went wrong. Just another malfunction around the house at the same time. What else could happen? Right on cue, the living room lights flickered. It was like someone had unscrewed the bulb only a little. It flickered off and then right back on.

"Okay, what the hell is going on?" she said out loud, lowering the gun to her side. A noise on the outside balcony caught her attention. She brought the gun back up to her torso and inched towards the sliding glass door. A chair on the balcony had slid across the concrete, creating a loud scraping noise. It could have been the wind pushing a chair. They got some strong winds off the beach sometimes that would push the furniture around slightly. With all the weird things happening, she wasn't taking that chance.

Cara pushed the curtain aside and peered out on the balcony. There was no one there. Her mind told her again that it had been the wind. The lights flickering could have been a minor surge on the power grid. The whoosh in the laundry room may have been the water heater. And Netflix unpausing could have been a program glitch. But the remote falling off the nightstand had no rational explanation that she could think of.

"Maybe I'm just jumpy from the unsolved show?" she asked herself. Though, Cara knew she didn't frighten easy.

Cara walked away from the curtain and headed back towards the couch. She decided she was being too jumpy and would ignore the little sounds around the condo. They weren't worth getting worked up over. Just in case, she pushed the handgun into the cushion next to her.

Settling in, Cara pressed play on the show and continued watching. After a few minutes, a glass shattered in the kitchen behind her. Cara pulled the gun from its hiding place and spun around in one quick movement. There was no one in the kitchen, but she could see the shattered remains of drinkware on the floor. Something had knocked it over and it couldn't have been a draft.

"Alright, who the hell is here?" she said aloud. "Quit messing around if you don't want to get shot. I don't know how you're-"

The television behind her turned off and she spun to face it. When she heard footsteps in the hallway behind her, she spun and pointed her firearm. There was no one there. "Okay, what the actual fuck?" she said with a tremble in her voice. There had to be someone here. Nothing else could explain it. She would have seen an intruder, though.

Cara went room by room, checking her entire condo. There was no one there. She tried to think of a logical reason the glass would fall off the shelf and couldn't. The ridiculous thought of a cockroach knocking the glass over crossed her mind before waving it on.

"Maybe someone slammed a door really hard downstairs?" she asked herself. It was flimsy at best, but it was all she had.

"Cara," a voice whispered beside her. She jumped and spun around to find nothing there. Her eyes glanced around the room, looking for any possible source of the voice. Not since Cara was a little girl had she believed in ghosts. And even then, she had been led to believe that any experience that seemed paranormal had been nothing more than a figment of her imagination. Now, she was starting to wonder about their existence again.

As her eyes fell on the cable box, she yelled out "Shit!" all but forgetting the ghost encounter. "I'm gonna be late for work."

Cara raced into her bedroom and changed out of the sweat stained workout clothes. She did so in record time. Seconds later, she emerged in a new pair of jeans and a black, tight-fitting shirt. Her hair was still pulled back but there was no changing it now. She had to go. Cara slipped the gun into her waistband. Grabbing her keys, she headed out the door. It could have been her imagination, but she swore she heard laughing as her front door swung shut.

Chapter 10

Jeffrey laughed as he made himself at home. The luxury of the living room was lost on him, but he dropped down on the couch and put his feet up on the coffee table. The television across from him showed the pause menu to some unsolved mysteries show on something called Netflix. He stared at the thin television and the strange looking remote resting on the couch and wondered just how much had changed since he died.

The world of the living was rapidly changing. Most spirits didn't notice or never took the time to care. Jeffrey among them. Both planes of existence were different from each other. Jeffrey only noticed the difference when he materialized into the world of the living so he could be seen. Their plane was crisper and clearer than his. Like they were viewing the world behind a clear sheet of glass. But in Jeffrey's world, everything was more muted with grey coloring. Like streaks on a window. It was something he hardly ever noticed, but it was there.

"So, this is y'all's place Ms. Cara Brown?" he said, craning his neck to look around. It was neatly decorated, and everything seemed put away in a tidy place.

"Lady might be a clean freak."

Jeffrey looked around the condo for a good place to wait while Dominic and the Sluagh did their business. He would have to ambush them once the Sluagh started to feed. Death might be unhappy with the results, but this was the only way. She said so herself. It could only be reaped while it fed and for a few seconds after. There would be no other opportunity to kill it.

Letting the woman die didn't bother him so much. The living and their mortal problems didn't register on his radar. But letting her soul be swallowed by the beast was tough. Ultimately, he had no choice. He couldn't let Dominic obtain any more spirits than he already had.

"Suppose I could lure it to another spirit to reap," he thought out loud. "That might take time to set up. Time I ain't got."

He shook his head. Cara was his next victim. Luring Dominic to some lost spirit wouldn't be so easy this time. The man might not fall for that trick twice. Besides, Jeffrey had the upper hand now. Dominic couldn't know that

Jeffrey would be here waiting for him. The Sluagh would feed on Cara and he would put it down. Her sacrifice wouldn't be in vain.

An eternity of nothingness. That would be her fate. At least there was solace in the fact that her spirit would not know pain or suffering once it was over. Sure, she would cease to exist. But she wouldn't know she no longer existed, so less harm done. Jeffrey knew this was only a justification for his future actions, but he didn't care. This was the way it had to be.

The thought of no longer existing crossed his mind. The idea sent a panic through his spiritual body. He had just spent time telling himself it wouldn't be so bad, and yet the idea scared him. Jeffrey enjoyed his afterlife. No longer existing was a scary concept. Everything would be gone. Nothing left. And worse, his spirit would help power up some damned sack of skin and organs to stay alive for a few decades longer. What a shameful death it would be.

Chapter 11

The events of the early morning were almost forgotten by Cara now. Her mind was focused on her job. Without a clear mind, people could get hurt or worse. She always had to have her wits about her. The life of a professional bodyguard was not an easy one.

As a woman, it came with its own struggles. Many people assumed she could not provide proper protection because of her gender. Of course, this was far from the truth. Most people pictured a large, burly man when they thought of personal protection. However, the better a bodyguard could blend in, the better. Movies may have portrayed most in her line of work as muscular men in flashy suits. That only served to make for a better target.

Cara could blend in well. While providing protection for a family, she could pass as a caregiver or a nanny. Her plain clothes did not betray her as a well-trained fighter or armed guard. All of this meant less attention, which is exactly what a personal guard would want.

Now, Cara was standing in a hotel suite ready to move. The room was one of the fanciest hotels in Miami. Her entire condo could fit inside the single hotel suite with room to spare. Truly a palace on the go for the ultra-rich. Cara didn't see the fancy chandeliers and marble flooring. Her mind was focused on her job. She saw windows and doors as potential entryways and ambush spots. Ornate decorations became usable weapons for an assailant.

A young woman poked her head out of one of the bedrooms before pulling a suitcase through the doorway. She dragged it behind, letting the floor leave scuff marks on the bag. No more than sixteen, she was in her rebellious stage. With a father as rich as hers, it was no wonder she cared little for keeping things nice.

The teen flopped down in a chair and pulled her phone from her pocket. While Cara waited by the door, she spotted the teen opening a social media app and press record. Cara rolled her eyes and approached the girl as quick as possible.

"Let me see that," she said, snatching the phone.

"Hey!" the teen yelled.

"You can't post anything about where we are or where we're moving to. Your father is paying me to protect and that's what I'm going to do."

"I wasn't gonna post-"

"Oh really, you weren't about to post something to Tik Tok?" Cara smiled.

"I mean, yeah, but not about where I am or where we're going. I'm not stupid."

Cara laughed.

"Honey, your shirt says Miami Beach right on it. I think they'd figure out where you are."

"Okay, but not the exact place, right? It's not like I said the name of the hotel or anything."

"You know I follow you on Tik Tok, right Amanda? You've said the name of the hotel like twice in the last twenty-four hours."

"Oh."

"Yeah, oh." Cara laughed and tossed Amanda back her phone.

"Don't beat yourself up over it, kid. You're just down here enjoying the sights while your father works. I've seen plenty of tycoons wanting to hire protection for their families who don't need it. Money can make people paranoid."

Amanda nodded.

"I told him we didn't need a stupid bodyguard for the weekend."

Her eyes went wide when she realized what she had said.

"I didn't mean it like that. You're not stupid. You're awesome. I mean, seriously. You're kind of a badass, you know? Like-"

Cara let out a laugh and leaned against the table next to Amanda.

"Don't worry about it. No offense taken. I get your meaning."

"Thank God," Amanda said as she scrolled through more videos on her phone.

They would be leaving soon to meet Amanda's father at the airport. The whole process couldn't be more routine. Though, Cara hated getting into habits and routines while working. It was the best way to let her guard down and something go wrong. Despite that, she couldn't help but agree with Amanda. She didn't need a bodyguard to move her from the hotel to the airport. Her father had seen one too many movies. Because he was rich, he assumed there would be swarms of gang members chasing after his daughter for ransom money. While those things did happen, they were less common with someone of his standing. He was rich, sure. But the real threat was power. Amanda's father seemed to be nothing more than a businessman.

"Hey, Cara, can I ask you something random?" Amanda asked, breaking through Cara's thoughts.

"Uh, yeah, sure. What's up?"

"Do you believe in ghosts?"

Cara almost fell to the floor. The memories of the morning came flooding back. She couldn't help but think how odd of a coincidence it was. Chills ran down her arms and the back of her neck. Little hairs stood on end as she suppressed a quiver.

"No. Not for a long time." She finally stammered.

"What does that mean?"

"Oh, you know, when I was a kid I believed in that sort of thing." A memory of a closet and a dark night flashed through her mind before evaporating. Something she couldn't quite remember.

"And you don't believe in them anymore?" Amanda asked.

"Why do you ask?"

Amanda shrugged and pointed to her phone.

"Because of this person I follow on Tik Tok. She does a lot of paranormal investigation videos and stuff. She's pretty honest about what she finds."

"Oh."

Cara felt a surge of relief. Amanda was only looking to make conversation. It was nothing more than a coincidence. With the events of this morning, she could only feel relieved.

"We need to get moving," Cara instructed. She wanted to make sure this conversation did not continue.

Amanda stood from the table and slipped her phone back in her pocket. Cara approached the windows and scanned the street below. She had just finished telling Amanda there was no need to be paranoid. Even though she believed there was nothing to worry about, she was still a professional. She would treat this job like any other. Not cut corners.

"Street clear. We move to the elevator. Stay behind me and do exactly as I say at all times, understood?"

Amanda didn't say a word. She only nodded. Cara could tell she was scaring the girl, but it didn't matter. This was her job. And it could potentially save Amanda's life. It would most likely turn out to be the least exciting job of her career but better safe than sorry.

They moved down the hallway as a pair. Amanda trailed less than a foot behind Cara. She walked with a nervous gait, her luggage dragging behind her. Cara could have been a model on the runway. She walked with comfort and purpose. Her confidence radiated.

As Cara had predicted, there was no incident from the hallway to the elevator. The pair rode in silence as it descended to the first floor. An odd feeling of being trapped inside the small box like a prison washed over Cara. It was not a position she ever wanted to find herself in. Once the doors opened, the pair stepped out and headed towards the concierge desk. Amanda checked out as Cara scanned the lobby. No threats here. All exits were covered. She was confident everything would continue to go smooth.

When Amanda was finished checking out, she fell back in line with Cara as they marched towards the front door. Their car sat out front in the valet spot. A four door, grey sedan. The perfect mundane car to blend in with the rest of traffic. Of course, her windows were a little darker than most others to keep from being seen.

Cara stepped into the revolving doors first. Amanda stepped into the same section, keeping close. There wasn't much room, but they wouldn't be here long. Cara would prefer her to stick close, no matter the discomfort.

They stepped into the morning air. Cara took in a lung full. It was crisp and clean. She could taste the salt in the air from the beach just behind the hotel. Living on the beach was her favorite thing about Miami. How anyone could live in a city not on the beach was beyond her.

Before they could reach the car a few feet from the exit, Cara noticed something was wrong. A man was approaching from the right at a quick pace. She spotted him from her peripheral vision. He wore a black hoodie and a determined look on his face. This was certainly trouble.

Cara reacted before Amanda knew what was happening. The man in the hoodie lunged forward. A hand sprung out from his pocket revealing a knife. Whether his intention was to grab Amanda or hurt her didn't matter to Cara. She gripped the man by the wrist and gave a firm twist. The knife pointed away from Amanda and back at the assailant. With a clean sweep of her leg, she kicked the man's legs out from under him. The top half of his body swung back like a pendulum and his legs flew straight up into the air. He landed with a loud thud on the concrete below. Several people in the area gasped.

The whole scene lasted less than a second. Cara had already secured the knife and pressed a knee into the man's sternum. She had drawn her sidearm in the same moment she had leapt on top of the attacker. Her eyes darted back and forth, looking for other attackers. Amanda stood with her eyes wide open, mouth agape. A classic pose of someone frozen in fear and shock.

Without missing a beat, Cara pulled a zip tie from her back pocket and twisted it around the man's wrists. He struggled to get free, but she pressed down harder. She shouted at a nearby valet to call the police.

"What the fucking hell was that?" Amanda cried out. Her shock finally breaking.

"Get in the car, now," Cara demanded.

Amanda did as she was told. She climbed into the passenger seat and locked the door. Cara would have to stay until the police arrived. As long as Amanda was secure in the car, she would remain safe. And since the attacker seemed to be alone, there was nothing more to worry about.

"This was supposed to be an easy job, asshole. Killing that young girl really couldn't have been worth prison, could it?"

"I ain't talking to a lady, pig," the man spit.

"Yeah, not a cop. And the lady part really isn't as offensive as you think it is. But it's fine. The police will be here soon. You can talk to them all you want."

Cara was beyond frustrated. When the police arrived, there were going to be all sorts of questions. A simple transport job had become much more involved. They should have been at the airport by now and the job over. She rolled her eyes. This was going to be a long day.

Chapter 12

Jeffrey had waited around all day for something to happen. It wasn't until after the sun had gone down he heard footsteps in the hall outside the condo. They were heavy thuds unlike something Cara's smaller frame could produce. He recognized the footfalls as Dominic's. He was here and ready to hunt his prey. Jeffrey stepped out of sight in case the Sluagh had come with him. Though, he guessed it would only show up once Cara was dead or dying.

The front door creaked open. Jeffrey peaked out of the doorway to Cara's bedroom to see if the man was alone. He was. Jeffrey stepped from the doorway and gazed at the brute. Something about him seemed different now. The blurry haze which most of the living shared seemed less prominent. Somehow, Dominic had become clearer to Jeffrey. He didn't have to concentrate as hard to see him in full detail. That could only mean one thing. He was close to stepping through the veil and being able to see the spirit world. Death had warned him of this. It would bring nothing but disaster.

Dominic searched the condo, looking for his victim. When he realized she wasn't home, Dominic looked for a place to hide. Jeffrey wished he could kill the man here and now. If he could lure the man to the balcony, Jeffrey could conjure enough energy to give him a nice shove over the railing. He gave it some thought before realizing he needed to ambush the Sluagh too. If he tried to kill Dominic now and it failed, he'd miss his chance to reap the Sluagh later. He had to choose one or the other. Reaping the winged creature and then killing Dominic was the better option.

As Jeffrey waited for Cara to come home and the show to start, he wondered what would happen if she got the upper hand and killed Dominic. She did have a gun, after all. Dominic was still a mortal and weapons could still kill him. If Cara could get a shot off and kill the man, his work would be a lot easier. Jeffrey wondered if he should have spent his time warning Cara to the danger coming rather than messing with her like he had. He knew there was nothing he could have done that wouldn't have caused her to run away screaming. If he wrote a ghostly message on the mirror or appeared before her like an apparition, she would have bolted.

Dominic wandered down the hallway and hid in a small room. Given his size, he wondered how the man could fit through the doorway. And how was he planning to sneak up on Cara? His footfalls weren't exactly silent. That wasn't Jeffrey's problem and he decided to stay focused on his part of the plan.

Jeffrey went into the bedroom and sat on the bed. He put his feet up and waited for the show to begin. Soon, things would turn violent. As he waited, he thought of ways to tip off Cara to the intruder in her home. Maybe once she came in through the door, he could make some sort of noise to put her on edge. He couldn't stop thinking about how a single bullet could do his work for him. Then he would be waiting there for Dominic's spirit and reap the son of a bitch.

It was decided. Jeffrey would wait for Cara to come home. Then he would make his way to Dominic's hiding spot and do his best to give him away. If Dominic never got the chance to kill Cara, maybe the Sluagh would never show. Or maybe it would show and kill Dominic. There was no telling for sure. The best Jeffrey could do now was try to interfere. She would either kill Dominic and make his job easier or she would die and the plan would continue. As long as Dominic ended up dead and reaped.

The front doorknob started to shift. Jeffrey peeked out of the doorway and caught the sight of something in the corner of his eye. There was a dark shadow on the outside balcony. Jeffrey looked at the figure while the front door opened with a creak. It was then Jeffrey realized the dark figure was that of the old man he had seen in the cemetery before. His skin sagged from his bones and he gave Jeffrey a grin.

"Shit," Jeffrey said, pulling his knife from its sheath. The Sluagh was already here and it had seen him. It wasn't going to just lay down its life. Jeffrey had a fight ahead of him.

Chapter 13

The condo was just as she had left it. The events of the day still whirled around in her mind like a merry-go-round. She had all but forgotten about the strange events of this morning. They were overshadowed by the man who had tried to stab the teenager she had been paid to protect. As it had turned out, the man was someone her father had screwed over in a business deal. He had lost everything. His house, his wife, and all his money. He blamed Amanda's father and snapped. People were strange and terrible creatures sometimes.

Cara tossed her keys on the dining room table and plopped herself down on the couch. Netflix still cycled through ads for their different shows. She had left in such a rush earlier that she had forgotten to turn off the TV. She clicked enter on the remote and her continue watching list popped up on screen. Unsolved Mysteries. She thought about finishing the episode before deciding on The Office. She needed a peaceful show to destress from her day.

The show started up with the familiar intro theme and Cara started to relax. None of the day's events drifted through her mind as she watched Jim pull another childish prank on Dwight. Her eye lids started to grow heavy as the show she had seen at least three times through continued to play. There was a good chance she would be sleeping on the couch tonight. Getting up and walking to the bedroom seemed like too much trouble.

A noise broke her from the hypnotic state. Her eye lids shot open. It sounded like the shower curtain in her bathroom. She stared at the TV wondering if the sound had been real or imaginary.

The noise echoed through the condo again. No doubting its authenticity this time. Something was moving the curtain in the bathroom. A logical voice inside her head told her it was just the air vent blowing the curtain aside. Since she had never heard it happen before, that explanation didn't make much sense. Besides, her air vents couldn't have pumped out air fast enough to cause the curtain to move much.

"Please let it be a *fucking* rat," she whispered as she stood from the couch. A rat would not be a welcome sight in her home. Nor had she ever seen one. Compared to the alternative to an intruder, she would gladly take the rat.

Cara removed her firearm from her waistband. If there was someone creeping around in her condo, they were in for a hell of surprise. She wasn't about to be some helpless victim plastered all over the news tomorrow morning.

Like before, Cara held the gun tight against her body. She advanced down the hallway with caution. If someone was there, she didn't want to make a lot of noise and alert them to her presence. If Cara could catch the intruder by surprise, she would have the advantage.

Just before she reached the bathroom door, her worst fear came to life. A man burst free from the bathroom and lunged at her. Cara had no time to get her finger on the trigger before he had slammed her to the floor. The gun was knocked free and slid down the hallway towards the living room.

A large fist rammed into her stomach. An involuntary cough burst from her throat. Before she could recover, another large hand gripped around her throat. Panic set in as she tried to gulp for air. Her temples throbbed and pulsed to the increased rhythm of her heartbeat. In less than a minute, she would be unconscious.

In a desperate attempt to get free, Cara struck the man square in the nose with one clean jab. His head cocked back for a second, but he didn't let go of her neck. Cara didn't let up. She swung with her other arm. This time, she hooked his nose from the left. He still didn't let go, but his grip loosened for a second. It was the opening she needed.

Cara twisted sideways and gripped the man's arm, giving a heft yank. He toppled forward towards the floor. She wasted no time rolling out of the way and jumping to her feet. Instead of running towards the handgun across the room, knowing the man would make a grab for her feet, she delivered a kick to the man's side. When he recoiled in pain, she kicked again. She wanted to hear the sound of ribs cracking before she turned for the gun.

She went for another kick, but the man anticipated her move and grabbed her foot. Cara felt her body lift from the ground and fall backward. Air rushed from her lungs as her back connected with the floor. She panted hard, trying to catch her breath. It would all be over in a matter of seconds if the man pinned her down now.

Instead of trying to catch her breath, Cara lunged away and out of the grasp of the assailant. The movement burned her lungs as she fought to breathe and move. She heard him grunt in frustration as her foot missed his grasp by inches. Climbing to her feet, she ignored the white-hot pain in her chest and pushed herself towards the living room.

Cara gasped for air as she ran towards the gun. It felt like her lungs would explode any second. There was no time to catch her breath. She needed her handgun. It lay there next to the couch only a few feet in front of Cara. She could hear the man standing up behind her. It was now or never. She dove for the gun and felt the familiar polymer grip in her hand. Before she could swing around and aim, she was picked up off the floor and tossed across the room.

Her body smashed against the television, and she collapsed to the floor. The shattered television landed on top of her. To her surprise, she still held a firm grip on the gun. Cara coughed under the debris and prepared for another attack. He flipped the flat screen from her body and tossed it aside. His eyes bulged in their sockets when he spotted the muzzle pointed at his chest.

Cara wasted no time squeezing the trigger twice. Both rounds buried in the man's chest. He stumbled backward as two pinpoints of blood appeared on his shirt. His body fell to the floor. Cara could have sworn the condo shook like it had been hit with an earthquake. She panted hard and caught her breath before standing. She would need to contact the police. But there was time to catch her breath.

She looked at the man's body sprawled out on her living room floor. He was a beast of a man. Cara was confident in her abilities as a fighter, but it surprised her one punch had not knocked her out. The fact that she was still alive had been due in part to her skills and part miracle. If it had not been for the handgun, she would surely have died.

"Someone will have heard those shots," she said. "I should probably call the pol-"

The man's chest began to heave like he had taken in a huge breath. Cara stumbled backwards in surprise, almost tripping to the floor. The two bloody marks on his chest sat just over the heart. It was impossible to survive a shot like that.

He started to stir and sat up. His eyes seemed glossy for a moment until life sprang back into them. He shook his head and stared at Cara like a grizzly ready to attack. Every ounce of training and reflex flew from her body. Nothing had prepared her for the dead to rise again.

"Looks like my spirit is strong enough to keep my mortal form alive," the man said. A smirk crossed his face. Cara, oblivious to what he meant, raised the gun once again.

"Don't come closer," she warned. The barrel shook in her hands, betraying her.

"I think you tried that already. Didn't work."

"I'll empty the mag into your skull."

"You're welcome to try."

A shiver flew down her spine and a cold chill passed her body. It felt like a small breeze had fluttered by. A picture fell off the wall and shattered on the ground to her left. Cara jumped.

'What the fuck is going on here," she yelled.

The man took one large step forward and stopped.

"I think my companion is here. Don't worry. You'll meet him soon enough."

He readied to lunge forward when things all around the condo began to move and break. Cara's eyes darted around the space, watching everything topple over by themselves. It looked like an invisible fight was happening all around her. Chairs were knocked over, items on the counter flew to the ground, and a crack appeared in the wall.

"What the hell is happening?" the man grumbled.

The figure of a man appeared in front of Cara. She screamed and jumped backwards, her back hitting the wall. None of what was happening made any sense. It was a nightmare she couldn't wake up from. The transparent face before her made a motion with his hand. The ghostly figure pointed towards the door.

"Run!" it yelled, and Cara found herself broken from her shock as the image vanished. There was no time to question what was happening. She bolted towards the door. The sound of the man's thundering footsteps boomed behind her.

She raced down the hall with the pistol still grasped in her hand. Her brain no longer registered its existence. Now, it was a useless thing. It was a fact her mind had yet to process. Somehow, the bullet had struck the man in the heart and yet he sat up like nothing happened.

There was no time to think about it now. His thundering footsteps were close behind her. One wrong step and he would swoop her up and break her neck. There was no doubt in her mind it would happen quick.

Cara turned the corner and spotted the elevators. She'd never make it in time. Her only option would be the stairwell. Lucky for her, the door was next to the elevators. This would be where she could gain some distance between herself and her attacker. Cara was lighter and in much better shape than the man. She could take the stairs much faster than he could.

A cold breeze swooped passed her again and she saw her new invisible friend appear at the staircase. He motioned for her to run faster. Cara had to shake her head to make sure she wasn't imagining things. The scene was the most bizarre thing to ever happen to her.

"He's gaining on ya," her invisible friend said with a thick country drawl. "Best get down those stairs-" Something unseen yanked him from the doorway, and he disappeared once again.

"Jesus Christ," she said, panting. "I've lost my fucking mind."

Slamming her body against the door, Cara entered the stairwell. She made it down half a flight before the large man barreled in behind her. He panted hard but kept up with her. Losing him would be harder than she thought. The gun in her hand felt heavy. Her instinct told her to raise the barrel and fire a few rounds at him. After the incident in the condo, she decided against it. All she would do is waste ammo and possibly injure someone in their own home.

"Quit running," the man exclaimed between wheezing pants. "You're only making it worse."

His threat fell on deaf ears. Cara was only focused on the staircase below her feet. She descended three steps at a time. One wrong step and she would tumble down the stairwell. If the fall didn't kill Cara, her pursuer would.

Her invisible friend appeared next to her on the steps causing her to almost lose her balance. Even though he descended the steps with her, he did not appear to be using the stairs. It looked like he floated above them. Cara could not explain the bizarre sight. Somehow, she had stumbled into the Twilight Zone. Or a superhero movie of some kind.

"You got a plan to get out of this, ma'am?" the floating spectral of a man asked. There was no strain in his voice to indicate he was running.

"Yeah..." she panted. "Run...until...I...get...to...my...car."

Then it hit her. Her car keys were not in her pocket. They were still inside her condo. Her eyes flashed to the useless gun in her hand and realized how upside down everything had become. The weapon in her hand was as useless as a paperweight. The real life saving tool sat somewhere in her condo.

"Shit...my...keys."

"On it," the man said and disappeared.

Cara continued to fly down the stairs, doing her best to not slip and fall. The sudden disappearance of her new invisible friend made her shudder. This had turned into the strangest night of her life.

Chapter 14

Jeffrey had managed to slip away from the creature Death had called a Sluagh. It wouldn't take long before it found him again. The thing had some sort of connection with Dominic. Wherever he was, the beast would be close. He was safe for now. The same couldn't be said for Cara. When he had left her, she was running down the stairs and looking like she would collapse at any moment. If Dominic caught her, it would be all over. Jeffrey couldn't let that happen.

The man's powers were already growing. When Cara had pulled the trigger and shot Dominic, he had nearly cheered. His job was done for him. He had readied himself to reap Dominic's spirit. But when he had sat back up, he knew everything had hit the fan. Mortal weapons couldn't kill the man. His spirit had become too powerful. With the Sluagh still lurking around, there was nothing he could do. Cara would be more useful to him alive.

Jeffrey wouldn't admit it, but he had developed a newfound respect for Cara. The woman had stood her ground against one of the biggest adversaries Jeffrey had seen in a while. And she managed to inflict real damage. In fact, she would have bested him if not for his ability to cheat death. A good fighter was a terrible thing to waste. Even if they were one of the living.

He passed through her condo door and looked on the floor for her keys. If they were here, he had to find them fast. She wouldn't last much longer out there by herself. He felt bad for her. Such a strong woman and yet she was limited by her human body. If she were a spirit, there was so much she could accomplish. Probably be the second-best hunter on Death's roster. Behind him, of course.

"Maybe I'll talk her in to letting the brute kill her," he said out loud while he searched. "Get myself a protégé. Kinda like the sound of that."

He spotted the keys under the couch. Jeffrey wasted no time rushing over and picking them up. Not bothering to open the front door, Jeffrey phased through the wood. The keys did not make the journey. Instead, they clanged against the door and fell to the floor. He looked at his hand for a moment and then laughed.

"Oh yeah, physical things. Annoyin'."

He opened the door and swiped the keys from the floor and turned to head back towards Cara. At the end of the hall, he spotted the Sluagh. It stood in what he could only assume was an attack pose. The damn thing had almost killed him several times tonight. He wasn't aching to cross it again.

"Look, I don't know what kind of deal y'all struck, but how about you and I strike one of our own, huh?"

The Sluagh stood in its human-looking form. An old man with skin sagging like water filled paper bags. It was a revolting sight.

"You let me go now and leave that bastard for good and I won't reap your nasty soul. Deal?"

The Sluagh only stared.

If this hideous creature was up here with him, it meant Cara was still safe. There was still time to get the keys to her and escape from this beast. He wished he could load her up in his car and drive off. Unfortunately, it would take too much energy to give the car enough mortal mass to keep her as a passenger.

It now stood between him and the stairwell. Normally, he would pass through the floor until he arrived at the bottom, but the physical keys stopped him from doing so. They needed to get far away from here so he could develop a plan.

"You are an ugly sonofabitch. Anyone ever tell you that?" Jeffrey said, stalling for time. "Why are you letting a meat bag like Dominic control you? Aren't y'all supposed to be ancient spirits or somethin'?"

He knew the Sluagh wouldn't answer. In typical Jeffrey fashion, he was stalling for time while he tried to think of what to do next. When an idea did cross his mind, he had to suppress a smile. It was crazy, but it might work.

"Well, I'm gonna get passed ya one way or another 'cause I can't look at all of this anymore. I didn't think spirits could vomit but you're gonna get me there." Jeffrey laughed.

The beast took a small step forward. Jeffrey knew this was it. He had to make his move now. Cara might be safe from the Sluagh, but she was far from safe from Dominic. He needed to get down there fast. Jeffrey took a large step forward to mimic the creature. It moved again and so did Jeffrey. They seemed to be locked in a sort of otherworldly dance. Each took steps forward in unison. Jeffrey suddenly broke off into a full sprint straight towards the

Sluagh. He watched as the features started to change into its hideous crow-like form before Jeffrey passed through the wall to its right. He kept his left hand outstretched into the hallway, the keys dangling from his fist.

He heard it groan in frustration as he ran by. It had not anticipated Jeffrey's little dodge and Jeffery hadn't anticipated the creature's speed. A claw wrapped around Jeffrey's exposed hand and yanked him free from the wall. The force flung him down the hallway towards his destination.

"God damned keys," Jeffrey mumbled as he picked himself up.

The Sluagh had already advanced at an alarming speed. Jeffrey tightened his grip on the keys and flung himself towards the stair well. He was able to glide down the stairs without taking each step. It helped save on time. But the monster wasn't far behind. The small space kept its wings confined but it still moved faster than Jeffrey liked.

He needed a faster way to get to the ground level. Cara's life, and his only lead, depended on it. An idea struck him as he came to the next floor down. Without a second thought, Jeffrey barged through the door and into the hallway. It felt strange using the door like a living person, but there was little choice.

Jeffrey had no reason to be picky. Any condo would do. He only needed one window to make his escape. Since the Sluagh could fly like a disgusting bird, Jeffrey hoped his plan would work. Hopefully, the creature wouldn't pick him out of the sky as he fell. At least he didn't need to worry about the landing. No fall could hurt him.

Jeffrey dove through the first door he saw. The keys slammed against the wood and stayed behind. He cursed himself for forgetting about the damn keys. There was no time to open the door and retrieve them when the Sluagh melted through.

The condo seemed empty, at least for the moment. The humans who lived here were probably fast asleep. Jeffrey wanted to retrieve the keys and escape the condo before they were alerted. If the Sluagh found another victim, it could just as easily pass their essence on to Dominic. Though, Jeffrey wasn't quite sure how it all worked. He assumed Dominic had to kill the living person before the Sluagh could kill the spirit. It didn't seem capable of harming the living. Or, at least, it didn't bother itself with doing so.

These were questions to ponder at another time. He had keys to retrieve and a condo to escape. He turned to face the creature and pulled his knife free from the sheath. It wouldn't cause any lasting harm to the monster, but it would buy Jeffrey enough time.

"I've really got to do the world a favor and reap you," Jeffrey taunted as he twirled the knife in his right hand. "I mean, you're one ugly sonofabitch."

The Sluagh snarled and gave a startling screech. Jeffrey advanced towards the winged beast as fast as he could muster. It charged forward. As the pair collided, Jeffrey plunged the knife deep into its chest and twisted. The creature howled in pain but did not back down. It wrapped its leathery wings around Jeffrey and twirled through the air away from the front door.

They landed with a thud on the opposite side of the condo near the balcony. Jeffrey wasted no time using his momentum to fling the Sluagh away. It phased through the sliding glass door and into the darkened void of the night outside.

Not wasting any time, Jeffrey flung himself towards the front door and ripped it open. He grabbed the keys in his hand and turned to face the balcony. The silhouette of a giant winged bird cut across the sky and dive bombed the glass door.

"Ah, shit," Jeffrey said as the door shattered and the Sluagh flew into him at full force. The pair collided with the opposite wall and bounced towards the floor. The creature oriented itself and landed on its feet like a demonic cat. Jeffrey was not so coordinated. His limbs sprawled across the floor like a twisted pretzel. The keys were still in his hand. Which meant there was only one thing left to do.

The occupants of the condo came rushing from their bedroom in nothing but robes. Jeffrey barely noticed them and the Sluagh seemed uninterested. It started at Jeffrey like it knew what his next move would be. Its black beady eyes almost dared him to take the leap. The monster could fly. Jeffrey could only fall. It would have the advantage.

With no other options, Jeffrey ran at full sprint towards the shattered sliding glass door. He knew he was leaving behind a confused couple. What he would have given to stick around and see the look on their faces. It almost made him grin. But the fear of an imminent death kicked back in.

Wings flapped behind him as the creature took flight. As Jeffrey leaped over the banister, he felt a gust of wind rush past him, missing by only inches. Jeffrey wasn't sure if he had been lucky or if the Sluagh was playing another game. Either way, he kept his eye on the street below.

The ground was coming fast, but the Sluagh was advancing faster. It swooped after Jeffrey and narrowly missed slashing him with its razor-sharp talons. Jeffrey held the keys tight in one hand and his dagger in the other. Jeffrey took swipes at the flying creature. He hoped to keep it at bay long enough to get on his own two feet.

While he descended, he spotted Cara crouched behind a car on the opposite side of the street. Dominic walked slowly down the road and searched around every parked car. He was running out of time to get the keys to her.

Jeffrey landed on his feet in the middle of the road. Since gravity worked differently for spirits, he didn't have to worry about landing too hard or coming to a violent stop. Before he could move, something slammed into his body like a freight train. Together, Jeffrey and the Sluagh went sailing back towards the condo.

The creature pinned him up against the wall and reared back its beak, ready to strike. Jeffrey rammed his knife into one of the creature's doll-like eyes. It screeched in pain and pulled back. Jeffrey fell to his knees but recovered fast. There was no time to gain his composure. He had to move. The beast would heal and would be on top of him again.

He spotted Cara weaving between parked cars as she continued to put distance between her and Doninic. She moved with a certain grace that could only come from someone with experience. He thought about the way she had handled the firearm in her condo and started to wonder about her story. She had some sort of self-defense training, that was for sure.

Jeffrey hurled the keys and watched as they landed right next to Cara. He smiled and put himself between Dominic and Cara. Revealing himself to the brute, he smiled.

"Hey there, buddy," Jeffrey said.

"You again? Why hasn't that thing killed you yet?"

"Your little pet's busy regrowing an eye." Jeffrey smirked again. "Don't worry, I'm sure it will grow back."

"What do you want with me?" The man took a large step forward, but Jeffrey remained still. He might be able to heal from any infliction done to him, but that didn't mean he could hurt Jeffrey. At least, not yet. A few more absorbed spirits and maybe...

"Why are y'all so desperate to get this woman? Couldn't you and this *thing* go after anyone? Grab a few random drifters off the street and be done with it. Or hell, why not some wandering spirits? Saw it do that before."

Dominic tilted his head to one side like a dog listening to its master. He took a small step forward. His eyes were fixed on Jeffrey.

"Are you wondering about how to use the Sluagh for yourself? You want to power up your spirit, eh?"

"Not quite, friend. You see, I've seen what happens when spirits get too much power."

He flashed the knife in his hand.

"Death usually sends me to reap 'em."

"Wouldn't you like to be all powerful? Answer to no one. Live forever!" Dominic raised his hands to the sky like he was worshipping some invisible being.

"Hate to break it to ya, but we spirits already live forever. You're fighting for nothing. Fighting so hard to stay alive when life after death ain't so bad."

"A spirit isn't forever. Not really. Not when there are creatures like the Sluagh out there that can devour the soul. Not when there are people like you with the power to reap. I want to never fear of vanishing from this world. I want to never truly die."

Somewhere behind Jeffrey, a car roared to life. Cara had finally found the keys and climbed behind the wheel of her car. It would be a matter of seconds before she drove off and away from this crazed man. If they could put some distance between them, he could come up with a plan to reap the Sluagh and Dominic.

"Death is coming for y'all. One way or another," Jeffrey said as he vanished from site.

Cara's headlights blinded Dominic as the car headed straight for him. At the last moment, he leaped to safety. The car continued to speed on and slid around a corner. Within a few seconds, it was gone.

Jeffrey sat in the passenger seat next to Cara but remained unseen. She was panting hard as adrenaline pumped through her veins. He wanted to give her a moment before revealing himself to her. Jeffrey checked the sky for signs of the winged creature but saw nothing. Perhaps the eyes were harder to heal than the rest of its body.

"Glad you're okay," Jeffrey said as he appeared in the passenger seat. Cara screamed and swerved the car, narrowly missing a telephone pole.

"What the fucking hell?" she screamed as she glanced over at Jeffrey. "Who the hell are you and how did you get in my car."

Jeffrey laughed.

"Ya keep your eyes on the road and I'll tell you everything."

Chapter 15

"I'm going crazy." Cara yelled as she sped down the road. "It's a brain tumor. Yeah, that's what it is. My brain is being scrambled and sending me strange visions about ghosts and crazy lunatics."

Jeffrey gave a chuckle from the passenger seat.

"If ya do, you'll see how we live on the other side soon."

Cara flashed him a concerned look. Jeffrey flashed a smile back.

"Oh, come on now," he said. "I was just joking with ya."

"Let me get all of this straight. You are a ghost who hunts other ghosts under the employment of Death. *The* Death. And this gorilla of a man is chasing me because he wants to drink my spirit in order to stay alive longer and grow all powerful. And you are here to stop him from doing that? Did I get it all?"

Jeffrey nodded. "A nice sum up. Honestly, not sure what's got ya so bothered with all this."

Cara slammed on the brakes and pulled the car to the side of the road. A car horn blared from behind as a car swerved to avoid a collision. Cara paid it no attention. She stared out the windshield for a few moments before slamming her fists against the steering wheel. Jeffrey remained silent.

Finally, Cara fell silent and collapsed against the wheel. It was all too much for her to bear. From the moment the man had stood back up after being shot, nothing had made sense. The least strange event had been someone trying to murder her in her own home. Now there was a ghost hunter sitting in her car who was a ghost himself. This took those paranormal investigation shows to whole new level. She had always believed they were full of scripted moments. Now, she wasn't so sure.

Cara lifted her head and looked over at Jeffrey. He smiled and gave her a wave. He was a strange looking man, or ghost. She wasn't sure what to call him. His pointed chin was covered with a thin layer of hair. Somewhere between a five o'clock shadow and a beard. It made her question whether or not ghosts could groom or if their hair still grew. He had the wrinkles and creases of an older man but still maintained a bit of youthfulness. The telltale signs of a hard lived life. She watched as he brushed debris from his brown leather jacket.

She chose to believe her eyes and not her ears. This was a man sitting beside her. Not a ghost. No matter what he said. It was a prank. Or a fever dream. It would explain all the strange events of the night.

"I can see you're struggling with everything. Like a wheel movin' in your head. I can almost see it turning," he said in his raspy, yet higher octave voice and southern drawl. "Let me help you out here."

For a moment, she didn't understand what she was seeing. Jeffrey was visible, but not completely. The details of his body seemed to fade away until only the outline of his body could be seen. He looked like a cartoon character made up of mist. He leaned over and passed through the door like he was nothing more than a projection. Once outside the car, he turned and faced the passenger window, looking like a solid person again. Jeffrey gave her a smile then bent down and knocked on the glass.

"See. Spirit," he said, pointing to himself.

Cara flung open her door and fell to the asphalt. She jumped to her feet and stared at Jeffrey over the roof of her car. Her heart thudded in her chest so hard she feared it would stop at any moment. The experience was almost too much for her. Inside her head, something fought for sanity. A little voice told her what she had seen was false. All an impossible trick of the light. But Cara knew enough to trust her own senses. It was real. All of it.

"Holy shit," she said, placing her palms flat on the car roof.

"I can see ya might be comin' to terms?"

"This is real, isn't it? You're a *fucking* ghost."

"I have been tryin' to tell ya."

"I still don't know if I believe it all. I mean, how the hell could any of this be real. And why the hell am I caught in the middle of it? What does that large fuck want me dead for?"

"It's funny, I asked myself that same question."

"You said he's stealing souls. Drinking them or whatever. But why me?"

"Question of the day," Jeffrey said. "But I know just who to ask. Wanna meet Death?" Jeffrey smiled. Cara recoiled in horror.

"Aw, hey now," Jeffrey said. "She ain't that bad."

Before Jeffrey could say another word, a woman appeared before them. She was a beautiful and petit woman with pale skin and a dark black dress. It clung to her like plastic wrap. The stark contrast between her skin and dress was almost mesmerizing. This was not the image of Death she had pictured. There were no skeleton hands, no black cloak, and no large scythe.

"You can't...I mean... you're not really...is it even possible?" Cara stammered.

"I would not normally reveal myself to the living," Death said. Her voice was cold and lifeless. Nothing at all like a human. More machine-like. She spoke in a matter-of-fact tone unlike anything Cara had heard before. It was somehow comforting. "But it seems the situation here may be dire."

"Ma'am, meet Death," Jeffrey said, motioning towards the woman in black.

"I...uh..." Cara couldn't find the words.

"Don't worry. She's star struck," Jeffrey joked.

"Jeffrey, the matter is serious. I can sense the man's powers have grown. He can no longer be killed by mortal weapons."

"Yeah, I shot him and he stood back up like it was nothing more than a bean bag."

"It is only going to get worse if he is not stopped. Time is running out. Too many more spirits and he will become all powerful," Death said.

"I'm sorry, but is there a reason you don't just step in and kill him? I mean, it's in your name, right?"

Jeffrey turned to her and said, "It don't work like that. That's why I'm here. Kinda my job."

"Okay, so let me just let this all sink in here. You're Death, but you can't kill people. Isn't that *your* job? Isn't that like you're whole thing? Reaper of souls. My God. I'm talking to my hallucinations. I've gone crazy."

"Death ferries the spirits of the livin' to where they will spend their eternity. She doesn't kill anythin'. People die naturally. She's more like a guide."

"A guide?"

Jeffrey nodded. Cara took a step back and leaned against her car. This was all too much to take in. Death, *the* Death, was real. The afterlife was and ghosts were real. To top it all off, a crazed man juiced up on the energy of absorbed spirits was chasing her down, ready to kill her. It was the plot of a horror movie, not real life. She began to feel nauseous.

"Death, I've got a question. Why's he so fixated on the lady here? Why not pick off a random person, ya know? He did it with that drifter in the cemetery."

"Drifter?" Cara interjected.

"A type of deadly spirit. Moves from place to place. Preys on the livin' when it can. You've probably seen 'em before. That little black shape in the corner of your eye. Moves when you look at it. Drifter."

"Oh," she said.

"I do not know for certain," Death said. "The Sluagh is known for preying on the sick and dying. Perhaps it is bound by rules like I am."

"Hang on. Are you saying that I might be dying? That's why this thing is after me?"

"No, you are not." Death said matter-of-factly.

"Oh, well I guess you would know." Cara said and Jeffrey snickered.

"Maybe it's got nothing to do with the Sluagh thing. I know how Dominic picks his victims. I watched him find her name on the little screen device on his desk."

"Little screen device?" Cara asked.

"Yeah. Little thing with a screen like a TV. All sorts of people's faces on it."

Cara laughed.

"It's called a smart phone and he was probably browsing Facebook. How long have you been dead?"

"Smart phone? The hell does that even mean? Phones make calls. Ain't nothing smart about 'em."

"Never mind," Cara said.

There was an awkward silence between the trio, now. Cara was still letting the events and the news of everything she had learned sink in. Somehow, they had to kill someone who could no longer be killed. Not to mention, the beast that followed him around. It seemed to be unkillable as well. The odds were stacked against them for sure.

"I don't see how I can be much help in this," Cara said. "This guy can't be killed. I mean, I shot him and he just walked it off. What the hell can I do?

I should just take off and hide until all of this is over. Maybe if he can't find me, he won't get more powerful. Should buy you some time, right?"

Jeffrey shook his head but didn't speak. He looked down at the ground like a thought was formulating in his mind. If spirits even had minds or thoughts. There were so many questions she didn't have time to ask. Jeffrey looked back up at Death.

"How do I reap him, now? If the body can't be killed, I can't get his spirit."

"The spirit will have to come out of the body in order to be killed."

"If his body can't die, why would he ever come out of his body?"

"Along with the ability to keep from mortal harm, he has gained the ability to utilize his spirit. It is like an extension of himself. Something quite rare for the living. He may be able to detach his spirit from his body completely."

"That could come in handy for a lot. Like sneakin' in somewhere unnoticed. His body is more like a ride now. Or a shell."

"Yes."

Jeffrey turned back to Cara.

"There's nowhere you can hide where you'd be safe. Ya might not see him comin'. Safest place to be is with me."

Cara felt lightheaded. Here they were, discussing ghosts trying to kill her like it was an everyday occurrence. Maybe for them it was. For Cara, it was anything but.

"Okay, so let's say I stay with you. How the hell are you going to keep me safe if you can't even kill this creature hanging around him, not to mention the guy?"

"The creature should be easy. It can be reaped while it feeds. So, we give it some food." Jeffrey smiled.

"Food? You mean a person?"

"Well, a spirit. Could be from the livin' or dead."

"This man has upset the balance enough. I would prefer no more of the living be harmed by him," Death said.

"So, what are we going to do, then?" Cara asked.

Jeffrey turned and gave her a wide smile like he hid some big secret. He probably knew a lot of things she didn't. This whole world beyond the veil was new and confusing. There were thousands of questions flying through her mind. She hoped she would get answers to them all.

"Maybe I can let this man do my job for me," Jeffrey said. "We find ourselves a lost spirit, lead him and his pet to it, let the thing eat it, and done. It eats, I reap. Simple, but effective."

Cara watched as the pale faced, attractive woman claiming to be the grim reaper held out her hand towards Jeffrey. Without a question, he placed his strange looking knife in her hand. It vibrated and gave off a faint glow as her hand gripped the handle. Within seconds, the knife was returned to Jeffrey and slipped back in his holster.

"Yeah, um, anyone want to explain to me what that was?"

"We just got our bait," Jeffrey said and smiled.

Chapter 16

Dominic was smart enough not to hang around after his target slipped away. He would catch up to her in time. For now, there were other sacrifices to be made. The Sluagh would not allow him to skip over Cara. Once a sacrifice had been chosen, the Sluagh demanded it be done. He could buy some time by moving on, but eventually it would want what was owed to it. There was no logical explanation for how he knew this. Only that he did.

All Dominic needed to do was find a candidate for sacrifice and the Sluagh would lead him directly to them. It was an odd feeling like nothing else he had experienced before. There was a strange connection between him and the creature. Like an unholy bond. Dominic could only guess that the creature exhaled a small part of its own spirit every time it fed him. It was like the Sluagh's own soul was imprinted on Dominic's. There was no handbook for this thing, so it was all he could guess on his own.

He drove with purpose, making sure not to draw attention to himself. The next sacrifice had already been chosen. A sub-conscious voice showed him where to go, though it didn't truly speak. It was like Dominic could see the directions in his mind's eye. He wished he could pick a person and let the Sluagh carry out the deed. But it didn't work this way.

The day he had met the Sluagh had been the scariest of his life. He was dying. Dominic had collapsed to the floor with a throbbing pain in his chest. His heart was giving out. There would be no help coming for him. Dominic lived alone and his phone was not in his pocket. He would die in this tiny apartment on the dingy kitchen floor. His body wouldn't be found until it started to smell. He didn't have any friends or a special someone in his life. Both his parents died when he was young. He was alone.

He gasped and coughed on the floor as he struggled to get up. That's when he saw it. At first, he thought he was hallucinating. A lack of oxygen to the brain had caused bizarre visions. This strange, elderly man walked through Dominic's living room and stared down at him. Dominic reached up with a weak hand, begging for help. But the old man stood there without saying a word.

As Dominic's world started to grow darker, he saw the old man start to change. The sagging skin stretched out and became leathery skin in the shape of a bird. His face contorted until it resembled a beak. Two black, beady eyes stared down at Dominic as he started to slip from this world.

Dominic felt a heavy weight fall from his body like he had taken off a lead-lined jacket. He had never felt so free in his life. When he looked down, he realized why. His motionless body sat on the kitchen floor below him. His face was contorted into a grimace of pain and fear. He was dead.

A feeling of immense fear welled up inside him. It shocked him that the dead could feel these emotions. He had always thought emotions were mortal reactions and would be cast away in the afterlife. The looming beast advanced on Dominic's new spirit. He stumbled backward to avoid the hideous beast's talons. If this was the grim reaper, the universe had a sick sense of humor.

Somehow, he knew what the creature wanted. He knew what it was here to do. It stared down at Dominic, ready to pounce. Whatever the afterlife was, he would never see it. This thing was here to prey on his soul. So, he did the only thing he could think of.

"Please, whatever you are, don't do this." He dropped to his knees and was surprised to feel the impact but with no pain. "Please, I'm not ready to die. Not like this. Anything but this," he pleaded. But the creature seemed to not understand or care. It advanced once again. It's doll-like eyes fixed on Dominic.

"I'll do anything. Anything! Just let me live. I can't die here. I'm not ready. I'm not ready!" Dominic yelled and begged, but the thing did not listen. It crept forward and its beak hung open like it was ready to eat.

"I get it. I-I understand," he stammered. "Food?" He said and pointed at himself. "Ghosts or souls or whatever you call them are your food. You eat us. Let me live and I can help you eat. As much as you want. Put me back in my body and I will give you all the souls you can eat!"

The creature stopped moving. It stared at him for a moment. Dominic could almost hear the thoughts in its mind as it considered the deal. He would do whatever it took to stay alive, to keep this horrible fate from befalling him. If he had to sacrifice a few unlucky people, so be it. The thought of no longer existing petrified him. Eternal darkness could not be how everything ended.

His parents' sudden death in a terrible car accident had left him with a fear of dying. His mortality would randomly flutter into his mind and an icy cold feeling would envelop his blood. His constant worry and anxiety over his own mortality had caused him to avoid things many others would have done. Having friends, creating a family, having adventures. He preferred to stay home where it was safe and less chaotic. The outside world was unpredictable. Just a walk down the street could end his life. A random car could slip from the road and strike him down. A loose brick could fall from a roof, crushing his skull. The anxiety of it all was too much. Death was everywhere.

Here was his chance to overcome death. To beat his own mortality. And he would not let it go to waste. His fear of death had lessened when he learned of the existence of the afterlife. But the monsters that inhabited it only skyrocketed his fears. Eternity meant nothing if he no longer existed.

The crow-like features started to subside. The old man with the sagging skin returned. Dominic fought back the urge to thank it profusely. Instead, he climbed up from his knees and gave the old man a nod. As he did, an understanding overcame him. The creature did not talk with words but seemed to communicate telepathically. Without hearing a word in his head, he knew exactly what the creature wanted and what it could do. For starters, it could put his spirit back in his body.

Dominic understood he would have to make sacrifices to the Sluagh in order to stay alive. It would be simple enough. Find a person and take their life. The Sluagh would do the rest. In doing so, the Sluagh would share the essence of the spirit with Dominic. This would keep his spirit tethered to his mortal body. It came with a side effect that the Sluagh seemed either unaware of or indifferent to. Dominic's power over his spirit would grow. He never stopped to think the creature may have been fattening him up like a thanksgiving turkey. The thought would have driven him mad.

The vision slipped from Dominic's mind as he pulled into a dark parking space. That day had changed his life forever. He was now a slave to this terrible creature, forced to kill for it. But he was still here. And the more lives he took, the longer he would stay. And that was worth each sacrifice to him.

Dominic sat behind the wheel and watched the main doors of the airport, straining his eyes to see through the darkness. He knew his next victim was due in any minute. He hoped the flight was either on time or running late. The distraction with the Cara woman had almost put him behind schedule. If Dominic missed the flight, it would take longer to track her down. That would not make the Sluagh happy. It was already upset enough at missing its last meal.

He waited in the short-term parking lot. There were cameras in the parking lot which could be used to identify him if anyone thought to check. Since he wasn't planning to make the sacrifice near the airport, he figured no one would ever think to look there.

While he waited, Dominic pulled his phone from his pocket to see if there was an update on his victim's Facebook page. She had checked in at an out of state airport several hours ago. He calculated the flight time in his head and checked the clock on the dashboard. He was in luck. Her flight must have just landed or would be landing shortly. He hadn't missed it.

"This is why you don't put so much on social media," he said as he tossed his phone on the seat next to him.

If she had not checked in at the airport, she would have been harder to track. It may have been a good way to let friends and family know they had safely boarded a plane or landed. But it also let anyone else know her location. Someone, like Dominic, could use that to harm her. If her profile had been locked down and private, she would have survived this night. Though, Dominic was thankful for her lapse in judgement. Her sacrifice would be his reward.

Dominic drummed his fingers against the steering wheel in impatience. Finally, he spotted his victim emerge from the airport. She looked around like she was waiting for a ride. An Uber was likely on its way to pick her up.

He shifted into reverse and pulled out of the parking spot. He would need to get up to the terminal before she departed. Dominic didn't know where the woman lived so he had to follow her home. At least she was smart enough to keep that information private. Not that it mattered much. If he lost her, the Sluagh would be able to point him in the right direction. Or perhaps it would kill Dominic and be done with everything.

A black sedan pulled up in front of the terminal exit a few yards in front of Dominic. After a second, he watched Nicole, his victim, climb inside. Finally, the next part of the venture would begin. He was tired of the waiting. Like ripping off a band-aid, he just wanted it over.

The drive was long and uneventful. Dominic made sure to keep far enough back that the Uber driver never became suspicious. It would be unfortunate to go through such careful planning to find and follow his victims, just for an astute Uber driver to call the police.

The Uber driver pulled in a neighborhood, stopping in front of one the houses. Dominic followed, being sure to stop a few houses away. He killed the engine and shut off the lights, hoping the driver and his passenger would not notice him. Nicole climbed out of the car, gave the driver a police smile, grabbed her luggage, and headed off towards the front door. When she was safely inside, Dominic climbed out of the car.

As he walked, he made sure to take note of the houses on either side of the street. Judging by the lack of interior lights, Dominic assumed the neighborhood was fast asleep. A single nosy insomniac was likely to give Dominic's description to the police once the body was found. Lucky for him, he'd be long gone by the time Nicole's body was discovered. If his description was given to police, it would mean the end of his reign in Florida. He would have to start hunting elsewhere.

Dominic snuck across the yard, making his way to the backyard gate. He let himself in the backyard with a sigh of relief. Now that he was behind the fence, he was less likely to be spotted by the neighbors. He felt safer. He crept through the darkness shrouded backyard until he reached the backdoor. Dominic crouched down low and placed his hand on the doorknob. He would be able to unlock it from the other side with his new ability, but he wanted to test the lock first.

"I'm kind of glad it's locked," he whispered to himself.

As he did at the hotel room, Dominic focused his mind and pushed against the knob. His hand remained still but a glowing force exited from his palm and reached through the door. He could feel this burst of energy like an extra hand. From the inside, he craned his ghostly appendage around and unlocked the door. Then, he pulled his hand free of the door and the energy dissipated. Dominic looked down at his hand and smiled.

"This is getting fun," he said as he let himself in the house.

Chapter 17

The house was dark and quiet. Nicole was probably tucked away in bed falling asleep or already out. If she were asleep, it would make sneaking through her home that much easier. There was no telling how many little creaks and moans the floor would give off as Dominic walked around.

The door he had entered through led directly into the kitchen. The kitchen was compact like a hallway. At the opposite end it opened into the dining room. To the left of the dining room, he could see a small hallway which had to be where the bedrooms were at. Dominic ignored the living room sitting in darkness beyond the dining room. If all went well, he wouldn't need to step foot there.

The wooden kitchen floor creaked under his feet. Dominic stopped for a moment, hoping he hadn't alerted the woman to his presence. The counter to his right jutted out from the wall to form a small bar between the kitchen and the dining room. He crouched behind it for a moment and listened. There was no noise coming from the bedroom. It appeared she was sound asleep.

Making his way across the dining room, Dominic stood in the small space that served as a hallway. Here there were three doors. One in front of him and two on either side. He wasn't about to leave anything to chance. Opening the wrong door could wake Nicole up, giving her time to call the police. Though he wasn't worried about her fighting back, or harming him for that matter, he was worried about rushing. Sloppy would get him caught. Sure, the police wouldn't be able to shoot him, but rotting in a jail cell for the rest of his life was not how he wanted his story to end.

The door in front of him had to lead to the bathroom. It was a smaller door than the other two. Which only left the doors on either end of the hallway. Up until now, he had only used his new power to extend a hand and unlock doors from the other side. Now, a more useful use was clear to him.

Dominic took a quiet step to the right and pushed his face as close to the door as he could manage without touching it. He focused his thoughts and envisioned himself pushing his face through the door. It was harder than reaching through with a single hand. His concentration was pushed to the brink. He thought of nothing else but pushing his spirit through the door.

Finally, he felt his mind disconnect from his body. It was a strange sensation. The lower half of his body felt heavy and cumbersome, while the top half felt light and nimble. His spirit was leaning free of his body.

The strangest feeling came when Dominic craned his neck back and peered at his own face. His body stood motionless like a wax figure. Dominic turned the extension of his body back to the door and peered through. He saw nothing but boxes and items of storage. Nicole's bedroom was behind the other door.

As Dominic pulled back into his own body, he smiled at his genius. His powers were growing. He could feel the energy coursing through him. There was no telling what he would be able to do next. His mortal form could already survive gunshot wounds, which meant he could survive most everything else. He had not put this to the test, nor was he eager to try.

He almost peeked inside with his newfound ability but decided against it. There was no need. He knew what was behind this door. It was better to get it over with. The quicker he could leave, the better. These sacrifices were best done as in and out trips. The victim's home was not ideal. In a rush, it would do.

Without stalling any longer, Dominic burst through the doorway. Nicole was on the bed, still wearing the same sweatpants and tee shirt he had seen her step out of the Uber with. When she heard the intruder, she shot up in bed like a rocket. Dominic was too fast. He scooped her out of bed and wrapped his fingers around her throat.

She sputtered and choked as her hands probed the darkness. Dominic pinned her against the wall and used his other hand to grab her by the wrists. Her eyes grew wide with fear. After the events at Cara's condo, Dominic wanted this to be quick and painless.

Nicole's legs flailed out as she tried to kick Dominic somewhere sensitive. He thrust his lower body backward and out of her reach. Her face had already turned blue. It would be over any second. Nicole's eyes shut and her body went limp. She had finally passed on from the world of the living. He let her go and her body slumped to the floor with a *thud!*

Dominic's heart was racing in his chest. Though he still had not grown accustomed to taking another life, the action was now filling him with adrenaline. Each life taken meant a step closer towards immortality. Whatever horrors waited for him in the afterlife would be no more. Every spirit consumed crept him farther away from his fears.

He started to wipe down any surface he may have touched, including the bedroom doorknob. He wasn't a forensic expert, but he knew enough that a single fingerprint could get him caught. Even a well-placed footprint. As he cleaned and wiped down surfaces, he thought it was strange the Sluagh hadn't shown up to deliver the woman's essence to him. He couldn't help but wonder if the creature was now betraying him. Had it seen his new abilities and realized its mistake? There would be no way of knowing. He couldn't see the creature unless it appeared before him. Walking in the spirit world was impossible. At least for now.

As he stood in the dining room contemplating what to do next, a streak of light snuck through the curtains in the living room. His eyes darted to the window. A car had pulled into the driveway. He glanced at the time on the cable box. It was past midnight.

"Were we expecting late night visitors, Nicole?" He mumbled under his breath.

A surge of fear pumped through his veins as his brain told him it was the police. Perhaps someone had seen him lurking around the yard. Dominic tiptoed across the living room and dared a glance out of the curtain. The headlights went dark, and a man stepped from the driver side. It didn't look like a police car, but he couldn't be sure.

He wondered if Nicole had a boyfriend or a husband. If he had a key, he would be as good as caught. To buy himself a couple minutes, he ran back to the bedroom to shut the door. If he could keep the body hidden for a few seconds, he might be able to slip out the front door while the man was distracted.

When he arrived at the bedroom, his blood ran cold. The body was no longer there. An audible gasp escaped his lips. She hadn't died. The woman was alive in the house somewhere. No wonder the Sluagh had not arrived. Dominic hadn't finished the job. And now the woman had probably run off to a neighbor's house and called the police. Maybe the man outside was a cop and she already called them. A record for police response time.

A soft knock came at the door followed by a whispering voice.

"Nicole," it said. "I know you said I didn't need to come over, but I decided too anyway. Are you awake?"

Dominic drew in a deep breath of relief. It was a boyfriend. He knew nothing of what had happened to Nicole. Yet, that didn't solve his current problem. Where had she gone?

A noise came from the kitchen. Dominic bolted towards it and found Nicole flat on her stomach, reaching up for something on the counter. His eyes followed her reach and spotted the knife block. He had to stifle a laugh. She had not screamed for help which meant he had damaged her vocal cords. Judging by the sharp wheezes as she inhaled, he assumed he had crushed her windpipe. Without enough oxygen, she would soon blackout.

Nicole looked over at Dominic. He could see the tears in her eyes. She was scared. Of course, he understood. He felt bad for her, but he had a job to do now. The soft knock came at the door again. Nicole shifted her eyes towards the door and mouthed something. It seemed she was desperate to cry out for help.

Dominic grabbed a knife from the block and pushed it back so Nicole couldn't reach it. He advanced through the house and arrived at the front door. The man on the other side was mumbling to himself about wishing Nicole had given him a key. Dominic unlocked the deadbolt and flung open the door.

"Oh Nicole, final-" The man stopped speaking when he spotted Dominic in the doorway. "Who the *fuck* are you?"

Dominic wasted no time grabbing the man by the collar and yanking him inside the house. He slammed the door shut and flung the man to the ground. He took the kitchen knife and rammed it deep into the man's chest. There was a brief look of panic and a yelp of pain from the man before his head went slack and he stopped moving.

"This did not go as planned at all," Dominic said as he pulled the knife from his victim's chest. His head snapped to the side and spotted Nicole in the kitchen who had now pulled herself to her feet. She was reaching for the knife block again. Dominic walked over and rammed the knife into her back. She crumpled to the ground like a doll.

"You could have gone for your cellphone and called the police," he said, as he ripped the knife from her back. "Of course, I guess you can't speak so that wouldn't have done you any good." He rolled her over on her back and looked her in the eyes. "I am truly sorry that I have to do this." He pulled the knife up over his head and brought it down with all of his might. The blade buried deep in her chest. Nicole let out a whimper as her eyes bulged. Seconds later, her head went slack and her body limp.

He sat for a few minutes, trying to organize his thoughts. This had been nothing short of a mess. The second body wouldn't change things much. In fact, it worked in his favor. If he set the scene up right, he could make it look like the boyfriend had committed the murder. Nicole fought back. In the end, both lives were tragically lost. Then there was the added benefit of the Sluagh getting two spirits instead of the promised one. Perhaps that would make up for missing Cara.

Dominic went about cleaning the crime scene of any evidence that would link him to the bodies. He wiped the knife handles down and pressed both Nicole and her boyfriend's hands against them. He hoped it would look like they had fought over the weapon before stabbing each other. When he was finished, the Sluagh appeared in the kitchen. It stood over the woman's body in its bird-like form. It moved closer to Dominic and readied to share the life giving essence with him. Like before, it exhaled a glowing vapor that enveloped Dominic.

The vapor leaked into his mouth and nose. Dominic took in a deep breath. It was like inhaling mist. He almost choked every time. The cloud of mist was thicker this time around. It seemed the Sluagh had made a meal of both new spirits. Dominic did his best not to picture the horrific scene which had played out on the other side of the veil.

Once the creature was finished, it disappeared. Dominic often wondered where it went when it wasn't feasting on souls. Did it have a nest somewhere? Did it even live somewhere or did the damn thing just wander around? There was little he knew about the Sluagh or even the afterlife. And if he kept on this path, he would never have to worry about it. Soon he would be all powerful.

Chapter 18

Only the hum of her engine echoed through the cabin. Cara kept her eyes on the road, not sure if she should try to strike up a conversation with Jeffrey beside her. She peeked at him from her peripheral vision. He seemed unbothered by the awkward silence in the car. He went about picking under his nails with the odd-shaped knife. It raised more questions Cara had to suppress the urge to ask. There seemed to be more pressing matters than asking if ghosts got dirt under their nails or if it was some sort of nervous tick he carried from his human days. Still, the image of him cleaning his nails seemed familiar, though she couldn't quite remember why.

"So," she said, happy to break the silence. "There's ghosts everywhere?"

"Spirits."

"What?"

"We're called spirits. Ain't ghosts."

"Is there a difference?"

"A few letters of a difference."

This stumped Cara for a moment.

"Oh, okay. I get it. Very funny. So, there are spirits everywhere, then?"

"Yes ma'am."

"Like right now? Are there spirits just running around in that field over there?" She pointed out the passenger window into the darkness. Jeffrey laughed.

"We're not dogs or cattle. We used to be alive, same as you. What makes you think we want to wander the fields like some lost puppy?"

"Where do ghosts, I mean spirits, live then?"

"All over and wherever we want, basically."

"Like, in people's homes? You're telling me haunted houses are real?"

"Well, technically, they are. But the only real threats come from the wandering spirits. And a hellhou- I mean hunter like me takes care of them, so you have nothing to worry about."

"That's not true, now is it? There's some immortal lunatic out there eating souls and coming after me. I would say I have a lot to worry about."

Jeffrey stayed quiet at the mention of this. In the corner of her eye, she saw him furrow his brow. She assumed he was used to hunting things he knew everything about. This new prey was a wrench in the everyday workings. She thought it would be for the best to change the subject.

"You started saying something before. Hell something? What's that?"

She heard Jeffrey huff.

"Hellhound. Don't worry about it."

"What's a hellhound?"

"It's what everyone calls one of Death's hunters. I don't like the term."

"Why not? Sounds kind of cool, doesn't it?"

"Cause, I ain't Death's little puppy."

"I think you might be looking into it too much." Cara stifled a laugh.

"What is it you do, anyway?" He asked, clearly trying to change the subject.

"Like for work?"

Jeffrey nodded without looking over at her.

"Security," she said. "Personal protection, actually."

Jeffrey looked up from his nails and peered over at Cara. He seemed to be interested now. For some reason, her profession had piqued his curiosity.

"A bodyguard, huh?"

"Yeah, why? Don't think a woman can be a bodyguard?"

"What?" Jeffrey said, sounding genuinely confused. "Oh yeah, that's right. You livin' care about stuff like that."

"Stuff like what?"

"Gender roles. Race, religion. Blah, blah, blah. Y'all care about that shit. Guess that's a perk of being a spirit. Levels the playin' field a bit."

"Well, I wish people were more like spirits, then," Cara said, as she looked back at the road.

"I'll bite. What happened?"

"What do you mean what happened?"

"To you," Jeffrey said. "You said you wish the livin' was more like us spirits. So, what happened to you?"

"Nothing specific. Just your average sexism in the workplace, I guess."

"Lot of gents don't take kindly to a bodyguard with lady parts?" Jeffrey laughed.

"Do you know how many times I've been asked if I'm a lesbian because of my job? Every damn week I get asked if I'm into women or the men who hire me expecting to get a little something extra. I guess that's all a woman is good for to them. And most of the ones who don't say it just say it in other ways like in the ways they look at me. But I can always tell. I'm so damn sick of being made to feel I have more to prove than men in my profession."

"I never thought I'd give one of y'all a compliment, but you are a hell of a fighter. Took on that big fella by yourself. Impressive. One of the reasons I knew I couldn't let ya die."

"Uh, thanks. I think. And what do you mean 'one of y'all'?" Cara gave him a dirty look.

"Calm down. I meant the livin'."

"You don't care for people much, then?"

"Don't really see why I should. Their, I mean your, problems seem like nothing in the grand scheme of it all. These wanderin' spirits out here will kill any one of ya all the same. Doesn't care what color you are or what kind of person you like to sleep with. Some will rip y'all apart limb from limb. And then, you're just like the rest of us. In the spirit world."

Cara eyed him from the driver seat. He stared ahead as he spoke. Everything seemed so matter of fact in his statement. There were no emotions. It just was. She had to fight the feeling that he was a good and decent person. His progressive attitude didn't come from a place of understanding, but a lack of empathy for the living.

"I'm curious. If you don't care about people, why are you a hellhound? That's protecting the living, right?"

At the mention of hellhound, Jeffrey rolled his eyes. Cara smiled.

"Indirectly, sure. But I ain't out there protecting poor people in the alley from the scary ghosts they can't see. I don't remember much about my time as one of y'all. I remember being dead and seeing Death for the first time. She offered me a choice. Move on to the unknown other side," Jeffrey gave a slight shudder. "Or stay here and hunt for her. I can't describe it, but I wanted to kill these spirits. It sounded, I don't know, fun."

"Maybe you were a serial killer in your life," Cara joked.

"Not sure that would surprise me much. It seemed killin' was all I knew. Death sure seemed to think I had a knack for it. Otherwise, why offer me the job?"

"Haven't you asked her who or what you were in life? Or maybe I can Google you and see what comes up."

"Death can't, or won't, tell me about it. She's always talkin' bout protecting the balance and all that bullshit. I think she knows a bit more than she's letting on, though."

Cara didn't know what else to say. He seemed conflicted. On one hand, he wanted to know about his life as a living person. But on another, he didn't care. His disdain for the living probably came from his lack of knowledge about his own mortality. There was a disconnect there which kept him from connecting with the living and remembering his time as one. She wondered if he had died so long ago that he just couldn't remember. There was no telling how memory worked for the dead.

All of this sounded crazy to her. Even crazier to Cara, she was starting to become comfortable with it all. She had finally moved on from fighting the notion a ghost was sitting in her car with her as unbelievable. Now, she accepted it as reality.

"What *is* on the other side? You know, like when you pass on or whatever."

Jeffrey shrugged.

"No one knows. Death's not spilling those secrets either. You choose to stay or go."

"Do a lot stay?"

"They do. Mostly the religious ones choose to move on. They're certain what's waitin' for them over there. Not sure I'm ready to find out yet."

It was strange to hear a spirit speak of the afterlife as if it were something to fear. Cara imagined knowing there was life after death would make someone less afraid of it. Hell, she was learning there was an afterlife and her fears had subsided a little. Though, Jeffrey was right. If no one knew what was on the other side, maybe it was still a cause for concern. If there was a heaven and a hell, how would you know which one you would end up in. Or worse. What if there were neither and the afterlife was something terrible? Cara tried to pry her mind from these dark thoughts.

"How will I know when we're close to wherever it is we're going," she asked.

Jeffrey didn't look up at the road ahead. He looked back down at his nails like the outside world around him was of no importance. She supposed, to him, it wasn't. Most things about the living world around him would be trivial. He wouldn't care about the advancement people had made in technology or medicine. Neither of these things would affect him in any way. None of the accomplishments made in the last couple decades would have mattered to Jeffrey.

"We're getting close," he said with a brief grin.

"What happens when we get where we're going? I mean, how do you plan on capturing another spirit? Do you have a special medallion that can trap souls or something?"

"This would be a first for me so I'm wingin' it," Jeffrey said.

"Well, that's comforting."

Cara knew Jeffrey wasn't worried about her comfort. If something happened to her while on this hunt, he wouldn't care. As long as it wasn't that guy and his creature that did the job. She thought about ditching Jeffrey the first chance she got, but then thought better of it. If that man came for her again, she would have a better chance of surviving with Jeffrey around.

"This is the place. Right up here," Jeffrey said as he pointed towards a dilapidated building. Rusted metal sheets clung to paint peeling concrete. It was like a warehouse straight out of a horror movie or an episode of Scooby Doo.

"Why would anything want to live in such a rundown place?" Cara asked.

"This type of spirit is known as a Leech. They feed off the life force of the living around them. Like a vampire. I think it's where the legend of 'em came from. Anyway, when they ain't feedin', they're hiding out in places like this. I think they like the abandoned places. Not sure."

Cara parked the car and pulled the keys from the ignition. She reached for the door handle and stopped. Jeffrey melted through his door like it was only a projection. Logic and reason broke in Cara's brain for a moment as it tried to decipher what had happened. Though she knew he was a spirit and could pass through solid objects, it still defied all logic.

"One more thing," Jeffrey said as Cara exited the car. "Stick close to me. A Leech feeds off the livin' slow, but it can be painful. You might not like that."

"Noted."

Jeffrey advanced towards the rusted gate blocking the entrance to the warehouse with his curved knife out in front of him. Like the car door, he passed through the metal object and didn't look back. Cara pushed gate opened and winced at the grinding metal. Jeffrey shot her a glance of frustration. She mouthed "I'm sorry." Then she added in a whisper, "Not like I can pass through solid objects like you."

The inside of the warehouse was no different than the outside. Mold had grown in several places on the walls and water stains littered the ceiling. Trash littered the grounds from several years of teenagers coming here to smoke weed, have sex, and spray paint graffiti penises on the walls. Of which there were many.

It was a wide-open space with several rooms off the main one. Most likely, it functioned as some sort of shipping warehouse at one time. Cara could even see the loading docks in the very back of the building. The metal doors were rusted with several small holes which let in the moonlight. If there was ever a place for an evil ghost to hide, this was it.

Jeffrey stood still in the center of the large room and gripped his knife. He closed his eyes and tilted his head to the side like he was listening for something. Cara was intrigued. She had no clue how this mystical bond between Jeffrey and the knife worked. When this was all over, she would ask him many more questions about it. Hell, she had hundreds of questions she wanted to ask. But she doubted he would answer even a quarter of them.

A noise caught her attention from the farthest corner of the warehouse. Cara's heart began to pump faster. Under normal circumstances, she would not be afraid. She had been in countless worse situations than an abandoned warehouse in the middle of the night. Being a professional bodyguard had its hazards. This was different. This was supernatural.

"I think it knows you're here," Jeffrey said with a smile.

"Knows *I'm* here. What the hell does that mean?"

"It feeds on human energy. Which means it can sense it. Why do you think I chose to hunt a Leech?"

"Are you fucking kidding me?" Cara whispered. "I'm your bait?"

Jeffrey smiled again.

"My dear, you've always been my bait in a way."

Before she could come up with a retort, something rushed at them from the darkness. Jeffrey reacted quickly, diving at the creature that stormed towards them. Cara only saw a streaking blur of a shadow rush across the room before she felt herself being thrown through the air like a doll. She tried to correct her body and land safely, but there was no time. Instead, she crashed to the floor and felt the wind knocked from her lungs.

Jeffrey leaped into the air and tackled the unseen being to the ground. He looked as though he were wrestling with himself. As Cara caught her breath, she focused her eyes on the shadowy blur he fought. Some features of the creature began to appear. She spotted pale skin and razor-sharp teeth. Parts of the body looked rotten and decayed. Long black hair draped over its face in thin strands and left bald spots in several areas on the scalp. The vision of the spirit lasted only a few seconds before it disappeared again.

There wasn't much Cara could do. Helping Jeffrey would be impossible. She couldn't even see the spirit attacking them without intense concentration. But she couldn't stand by and be Jeffrey's bait or burden. She needed to do something. Cara needed to be useful. She wasn't used to the feeling of being the protected.

The Leech tossed Jeffrey across the room and his knife skittered across the floor. Cara thought about chasing after it but remembered Jeffrey had explained the knife would only work for him. In her hands, it would be useless. In this case, she already felt useless. There seemed to be nothing she could do.

"Jeffrey," she called out as he clambered to his feet. "Can you subdue this thing?"

"Workin' on it."

"I mean, if we can lure it somewhere, are you actually able to capture it?"

"Just need my car. I can keep it locked away in the trunk. Why?"

"Because, you need bait."

Jeffrey seemed to think for a moment before realizing what she was saying. She saw him shut his eyes for a moment and smile. A second later, she heard the growling of an engine outside the warehouse. Somehow, he had conjured a vehicle. She made a mental note to ask how it was possible later. Now, she needed to get to that car.

"Hey, you!" she screamed. "Hungry for a little fresh whatever the hell it is you consume from us?"

She could see the shadowy figure turn in her direction. Cara had its attention. Jeffrey stood still with his knife in his hand. He looked ready to pounce if the situation called for it. All Cara needed was to escape the warehouse with the Leech close on her heels. Once close enough to Jeffrey's car, she could use herself as bait to trap the creature in the trunk.

A shadow moved across the warehouse. The spirit was coming for her. With her heart pounding wildly in her chest, Cara turned to run. Her feet couldn't move quick enough. Something wrapped around her foot and pulled her to the ground. The concrete floor came up quick, busting open her lip. Blood leaked down her chin.

"Ah, shit," Jeffrey said from across the room. Cara didn't like the sound of it.

There was a whirlwind of commotion as the Leech pounced on Cara. It felt like a major wind had blown over her entire body. With the wind came a searing hot pain. She cried out in agony. Her body grew weak like all her energy and drive had been taken from her at once; like getting hit by the worst flu imaginable.

It was the worst pain she had ever experienced in her life. No amount of punches, stabs, or bullet wounds could ever compare to this. She felt like her body was being torn apart molecule by molecule. With each passing second, she only grew weaker and unable to escape her fate. Whatever this Leech was doing to her would likely kill her in a matter of minutes. But not before she suffered up until the bitter end.

As it drained her energy, Cara could see it clearer. The spirit straddled over her like a lioness pinning down its prey. The grey orbs in its eye sockets seemed to pulse and flicker with a dark energy. Somehow, Cara knew this was her own spirit being drained from her body and giving life to this creature. It snarled and hissed at her like it was proud of its actions. Spittle hung from its gaping maw.

Jeffrey rushed from across the room and slammed his full body into the being. The pair slid across the floor. Cara sat up and took in a deep breath.

Her body felt like hers again and the searing pain turned into an icy numbness. With her body back under her control, Cara tried to stand. She took one step and collapsed back to the floor. Her legs were weak and her body felt heavy. Jeffrey wrestled with the Leech on the floor. He gave her a quick look before turning back and plunging his knife deep into the creature's chest.

Cara let out a cry of disappointment. She watched as the spirit disintegrated into a thick cloud of mist. The knife seemed to pulsate at this, and the mist cloud began to float towards the blade. In seconds, the knife absorbed the entire cloud of water particles as if it had never existed.

"What the hell did you do that for?" Cara snapped between shallow breaths. "We could have caught it."

Jeffrey shook his head.

"We wouldn't have. The moment it drew your blood, it was over. A Leech feeds on the livin' slowly. But when it injures someone and draws blood, well, you saw what happens."

"More like felt it," Cara said propping herself up on her knees.

"Exactly. It wasn't gonna stop until you were gone. I had no choice."

"Damnit, we were so close. What are we going to do now?"

"Guess we'll have to search for more bait. We need something for that Sluagh. I can't reap it if it doesn't feed."

"And they always turn to mist when you're-"

Cara stopped in her tracks. The image of Jeffrey shrouded in mist stuck in her mind. Something about it seemed familiar. Like the thought of him cleaning his nails in her car. She had seen all of this before somewhere but couldn't remember where.

A long-lost memory crept into her mind from somewhere deep down. It was something that had happened to her as a child which she had all but forgotten. As she stood there staring at Jeffrey, she remembered it all. It had been an episode the therapists had called sleep paralysis. It was common for people to see scary images or ghosts in their room during a sleep paralysis episode. Unable to move, they would be forced to watch the terrifying scene unfold. Somewhere along the line, Cara had accepted this explanation as truth and forgot the incident entirely. Until now.

"What's the matter? Ya look like you've seen a ghost." Jeffrey laughed.

"It's you...you were my ghost. You're the one I saw that night." She took a step back and almost stumbled over. "Everyone told me I was seeing things. Said it was a hallucination. But you're real. It was you." Her hands shook as she pointed at him. Buried fear had risen inside of Cara. "That is not something a six-year-old should have to experience. Alienated from her friends because she's now a freak, talking about the scary ghost that tried to drag her into the closet only to whisper boo and never be seen again!" Her hands curled into fists at her sides.

"Well, damn. I thought you looked familiar," Jeffrey said and smiled.

Chapter 19

Dominic felt different. The last two lives he had claimed seemed to have jump started something inside of him. He couldn't explain how he felt. There was something different about him now, that was all he knew.

Dominic wasn't sure what would happen once he tried to unleash whatever new power he felt inside him. He stood over the bed in his cheap motel and stared at himself in the mirror. There were probably a thousand better places to test drive, but he wanted to do this now. He couldn't wait until he was far away from here. He needed to know what he could do. If he ran into trouble in the future, it might be of use.

Besides, he had to track down the woman who got away. He couldn't let her live. At this point, it was no longer about feeding the Sluagh but about his own self-preservation. She could identify him. And sure, bullets couldn't harm him. But he could rot away in a jail cell forever. With this great power, he didn't want to waste it.

With his eyes closed, Dominic concentrated on this foreign feeling bubbling inside his mind. It was like commanding a limb to move but required a lot more concentration. He focused his mind and energy on this strange feeling.

He took a step forward, but something was different. His body had not moved. The front half of his body felt light and free while the back half felt heavy and weak. It was a strange sensation that sent a surge of anxiety through the parts of his body he could still feel. He was detaching his spirit from his body. He had been able to push part of it out before in order to look through walls or unlock doors. Now, he was able to shed his body like a suit of armor.

His spirit wasn't free from his mortal shell yet. Dominic needed to push further to see how much he could manage. If he could step completely out of his body, there would be nothing that could stop him ever again. With the ability to project some sort of astral form, he could get through any door, sneak around unseen, avoid being harmed by anything. This would change everything.

With as much power as he could focus, Dominic took a large step forward. His body remained and his spirit moved. There was a strange, disconnected feeling. Almost like he had stepped into a foggy, dream-like state. He glanced back over his shoulder and spotted his body standing there like nothing had happened.

"So, this is what an out of body experience feels like," he mumbled to himself with a smile.

There was a thin mist surrounding his spiritual form. It trailed back towards his body like some sort of tether. A thought of an old scuba diver with the brass helmet fluttered through his mind. This misty tether felt a lot like the tubes of air that connected to their helmets to keep them alive. He could only surmise this worked in a similar fashion.

He needed to test the limits of this newfound power. If there was a maximum distance away from his body that he could travel, he would find it. Dominic carried on towards the motel room door. Like it was natural to do so, Dominic walked straight through the door without opening it. He phased through it and found himself looking at the parking lot.

The world seemed strange now. Colors were less bright. The world was darker and hazier. Like an unseen fog had descended on everything around him. There was a man walking down the road in the distance, but Dominic couldn't make out his details. He was nothing more than a shadow of a person. It seemed he was no longer in the world of the living but in a place between reality and the afterlife. Or was this it? Is this what happened after death? When a person died, did they roam the world as a lost soul? Was there no heaven or hell? Nothing but chaos.

Dominic didn't want to think about it anymore. It was all too much to take in. The idea that he could now walk in the spirit world was overwhelming enough. He didn't need to figure out the rules of the afterlife as well. Best left for another day.

There was still farther he could travel. Somehow, he knew he could. He needed to push it to the limit. Dominic set off towards the road and across the street. He felt lighter as he walked. His feet barely touched the ground as he moved. There was no need to come in full contact with the solid matter of the world when you could walk through it. A car sailed down the road, directly towards him. Dominic tensed, worried the car would run him down before remembering he was not in a physical form. He let the car glide through his body like it was made of smoke.

Once across the street, he turned to face the motel. He could still see the thin vapor that connected him with his body. It trailed behind him like a streak in an oil painting. It was his tether back to his real body. He wondered what would happen if something were to sever it. *Could* something sever it? He didn't know but he didn't want to find out. He could only imagine it would mean death.

Dominic felt comfortable pushing himself farther. There was nothing around that could interfere with him and his practice. No living person could see his spirit form. Of that, he was sure. If there was a limit to how far he could travel out of his body, he needed to know. It wasn't the sort of thing he wanted to test in a bad spot.

He followed the sidewalk for a few yards before it dipped down beside a small bridge. He followed the winding sidewalk down and discovered a small stream running next to the sidewalk. A few more yards led him to an overpass. The occasional car echoed over head as it passed by.

The area under the overpass was a spacious area like a concrete cavern. Dominic could hear the bubbling stream below him. Like all places cut off from the rest of the world, graffiti littered the area. Most were silly images with little meaning. But there was on that caught his eye. A troll like face with dark, black eyes. There were two floating orbs painted under the troll and someone had written *have you seen the mini lights?* Underneath. It was rather odd and Dominic didn't know what to make of it. He shrugged, assuming it was some urban legend from the area. He had been many places since the start of his hunt for sacrifices. One thing he had learned, urban legends were abundant in every city.

As he scanned the dark space, he spotted a strung-up sheet in the far corner. Some poor homeless person had claimed this area as their own. Not one to waste an opportunity, Dominic thought about making this person his next victim. After all, it beat having to do research and finding the next one. Here was someone ripe for the picking. And he could help grow his powers. But first, he wanted to see what he was dealing with.

Dominic stepped forward, glancing over his shoulder. The trail of mist was still present, and he felt he could continue with no issues. Without a second thought, he carried on towards the makeshift shelter. He didn't bother with pushing the curtain aside. He wasn't even sure if he would be able to. Instead, he passed through the curtain without disturbing it.

If a homeless man lived here, he was out for the night. But the corner wasn't vacant. A strange looking creature with long, straggly hair and arms made of pure muscle stood in the darkness. It stared at Dominic with sunken yellow eyes. The creature looked like the cross between a man and a gorilla. If Dominic could have released his bladder, he would have.

The spirits mouth opened, showing off several rows of razor-sharp teeth. It let out a wail that could have shattered glass. Fear had frozen Dominic until this moment. He readied himself to run for his life.

Before Dominic could move, the spirit lunged and slashed with its claws. He felt the nails tear through his left arm but there was no pain. Dominic flung himself through the curtain and bolted from under the overpass. It surprised him to see the creature did not follow. Though, that did not stop him from putting distance between him and its lair.

He followed the sidewalk in the opposite direction as it snaked alongside the stream. It was only now that he noticed the other figures out for a walk. He almost mistook them for people before realizing he could see them clear as day. They were spirits. Though there weren't many, it was enough to bring the point home for Dominic. The living was seldom alone. Even a short walk in a park surrounded the living with spirits. Both seemed to be oblivious to on another.

He'd had enough for one night. Dominic walked back up the embankment to the topside of the bridge. The motel sat like a dingy beacon in the night. He saw a few ghosts mingling in the parking lot and one or two walking in and out of rooms. They could travel anywhere they wanted. Why hang around a dirty motel? There was much he wanted to learn about the spirit world. For now, he had to get back to his body and recharge. It was draining, being away from his physical body.

There was no need to push open the motel room door. The feeling was still foreign to him. As he approached, his hand went out towards the knob. He had to stop himself from gripping it. As he passed through the thin piece of wood, he kept his eyes open hoping he would see the interior of the door.

He saw nothing. There was a moment of darkness and then he was inside his motel room.

His eyes fell upon his body still standing just like he had left it. It was the most surreal thing he had seen all night. A thought about the most realistic mirror fluttered through his mind. As he approached, ready to combine his soul with his human form, he noticed a trickle of blood running down his left arm. There were three large scratch marks just below his left shoulder. Right where the claws of the spirit had scratched him.

"What the hell?" he asked no one.

Spirits couldn't harm each other, from what he could tell. But his case was different. Whatever happened to his spirit form would replicate on his human body. This rose a red flag for Dominic. If his body could be harmed when he was separate from it, could it be killed? There was no way to test that theory, but he could test something else. The gunshot wounds had healed. Had that been because of his spirit? He needed to know how vulnerable his body was when he left it.

Unlike leaving his body, re-entering was easy. With a simple thought, Dominic snapped back into his mortal shell like a rubber band. The force of it caused his physical form to tumble over and break his nose on the floor. He lay sprawled out on the carpet for several seconds. His body felt like gravity had taken a hold of him all at once. He was heavy and slow again. There was a white-hot pain in his left arm and a throbbing in his nose. Dominic lifted a trembling hand to his face and wiped a streak of blood away from his nostril.

"I guess that confirms it," he groaned as he sat up.

Lifting his left sleeve, Dominic saw the scratch marks were no longer there. The pain had already started to subside. The throbbing and bleeding in his nose stopped within seconds. When he returned to his body, his wounds would heal. If his body were to become mortally wounded, he could keep himself alive by returning. But it still meant he was vulnerable out of his body. There were pros and cons to using his spirit. He would have to be careful. One thing was for certain, he was getting closer to no longer needing the Sluagh. And when that day came, nothing could stop him.

Chapter 20

"Look, lady. We could stand here and bicker all day. It ain't gonna change anythin'," Jeffrey said.

"You were my ghost!" Cara screamed back. "I was petrified for years after that. You have no idea the kind of trauma I went through as a kid thanks to you."

"Thanks to me? I saved your life that night."

"You saved my life? By scaring me half to death? Not sure I follow that."

"Look, we don't exactly have an abundance of time right now. But listen. There are four types of wanderin' spirits. We call 'em Drifters, Augurs, Leeches, and the worst of them all Beasts. The one we just killed was a Leech. Y'all think what it did to ya was bad. Just wait until you encounter another Beast."

"What do you mean *another* Beast?"

"I mean, ya already encountered a Beast once in your life. I recommend not doin' it a second time."

"Are you seriously trying to tell me that I was almost murdered by a fucking ghost that night?"

"Yes ma'am. But so much worse than that."

"Worse? How could it be worse?"

"You don't know what a Beast can do. A fully powered Beast can do nightmarish things to the livin'. Not only can they kill you, but they can pull your spirit down to a place between the world of the livin' and the spirit world. Not even Death can reach ya there. A beast could spend decades or centuries tearing your spirit limb from limb over and over. And trust me, y'all would feel it. Beasts are the only ones that can technically harm another spirit. When one pops up on Death's radar, it always takes priority. That night, I was there to spare ya the worst kind of fate imaginable."

"I don't remember seeing any other ghost there except you!"

"And you wouldn't see 'em. But I bet you felt it. Cold air. An eerie presence like you were being watched. Lights flickering. That sort of thing."

Cara stood still for a moment. Jeffrey could see the gears turning in her mind. She was remembering that night and the events were revealing themselves to her. She would remember the little details and realize Jeffrey was right. There was a monster there that night and it wasn't him.

Jeffrey was less focused on remembering the Beast and centered on the memory of little Cara. The passage of time worked differently in the astral plane, but it still seemed like so long ago. He remembered the little girl spotting him across the room. Jeffrey could appear before the living at will. But a human being able to see a spirit with minimal effort was impossible or should have been. Jeffrey never understood how she had accomplished this.

The memory of the little girl sat with him for years until it eventually fell from his mind. Hunting wandering spirits always took precedence. Everything else always became background noise.

"Alright, even if what you said is true, that doesn't explain why you tried to scare me that night. If you really were there to save me, why would you scare me like that?"

Jeffrey laughed.

"Oh yeah, I remember now. Alright, maybe I see why you're mad. Just a bit of fun."

"And that's fun for you, is it? Scaring little girls out of their minds!"

"Relax a bit, lady. Just keeping the spirits light. How was I to know you'd need years of therapy because of my little joke?"

"You could have just not done it. Scaring a child for fun is hardly a joke."

"Look, there are bigger things at play here than something that happened to ya as a little girl. In case ya don't remember, there's a man killing people and reaping spirits out there and he's after you. What say you to tablin' this discussion for another time?"

Cara still seemed unhappy, but her expression said she understood. The living was so emotional. Jeffrey had a feeling he had never been such an emotional creature in life. For all he knew, he could have been the biggest box of emotions the world had ever seen. He envied Cara. At least she had a memory of her young life. There was nothing he could remember. If Jeffrey could have seen a therapist, they might have told him it was the reason for acting out against the living. Why he would go to great lengths to scare them or play with their minds. Jealousy. They had what he could never have. Memories. Since there was no such thing as therapists in the afterlife, Jeffrey would never learn this truth. Not that he would care to learn it anyway.

"Fine," Cara said. "I'll table it for now." She gritted her teeth on the last couple words. Jeffrey rolled his eyes.

We're a proper couple now he thought.

"So, what's the plan?" Cara asked. "We can't waste more time hunting down another spirit just to lose it again."

"Well, I do have an idea, but ya probably won't like it."

"Try me."

"Things might be easier if we focused less on the spiritual bait and more on the physical."

"You mean a *person*?"

"Indeed," Jeffrey said.

"What? Me? You're right, I don't like it."

"No, not you. Someone like you."

"Still don't like it."

"Oh, come on now. A bit hypocritical of ya, don't ya think?" Jeffrey said with a laugh. "You were all willin' to hand over a spirit to this guy so we could stop him. But a person is crossing the line?"

"Yeah, it is. That's what we living call murder. No one would come knocking on my door about a missing or dead ghost. Except maybe doctors from the psych ward."

"Okay, fair enough. What's your suggestion then?"

"What about luring him to a place already inhabited by a spirit? Then he's forced to deal with it."

"It's risky. It could come after us instead."

Any option they came up with would have its risks. He thought over her plan carefully. It would be more complicated than finding a living person. Every second they wasted trying to get a spirit in the right place at the right time lost them time. While they wasted time, Dominic could be out there growing stronger.

"Okay, so what? We use *me* as bait to lure this guy out. We meet him at some sort of abandoned warehouse or wherever we find another spirit. If it attacks me, then so be it. He will want to intervene to make sure I don't die and slip through his fingers, right? He'd probably send this creature after the spirit."

"And what happens when he decides to let the spirit kill ya and reaps it when it's done?"

"Then you step in and stop him."

"Right, 'cept we're forgetting about that Sluagh creature. In case you forgot, it eats other spirits. Which means, it could kill me. And maybe you're okay with dyin' but I aint."

"Uh, aren't you already dead?"

"Ya know what I mean."

Jeffrey started towards the door. There was no sense arguing the point anymore. Too much time had been wasted already. The best option was to find a suitable human they could use as bait. When Dominic arrived to kill him and the Sluagh feasted on the spirit, Jeffrey would reap the creature. Then there would be nothing between him and Dominic.

He was still unsure how he would stop Dominic. But one step at a time. If he weren't dealt with soon, everything could be shoved into chaos. Dominic's new power could allow him to dominate the spirit world. He could kill all those who oppose him and even walk in both worlds. It was too much power for any man or spirit to have.

"There's no way I'm helping you kidnap a person and sacrificing him to this guy. I can't do that."

"We could pick someone terrible. Scum of the Earth type. Like a pedophile."

"I don't care who it is. I can't do it."

"Look, I get it. But we have to think of the bigger picture."

"No, Jeffrey, I get the bigger picture here. I understand what you and Death have told me. If this man becomes all powerful it could be a dangerous tragedy for the living and the dead. But if I have to become the very monster he is to stop him, then what is worth saving?"

Cara followed Jeffrey as they made their way out of the warehouse and into the calm night.

Jeffrey, for the first time in decades, looked up at the stars. He always wondered about them. What was out there? Was Earth it? How much of what they did mattered? It made him feel small. Death probably held a lot of the answer to the universe, but she wasn't sharing. But Jeffrey wasn't exactly asking, either. He wondered if he should start.

Jeffrey leaned against his own car and looked back down at Cara. She was a determined woman. Almost too determined for her own good. But he admired her for it. Where most people would compromise on their values, she stood strong. It was a trait he liked a lot. Still, it was frustrating. He could see no other options to put a stop to Dominic's madness. None that didn't put them on the chopping block. And Jeffrey knew his importance. If the Sluagh killed him, there would be no one left to stop Dominic. Of course, Death had other hunters she could employ. None like Jeffrey. His name was well known among the other hellhounds and regular spirits alike.

"Alright, Cara. Ya don't want to find someone to use as bait and I can't let us use ourselves. So, what do we do next?"

Cara stood silent for a moment. Jeffrey knew she was processing all her thoughts. In the end, she would realize he was right. There was no other option they could take. Putting themselves in harm's way made no sense. But finding the right bait did. Especially someone who was expendable. Someone nobody would miss. A criminal already rotting away in his jail cell or a cartel boss that murdered and raped as he pleased. There would be no problem with removing a person like that from this world and perhaps even the next.

"What about a Beast?" Cara asked like the idea just sprang into her mind.

"What? You've gone out of your mind."

"You said it yourself, a Beast is the only spirit that can harm another spirit. Maybe we lure this man and his monster out into a place with a Beast and let it sort out the problem. Maybe we'll get lucky and he'll take both out with him."

"Lady, seems like you really like the plans that get us killed. What's wrong with you?"

"Technically, wouldn't we be at risk if we used human bait as well? What if he didn't fall for it and came after us instead? He can't be dumb. He might see through the plan. Which is why this is perfect. He'll never see it coming. Sure, he might suspect a trap, but I bet he comes anyway. And when he's attacked by a beast- "

"There's no guarantee the Beast will attack the one we want 'em to." Jeffrey said, rubbing his temples.

"And there's no guarantee Dominic won't skip the human we bait him with and come after us instead. But at least this levels the playing field. Without it, we have no protection from that creature of his."

The fact that she was right annoyed Jeffrey. His plan allowed them for no backups. If Dominic sent the Sluagh after Jeffrey, there would be no stopping it. While he fought for his life, Dominic would kill Cara. He would have failed on both counts. If he could get them all in a room together with a Beast, there would be a chance. It might get dangerous for Cara and himself, but at least it would be just as dangerous for Dominic and his pet.

"There are a few kinks to work out in y'alls suicide plan, dear. But I suppose if anyone can iron them out, it's me."

Cara smiled and asked, "What do we do next?"

"I need to have a chat with Death. Only she knows where a Beast might be hiding."

Chapter 21

Luring Dominic to their trap would be difficult. The man wouldn't be easily convinced. If Jeffrey played it right, he might be able to convince Dominic he was willing to give up on the woman. Luring Dominic to a beast would be the only option. Beasts weren't exactly friendly creatures. He would never get one to follow him out of its dwelling.

This all would have been so much easier if Cara had agreed to use a living person as bait instead. It would have been easier to convince Dominic as well. Jeffrey could have offered a new sacrifice as a sort of truce. If he left Cara alone, Jeffrey would give him someone else. The cover would have been perfect. There was no reason for Cara to be up in arms about it. He understood that she felt it was against her morals to let another person die. Not just die but cease to exist after the Sluagh devoured it. Someone terrible like a child molester would deserve it. How could she detest it?

He sat in the passenger seat of Cara's car, brooding over the choice. Death had given them what they were looking for. Now, they were on their way to the beast's location. Jeffrey thought about lying to Cara. He could give her directions somewhere else and find his human victim. Against his better judgement, he decided against it. He needed Cara's help now. He couldn't afford to make her an enemy.

Dominic had grown stronger since their last encounter. No doubt he had killed a few more people and absorbed their souls. It would be a struggle to reap the Sluagh without Dominic trying to intervene. As much as he hated to admit it, he needed Cara's help. She could distract the brute while he fought to reap the Sluagh. Without her, it would be an uneven fight. And he had seen the way Cara fought. She was not someone to be trifled with. He knew she could hold her own. At least for a while.

He looked over at Cara. She was remarkable. For the living, of course. He couldn't believe he actually admired the woman. He never cared about the living. Whether or not they lived or died was no concern of his. They were nothing but shadows to him. Death always gave him grief for letting the living die on his missions, but he didn't care much. They would all become spirits eventually. Why should he care?

But Cara was different. He viewed her crystal clear. It was strange, really. Jeffrey had to focus to see most other living. With Cara, he could view her like she was one of the other spirits in his realm.

"So, what's the plan when we get this guy there?" Cara asked.

"There are two positive outcomes we can hope for," Jeffrey said. "The Sluagh kills the Beast and I reap the Sluagh. Or the Beast kills Dominic and drags his spirit down to wherever it is they take things."

"And what happens if you can't kill the Sluagh? What then?"

"You'll probably be killed by Dominic and the Sluagh will absorb me, feedin' my essence to Dominic."

"Yeah, not ideal."

"At least that we agree on."

"Are you still upset that I won't let us use a person as bait?" Cara asked.

"Y'all gotta admit, it would be easier."

"How so?"

"We bring an offerin' to Dominic and tell him we will hand it over in exchange for peace. He agrees. We leave. I go back, unseen, and wait for him to murder the victim. When the Sluagh starts to feed, I reap that sonofabitch."

"I have to hand it to you, Jeffrey. It's a solid plan."

"Agreed. So, we're doin' it then?"

"Hell no! I'm not letting you damn some poor person to that kind of torment. They don't even get a chance at an afterlife. Just gone forever. And like I've already said, that doesn't look good for me. No one will believe me if I say 'Oh, I sacrificed that guy to a demonic creature so my ghost buddy Jeffrey could reap a person stealing souls to become all powerful.' I'd get locked up in jail. Or a mental ward."

"No one'd ever know you were involved."

"It's murder and I won't be a part of it."

Jeffrey let out a sigh.

"Hypothetically, let's say it was someone like Hitler we sacrificed. Would it be okay then?"

"There's no point dealing in hypotheticals since they can't happen."

"Fine."

"Hey, that does bring up a good question. What happens to people like Hitler when they die? Is that bastard just roaming around somewhere out there?"

Jeffrey smirked.

"Let's just say certain spirits don't get the chance to become lost before they're found."

With that, the conversation ended. Jeffrey couldn't help but think she had a point. The more corrupt and vile the person in life became, the easier it was for their spirit to become one of the lost ones. Jeffrey did not relish the idea of hunting down Cara's spirit and reaping her several decades from now.

"We're close," Jeffrey said.

"What's the plan once we get there?"

"First, we're gonna want to scope the place out. I'm not sure where this beast is at the moment. Could be an empty field for all I know. We don't want to find it right away, though. We need to get Dominic there first."

"And how do we do that?"

"I can track him down at any time." He flashed the knife. "Can still feel his presence."

"How will you convince him to come?"

"You insisted on being the bait. So, I was gonna offer him you. Here's what we'll do. I'll set you up somewhere far enough away from the beast that it doesn't come for you. Then I will go find Dominic and tell him I got ya stashed somewhere and y'all can have your fun together. When he gets there, I'll find the beast and provoke it, bringing it straight at him. As soon as you see me comin', run. Trust me."

"And what if Dominic gets there before you come back with the beast?" Cara asked. Her voice cracked on Dominic's name.

"Y'all gonna have to hold your own against him for as long as ya can."

She could hold her own against Dominic. Jeffrey had no doubt. He wasn't sure about how strong Dominic had grown since their last encounter. Things might be different this time around. There was no telling what the man would be able to do now. This was something they had never seen before. Jeffrey could only wonder at what type of abilities the man had obtained.

"We're about there," Jeffrey said, pointing down the street.

"Here? This is a neighborhood."

"Exactly. Perfect place for a beast. They take up residence with the living and torment the hell out of 'em."

"So, Amityville Horror, huh?"

"What?" Jeffrey asked.

"Nothing, never mind. Which house is it?"

"Just a few more down," he said as they continued driving. "There, that's the one."

He pointed do a dark house with a for sale sign in the front yard. What luck. They wouldn't have to worry about another family being in the house and waking. He was sure Cara would have words against the plan had an innocent family been involved. This couldn't have worked out better. At least, for now. He still hated that he had to involve a beast in their plans but there was no turning back now.

The house towered over them. The second story windows seemed to glare down at them in anger. Something terrible lurked inside, waiting for a victim to arrive. Anyone unassuming would think it was the perfect home to raise a family. A nice front yard with a large oak tree in the center. The clean white paint was bordered with a vibrant blue which gave it a homey feel. Any living family would be happy to stay here.

Jeffrey spotted a few spirits out for a late-night stroll. They hastened their step as they approached the beast's den. They could sense something terrible lurked there. Though, they were probably unaware to exactly what it was. Which was for the best. There was no fate worse than being taken by a beast. He almost felt sorry for the Sluagh. But that creature was a monster all its own. It would not be missed.

"I'm gonna go get Dominic," Jeffrey said. "Do not move from this car no matter what happens, you understand?"

"Trust me, I'm not going in there until I have to."

"Good. I can travel faster than Dominic so once I've set the trap, I'll come let you know. We'll find ya a nice place to hide and wait this whole thing out. Unless you never want to be seen again, don't step foot in that house."

Cara nodded.

"Stay put," Jeffrey said as he passed through the passenger door.

"Yeah, I get it," Cara mumbled to herself.

Jeffrey tapped on the glass with a ghostly finger and said, "Seriously. Don't."

Cara couldn't help but laugh a little, even though she was getting annoyed. She gave him the finger and he gave her a nod in return.

An engine roared from nowhere before Jeffery's car appeared from thin air like a mirage. He could see Cara's curiosity through the driver side window. She wanted to know more about his car. He would be more than happy to talk all about it. It was unusual for the spirit world. He loved to gloat about his baby, Mia.

He smiled as he climbed behind the wheel. He had spent too much time in the passenger seat of Cara's car. Finally, he would be able to drive himself. Freedom at last. The grin on his face widened as he shut the door and put the car in gear. Soon, Dominic would no longer be an issue. He took one last look back at Cara before driving off. He found himself hoping she listened and stayed out of the house. Based on her reaction, and Jeffrey's constant reminding, he assumed she would keep her word and stay out. He was surprised to find he was worried for her well-being. It was a strange feeling, caring for one of the living.

No, that wasn't it. He didn't care about her. He couldn't. He still needed her. But he knew that was a lie. Her part had been done for a long time. If the beast took her, Dominic would no longer have another victim to prey on. Cara being removed from the picture would be a good thing. And yet, Jeffrey couldn't stand the thought of the beast taking her or Dominic sacrificing her.

Before he drove off, Jeffrey looked back at Cara and the two locked eyes.

"Stay...out...of...that...house," he mouthed before driving off into the night.

Chapter 22

Cara was exhausted. It felt like days since she had last slept. She didn't want to look down at the clock on the radio for fear she would see it was almost morning. Her eyelids began to feel heavy. Invisible weights pulled them down further with every passing second. Cara fought to stay awake but was losing.

Her vision drifted from the car dashboard to the looming house. Somehow, the suburban dwelling looked menacing in the darkness. She could almost picture the garage door sliding up to reveal a mouth full of razor-sharp teeth and tongue flicking like a snake. The windows above the garage glared down at her like piercing eyes. She wondered if the house would still appear menacing had she not known what lurked inside.

As she stared at the house, she began to feel a sense of calm. Her thoughts drifted to nothing as her eyelids began to close. A swirling haze seemed to cloud her mind and her vision until there was nothing to see but the house in front of her. Cara pressed her forehead against the window and let her eyes close.

She fell into a deep sleep and began to dream. It was a peculiar dream. She was nine again and standing in front of her childhood home. She stared up at it in wonder. There were lights on inside and voices floating on the air indicating her family was inside and nothing had changed. It would be so nice to see them again after so long. She missed them.

Cara felt compelled to go home. To walk inside and embrace her mother and father. There was so much she wanted to tell them about her life. About what she had become. Sadly, they had never seen her accomplish her career. Both her parents had died when she was in her early twenties. It was a tragedy nobody saw coming, and one that no one could have ever predicted. Her parents had gone away for a romantic cabin getaway up north. During the trip, a violent snowstorm whipped through the mountain. The cabin was buried under the snow, and it took rescue workers days to clear it out. But her parents' bodies were never found. Search and rescue told Cara it was typical for people to abandon their shelter in severe storms like these and become lost in the snow. Not the comfort Cara had hoped to hear regarding her parent's death.

The world was chaos. Cara understood this better than most. She had chosen the career path of personal bodyguard to help keep people safe. It gave her a sense of control over an uncontrollable world. She always knew, no matter how hard you fought or how well protected you kept yourself, life could be over in the blink of an eye. Control was an illusion.

Her parent's voices still drifted on the breeze, echoing from inside the home. She couldn't help but wonder if she had been given a glimpse beyond the veil. Maybe her parents had stuck around to see her grow after all. Jeffrey had told her many chose to stick around to see the world or watch over their loved ones. Could her parents have done the same?

A desperate need to see them again filled her mind and body. Her childhood home beckoned for her to return. To step inside and embrace her parents after such a long time. She could see no harm in seeing them one more time. There was something important she was supposed to be doing, but she couldn't remember what that was anymore. The memory of her parents was too great.

Cara put her left foot forward and slid closer to the house. It was a funny feeling, like her feet were not under her control. She moved forward like a marionette doll. Looking behind her, Cara could see nothing but darkness. It seemed the only thing that existed in this world was her home.

The place she had spent her childhood no longer felt like the warm inviting place she had hoped. Something felt off. But there was no turning back now. She was compelled to move forward until she was face to face with the front door. Her hand reached out and gripped the cold doorknob in one hand. She gave it a slow turn and the door creaked open.

The inside looked the same as she remembered it. Except for the lingering darkness. There were no lights or happy voices. Everything was empty and silent. She struggled to remember why she was here. What was she supposed to be doing? Someone had told her something shortly before she had entered the house, but she couldn't remember what. She desperately searched her memory for an answer.

When she reached the center of the living room, the dream state began to wear off. Her childhood home melted away around her like a surreal painting. Fantasy dripped from the walls to reveal reality. She was not in her childhood home. Instead, she had found herself in the very house Jeffrey had warned her to stay out of.

Her neck snapped back towards the front door still open wide. Thoughts of running flooded her mind. Before she could move, the door slammed shut. Cara bolted across the room and gripped the knob in fear. It wouldn't budge. It seemed to be locked from the outside. Her heart thumped like a jackhammer in her chest. She had never felt fear like this before.

The house was empty. Not a single piece of furniture or decoration graced the home. She looked for anything she could use to break the glass and escape this nightmare. There was nothing. That wasn't going to stop her. Cara approached the window in the living room. She peered outside and saw her car sitting in the street.

The glass looked thin enough. A well-placed kick would do. She stepped back and flailed her foot out towards the center of the glass pane. It cracked but did not shatter. As she readied herself for another strike, the glass began to melt back into its original shape. The crack had disappeared. Cara's heart leapt up into her throat. This place was a prison. There was no escape.

A disembodied laugh echoed through the halls. It was as quiet as a whisper. But she had heard it. The memory of her bedroom closet flashed through her mind. Cara shut her eyes and tried to wake up from this nightmare. All of this was nothing more than a dream. Eventually, she would wake up and Jeffrey would be standing over her with that devilish grin on his face.

When she opened her eyes, nothing had changed. It was all terribly real. Somehow, the had been lured into the house in a dream-like state against her will. Now that she wanted to leave, she couldn't. Jeffrey had not mentioned that a beast had this sort of power over the living. She wondered if he even knew about it.

Down the hallway, a bedroom light began to flicker. She had seen enough horror movies in her life to know heading towards the room was suicide. She wouldn't be going anywhere near that bedroom. Cara exhaled and saw a stream of air pass her lips. The temperature had dropped significantly. Her body began to shiver like she had been dunked in a tub of ice. Half was from the chill and the other half from fear.

Cara spun around and tried for the front door again. When the knob wouldn't turn, she pounded a fist against it and screamed. Her only hope was a late-night passerby hearing her screams and liberating her. There was no such passerby. There was no one to rescue her. It would be the second time that night she stared her own mortality in the face. Only this time, she did not think she would have a chance to fight back.

From behind her, a sound like a knife scraping against drywall erupted in her ear drums. It grew louder with each passing second. Something was approaching her. Cara took short breaths and prepared to spin to face her attacker. When she had finally worked up the courage to move, there was nothing there. The house had grown quiet once again.

Somewhere, a door creaked. It went on for several seconds before slamming with a loud *thud!* More doors began to creak and slam. It repeated over and over until all Cara could hear was the sound of slamming doors. Her ears drums started to ache. Cara pressed her hands against her ears to block the sound. She could hear the muffled door slams as they repeated over and over again.

A dark shadow shot across the room at the edge of her vision. She turned to face it but saw nothing. The shadow darted at the opposite side of her vision and she spun to face it. Again, there was nothing there. Whatever this thing was, it was toying with her and enjoying it.

Cara tried the front door again. It still would not budge. She pounded a fist against wood and screamed. A putrid smell filled her nostrils forcing her to gag and nearly vomit. It was an overwhelming aroma of decay. She heard a disgusting sound that reminded her of a soaked cloth hitting the floor. It sloshed over and over. She was afraid to turn to face it but knew she had no other choice.

In the center of the room, a brown sludge dripped from the ceiling. Each drop made her flinch. A pile of brown goop had formed in the center of the empty living room. It pulsated in a rhythmic beat like a pumping heart. As more brown slush fell from the ceiling, it began to take on some sort of form.

It slowly resembled a person. A human made of clay which had managed to melt down to an amorphous blob. Features had begun to form. The outline of a face was visible. Empty eye sockets stared up at Cara with a disturbing glare. She had no idea what was forming before her eyes. It had frozen her in fear.

"Cara...sweetheart," the blob began to speak. Its voice was high pitched and scratchy like keys scraped over a violin.

"Nothing...will...harm...you...while...I'm...around," it said. Cara's breath became labored and panicked. They were the words of her father. "Daddy...isn't...afraid...of...anything," it moaned.

The disembodied voice laughed in her ears again. Somehow this beast was inside her head. It knew everything there was to know about her. Her past, her memories. It was all there for the taking. It could use it all against her. She wondered if this were the same spirit which haunted her room when she was younger. Jeffrey had said he reaped it, but what if he had been wrong?

"I'm not afraid of you," she said as her heart thudded in her chest. She knew it was a lie. And worse, she knew *it* knew it was a lie.

"I...love...you...Cara." The voice sounded more like her father now.

The echoing laughter returned with a whisper. It said, "He's in here with us. Come be with him again."

Cara flung her arms out instinctually. She was ready to fight back whatever monster had whispered in her ear. The blob on the floor continued to pulsate as she spun around to face her attacker. As before, there was no one there.

"Stay back!" she screamed. This thing would not drag her down to whatever horrible place it lurked without a fight.

The doors began to slam once again. Even the cupboards in the kitchen flapped like bird's wings. The rotten flesh smell became overwhelming. Brown sludge dripped down the walls and every light in the house strobed. Cara's senses were overwhelmed. She shivered in the cold but did not lose her nerve. She stood strong. At once, everything stopped, and an eerie calmness fell over the house.

With a thunderous roar, the beast burst from the back bedrooms, racing towards Cara. Long hair framed its sunken cheeks and bulging eyes. Its arms were like long, thick tree trunks. Its torso was thin and frail. Gray skin stretched over its frame revealing every rib in great detail. The mismatched proportions only served to make the creature look terrifying.

It was surrounded by a black cloud of smog that seemed to swirl around the creature as it moved. Cara found herself frozen in fear as the beast pounced on her. She felt it grip her by the arms and a white-hot pain shot out through her body. It was like the creature's touch burned her skin. Cara struggled to get free. The beast's hands slid up and down her arms, causing Cara to cry out in pain. It snarled and snapped in her face like a wild dog. Cara had never felt a fear as intense as this.

In the blink of an eye, the beast disappeared. Cara dropped to the floor and curled her arms inward. The burning sensation had dulled but had not completely vanished. It felt like a smolder just beneath her skin. Cara was not a stranger to pain. But this was worse than anything she had ever endured.

Before she could wonder why the Beast had disappeared, she heard the disembodied laugh once again. She understood what it was doing now. It was toying with her. It got satisfaction from the torture it inflicted on others. Jeffrey crossed her mind for a moment. He too liked to harass the living. He might not have killed people when he was finished playing, but the psychological damage could be just as bad.

Though she did not think she could, Cara forced herself to stand. The burning feeling in her arms had left her feeling weak and drained. Almost like the Beast had absorbed energy from her. Her legs swayed like palm trees in a heavy wind. Any moment, she feared she would topple back to the floor and become easy bait for this monster.

The banging began once again. Doors and cupboards all around the house opened and slammed shut. Lights flickered on and off. The strange black ooze continued to slide down the walls again. The goop pooled on the floor around her. Cara could only watch in horror as it began to giggle and slide closer. She didn't know what it was, but she knew she didn't want it to touch her. The circle of black tar closed in. Hands stretched up through the substance and reached out toward her. If one hand grabbed her, she knew it would be over. This would be how it dragged her down to that awful place Jeffrey had told her about.

Voices cried out around her from her memory. Her parents spoke in broken words like skipping records. Each word spoken felt like a knife and Cara's psyche. She flinched at every sound. Fear had almost immobilized her.

Beyond the blob was a clear spot of floor leading down the hallway. If she could manage to leap from her prison, she had a chance to break free. Cara slid her right foot back a few inches and readied to make the lunge. A hand reached out and swatted at her but missed. Cara moved faster than she had ever moved before. Fear giving her strength, she dove headfirst over the arms reaching from the disgusting blob. The clear floor moved up to meet her faster than she expected. She shielded her face and head with her hands, vaulting herself into a roll which brought her back to her feet.

When she was up, she didn't waste any time. The blob was only a few feet behind her. It would soon be after her. Cara bolted down the hallway and barricaded herself in one of the empty rooms. The beast would be able to get in, of that she had no doubt. But at least it bought her a few seconds to breathe and formulate a plan.

Except, there was no time to think. When Cara had turned around, she found herself staring at her childhood room. Everything was exactly as it had been. Right down to the Powerpuff Girls nightlight. The sight mesmerized her for a moment and the rest of her problems melted away. For a moment, she expected to hear her mother or father shouting from a different room to brush her teeth and climb in bed. She no longer felt like a thirty-year-old woman caught up in a fight against spirits and the Grim Reaper. Instead, she felt like a nine-year-old little girl who only wanted to snuggle up with her blanket and sleep.

The feeling overwhelmed her. The bed called to her. Deep in her mind, she knew to resist the urge, but she couldn't remember why. Her feet moved beneath her like they were under someone else's control. Cara didn't fight it. It felt good to let go. She wanted to sleep in her bed. Once the blanket was pulled up to her chin, she would feel safe again. Safe from what, she didn't remember.

Cara pulled back the pink comforter on her bed. The sheets looked so warm and inviting. She didn't hesitate to crawl in. Her head sank into the pillow and she felt at ease. The blanket was pulled up to her chin. Cara looked up from her cozy spot in the bed and saw a familiar face staring down at her.

"Hi daddy," she said. Her voice was that of a squeaky nine-year-old.

"Hey sweetheart," he said as he leaned down and kissed her forehead.

Something in the back of her mind told her this wasn't right. She ignored it. As her father stared down at her, the nagging feeling continued. She tried to mentally bat it away like a mosquito buzzing around her ears. There was no getting rid of the thought.

"Daddy," she said, not knowing what she would say next. Her subconscious mind had taken over. "Can you check the closet for monsters?"

Her father stood above her and smiled. The smile no longer seemed warm and inviting. Something was off about it. Cara was becoming suspicious of her surroundings with every growing second. She just couldn't place what.

"Of course, sweetheart," her father said and turned to face the closet.

He approached it and pulled open the door. He stood there for a moment like he was scanning the inside. Cara watched him closely, knowing something wasn't right, now. There was a memory of a house that wasn't hers. She could remember feeling trapped and scared. But she still couldn't remember why.

"Well," her father said. "There are no monsters in here." He turned around and stared at Cara. His face was no longer his own. It had contorted to an evil monstrosity. The eye sockets were sunken and empty. His cheeks melted off his face like cheese left on a hot surface. Something oozed from his mouth. It ran down from razor sharp teeth like a perverted river. "But there's one out here," her father's broken voice said to her.

Everything flooded back to Cara in that moment. The memory of the night was clear as day now. This monster had been tormenting her for what seemed like hours. The bed she had found refuge in no longer existed. It had been in her mind like the rest of her bedroom. Instead, she found herself sprawled out on the floor with this monster standing tall above her. It snarled and snapped like a ferocious dog. This was it. This was how she would die. Jeffrey had told her a beast was the worst fate imaginable. She could only hope he was wrong and that this beast would finish her quick.

There was a sound to her right. Like a small breeze blowing through the door. She couldn't look away from the slow advance of the beast before her. If she could manage to peel her eyes away from it, she wasn't sure she would want to. She no longer wanted to face the horrors of this house or this beast. She wanted it all to end.

"Ah, hell." She heard a familiar voice say.

Chapter 23

Jeffrey stepped into the empty bedroom and cast his eyes down at Cara. She was sprawled on the floor like she had tucked herself into bed. The beast standing over her snapped its head towards Jeffrey and gave a snarl. It didn't like being interrupted from its prey. Jeffrey knew he couldn't reap it. They still needed it for when Dominic arrived.

"You are one ugly sonuvabitch," Jeffrey said with a smile.

The beast did not respond. Instead, it lashed out with razor-like nails. Jeffrey dodged its strike with ease. After so many years of hunting these creatures, he was an expert at it. He was confident he could string it along for a decent amount of time. He just hoped Dominic and the Sluagh arrived soon. The longer he danced with the beast, the more likely he was to reap it.

Jeffrey dove backwards into the hallway and the beast followed. He wanted to lure it away from Cara. If the beast wanted to, it could kill her in a heartbeat. Jeffrey still needed her. Dominic might not stick around long enough if Cara was no longer there.

There was real danger taking on a beast, though it didn't come from a potential reaping and eternity of nothingness. The real danger came from the beast's ability to drag unwilling spirit down into its dark pit. If Jeffrey wasn't careful, he would suffer that fate. He had reaped enough in his time to know how to avoid it.

The beast chased Jeffrey down the hallway, flinging doors open as it moved. Jeffrey made his way to the living room and dodged another swipe of its long claws. Jeffrey kept his knife holstered. Wielding it would only increase the chances he would reap the monster prematurely. Instead, he opted to stay on the defensive. He dodged strike after strike as he darted back and forth around the living room.

After a few minutes of this spiritual game of tag, the beast began to grow impatient. It stopped striking at Jeffrey despite his best efforts to continue to antagonize.

"Come on, now," Jeffrey said. "I thought y'all was a killer. Can't even catch me. Pathetic."

This didn't seem to enrage the beast like Jeffrey had hoped. He could see in its sunken face that it understood something. Jeffrey was protecting the woman. It turned its head back towards the bedroom and snarled.

"Ah, shit," Jeffrey said as he lunged forward at the beast.

The two of them tumbled through the air. Sharp claws tore into Jeffrey's left arm and he cried out in pain. The wounds would heal like all other wounds Jeffrey received. But these would take longer and would hurt like hell. Too many slashes, and Jeffrey would be immobilized allowing the beast to drag him to its personal hell.

He grabbed the beast by the wrists and flung it across the room. It suspended itself in mid-air, reorienting. Even Jeffrey had momentarily forgotten that the rules of physics and gravity didn't always apply to spirits as expected.

It lunged at him again, taking a swipe at Jeffrey's midsection. He dodged it but the razor-like nails tore through his shirt. Lucky for Jeffrey, he avoided any injury. He couldn't keep this up for long. Dominic needed to arrive soon.

Then Jeffrey realized that Dominic might not come in the house at all if he could see or hear the struggle between him and the beast. Sure, they were fighting within the spirit realm now. But Dominic was gaining strength with every spirit he reaped. This meant he would grow more aware of the spirit world around him. He might even be able to walk in it. If he saw Jeffrey and the beast, it would be over.

"Guess we gotta leave the playground, bud," Jeffrey teased as he turned to run.

He ran down the hallway and into a different bedroom than the one Cara lay. There was no time to check on her to see if she were still unconscious. The beast followed behind Jeffrey, swiping and snarling all the way. Jeffrey did not stop when he reached the backwall. Instead, he passed through and made his way into the backyard. He was relieved to see the beast did the same.

The backyard wouldn't be good enough. Dominic or the Sluagh could scope it all out and spot them. He hated the thought of leaving Cara alone in that house. If Jeffrey didn't time it right, Dominic could kill her and the Sluagh could feast.

Jeffrey crossed the backyard towards a neighboring house. They would move their fight to another home's garage. That would buy him some time.

He just didn't know how long to spend toying with the beast. For all he knew, Dominic had already arrived. His knife could warn him if he grasped the handle, but he still did not want to risk reaping the beast. Their entire plan depended on it.

Once in the garage, he stopped and waited for the beast to come inside. It stepped through the garage door and stared down at Jeffrey. It looked wolf-like, now. It leaned forward and propped itself up on its long arms. He expected it to howl at him before charging. It didn't, of course. It galloped at Jeffrey on all fours, drooling and snarling.

There was no time to hesitate. Jeffrey lunged into the attack and fought as best he could. A few times, he was clawed by the beast. Each strike burned like he had been slashed with a hot poker. The beast was no longer toying with him. It was out for blood and it wouldn't stop until Jeffrey was injured enough he couldn't fight back.

Jeffrey had no choice but to continue this dance with the beast. He exchanged blows and accepted slashes to his body before delivering a kick to the spirits chest that sent it flying across the garage. It rolled across the floor as Jeffrey dropped to one knee. He panted and clutched at his wounds. With each passing second, he could feel himself growing weaker. Toying with the beast was taking too much out of him.

There was little choice now. He had to wield the knife. It would help to keep the beast at bay and give Jeffrey a sense of when Dominic arrived. He pulled it free from the holster and held it out. The beast rose from the floor and snarled at him once again. It did not focus on the knife but stared daggers at Jeffrey.

Dominic was close. He could feel it. This distraction with the beast only needed to go on a little longer. He could make it happen. His thoughts turned to Cara now. He hoped for her sake she had been able to pick herself up and make her way back to the car.

The Beast bent down on all fours like a rabid dog and charged. Jeffrey side stepped, pushed the beast with his free hand, and slashed with the knife. It cut through the beast's skin, and it howled in pain. Brown blood dripped from its wound to the concrete floor below. It looked down with wide eyes.

"Hey, now," Jeffrey said. "Fair is fair."

The beast did not seem to like Jeffrey's taunt, nor did it seem to like the level playing field. With little rational thought, the beast would continue to attack instead of running away. They had never been known for their critical thinking skills.

The knife handle grew warm and started to buzz in his hand indicating Dominic's proximity. Timing would be crucial now. If Dominic sensed a trap before Jeffrey could lead the beast to him, it would all be over. But Jeffrey didn't think he had to worry about it anymore. The beast was laser focused on Jeffrey now. It would be easy to lead him next door.

Jeffrey turned around and bolted for the inside of the house.

Jeffrey passed through the garage door and found himself in a small study. There was a sharp right turn into the kitchen. If the residents were awake and could see the beast and Jeffrey as they traipsed through the house, they would have died of fright. Jeffrey turned right and ran straight through the kitchen. The beast followed close behind. As they moved, things on the counters shifted slightly.

Jeffrey dove into the dining room to avoid a swipe from the beast's talons. He rolled across the large, oak table, knocking over one thin candle that had been sitting in the center as a display. It rolled across the table and dropped to the floor. There was no time to pause, the beast was already running through the table and straight at Jeffrey. Its claws would rip him to shreds if it caught him. That would hurt like hell.

The dining room let out to a wide-open living room, but Jeffrey did not stop to admire any of the furnishings or décor. Instead, he ran straight through towards the stairs. He could feel Dominic's presence closer now. He was either approaching the trap house or already inside. Jeffrey couldn't tell specifically. But he knew this chase would have to end soon.

The pair flew up the stairs and down the short hallway. Jeffrey did not want to risk popping into a bedroom with any of the living inside. The beast might change its target and go after them instead. He needed it focused on him. He let his body fall straight through the floor like it was made of water. He landed on his feet back in the garage. Seconds later, the beast dropped down with him.

"Hey there, buddy. Struggling to keep up?" Jeffrey smiled at his taunt. It seemed to work. The beast snarled with a snake-like flick of its tongue.

This was it. The final push. He would have to lead the beast back towards the other house.

Jeffrey dodged another swipe from the beast, though one nail still caught and dragged across his skin. It burned with excruciating pain, but Jeffrey pushed on. He started off towards the trap house. The beast was close on his heels taking swipe after swipe. Jeffrey could feel the wind from each attempted blow.

Out in the early morning moonlight, Jeffrey could see another car parked a couple houses down. It had not been there before. The trap had finally been set. But another sight caught his eye. The car Cara should have returned to was empty. Which meant she was probably still in the trap house with Dominic.

"Shit," he said as he increased speed towards the house. The beast snarled and barked behind him.

He wasted no time running straight through the wall which led to the living room. He stopped in his tracks and stared at the awful sight before him. Cara lay sprawled out on the living room floor. Dominic knelt over her with his hands on her throat. Cara's spirit stood close by staring at the scene in front of her. She seemed scared and confused. And Jeffrey understood why. The Sluagh was standing before her in its bird-like form. Its leathery wings shot out and wrapped around Cara's spirit like a blanket and the Sluagh went in for the kill.

"No!" Jeffrey screamed as he tried to spring across the room and tackle the Sluagh. But something shot straight over his head and dove towards the Sluagh and Cara. It was the beast. Jeffrey did not know if it had dived for Jeffrey and overshot or if it had recognized the Sluagh as a new, and worse, threat and adjusted course. Either way, he knew the outcome would not be good.

He tried to make it to them in time, but the beast tackled both Cara and the Sluagh. The Sluagh was unable to consume Cara's petrified spirit, but the beast would finish the job. Jeffrey could only watch in horror as the beast gripped both the Sluagh and Cara. Then the trio melted through the floor and disappeared.

Jeffrey dropped to his knees and yelled. The beast had taken them both to a place between the living world and the spirit. There would be no coming back. Cara was gone. The torture she would endure there would be unlike anything she could fathom or endure. But she wouldn't be able to die. Not for years or even decades. Jeffrey had failed. He cursed himself for being talked in to using her as bait.

He turned back towards Dominic who had just stood up from his fresh kill. He looked around, puzzled. The Sluagh should have been there by now to feed him his essence. Dominic turned and looked directly at Jeffrey. Though Jeffrey should have been confused as to how Dominic could see him, he didn't think about it. Instead, he glared at the man and gritted his teeth.

"You," he snarled and lunged through the air.

Chapter 24

The vast emptiness around her was overwhelming. It was a feeling unlike anything Cara had ever felt before. There was darkness all around her and yet she could still see. Only, there was nothing to see. There was nothing but an empty void to stare into.

It was like being in a deprivation chamber, except there were no sounds to hear. She couldn't hear her heartbeat or the rushing of blood in her veins. Both were things said to be heard in one of those devices. There was nothing but a deafening silence.

Anxiety kicked in and Cara began to shake. She couldn't remember anything before this place. She closed her eyes and thought hard. Nothing would come to her. For all she knew, this was all her life had ever been.

A ghostly image of a house materialized in her mind. She could remember it now. Jeffrey had taken her to this empty house to lure Dominic closer. Cara wasn't supposed to go inside, except she had wandered in. She did not know how or why. Something had controlled her.

Then an image of the beast rose in her head. It had brought her into the house. With the memory of the beast came the memory of what it could do. She then realized where she was. She was in a space between the living world and the spirit one.

"Am I dead?" she said aloud. The words echoed for what seemed like minutes.

"Dominic killed me," she answered herself. The memory had come back to her. Like the fog from a dream she could barely remember, the memory seemed far away. Cara focused on only the memory. She needed to remember how she got here. Maybe there was a way out.

She remembered waking up to find herself sprawled on the floor inside the house. There was a vague memory of her childhood and her father, but she couldn't remember why. When she realized where she was, Cara had run for the door. But something had stopped her. No, someone. Dominic had towered over her in the doorway.

He saw her and smiled. Cara remembered her heart sinking. It had actually felt like it had slipped from her chest and fallen through her body. Dominic was there and Jeffrey was nowhere to be found. Her first thought wandered to bait. Had Jeffrey decided it would be easier to let Dominic kill her and let the Sluagh feed on her spirit?

Dominic had smiled and said, "So, he was telling the truth. I expected this to be a trap." Cara had wanted to say it was a trap, but no longer believed it. Jeffrey and the beast seemed to be gone.

Cara heard movement in the abyss now. It came from everywhere and nowhere at once. She wasn't the only thing here. Her eyes danced around in the odd darkness, hoping for a glimpse of anything else. But she saw nothing. She let herself fall back into the memory of the house.

The memory floated back in like a cloud. Dominic had pushed into the house and shut the door. Cara attempted to scream for help, but Dominic had already pounced on her. She had been able to fight him back. A well-placed punch to his throat caused him to stumble backward. Cara had wasted no time delivering a powerful kick to his sternum. Dominic tumbled back and fell to the ground.

As she was about to drop down on top of him and pummel his face until he stopped breathing, something tossed her across the room like a piece of dirty laundry. Dominic had not moved from the floor. As her back struck the wall, she wondered if the beast had returned. Or had this monster Dominic traveled with attacked her?

She had looked up from the ground. Her back ached from where it had hit the wall. Dominic stood above her. Only he wasn't all there. He looked like a projection of himself. She could not see it for long before it started to dissipate. Her eyes darted over to Dominic's body still sprawled out on the ground. Dominic had learned to eject his spirit from his body. There would be no way to fight him.

Her foot lifted into the air by itself, and she was dragged across the floor. She tried to kick her unseen attacker, but it did her no good. With nothing to grip, she was at Dominic's mercy. Her foot dropped once she had reached the center of the room. Cara remembered looking around for some sign of her attacker. She could feel his gaze burning through her. It was the most uncomfortable feeling she had ever felt. If Jeffrey had returned then, he may have been able to reap his spirit and be done with everything. But he hadn't come back. The full memory flooded her mind.

Dominic's body had risen like a zombie. He turned towards her. Cara attempted to sit up, but Dominic was too fast. He had flung himself on top of her, hands around her throat. His body weight kept her from moving her legs, but her arms were still free. No amount of slapping, scratching, or punching had affected him. As her fingernails drew blood on his face, the wounds quickly healed. Again and again, she scratched until her body started to grow limp. She could feel her eyes bulging and her body fighting for air. In the end, Dominic had succeeded. She had died.

Cara remembered standing in the center of the empty living room, staring down at the whole scene before her like a strange movie playing out before her. She had felt weightless. Like a hundred pounds had been removed from her body. That's when the winged creature had shown up. She could only guess it was the Sluagh.

A noise broke the silence on the other side of the room. She turned in time to see Jeffrey pass through the wall and stop in his tracks. He had looked at the whole scene. She had seen something on his face she never thought she would see. Worry. But the sight wouldn't last long. The beast burst through the wall behind him. It had spotted the Sluagh standing over her and immediately attacked. She remembered it tackling the two of them together and the strangest sinking feeling had kicked in. It was like she was falling and standing still at once. She would have vomited if she were mortal.

That was everything then. She had remembered it all. The Beast had taken her and the Sluagh down to his domain. Which meant there were two monsters down here with her. There was no telling how long it would take for them to find her.

She felt an intense dread surge through her body. Cara couldn't explain it, but she knew it meant the beast was nearby. Of course it was. This was its world. She may have been lost down here, but she could only imagine the beast knew this world like the back of its hand. There was no time to consider the inner workings of this dimension. Cara had to find a way to escape. If the beast could enter this place, then it could leave. And if it could leave, so could she.

Something broke through the darkness ahead of her. Her eyes took longer than she expected to adjust to the scene. The Sluagh stared at her with its beak wide open. Cara didn't know if she could run away, but she turned around all the same. She was met by the beast, towering over her with drool sliding down its open jaw.

The two beings were in a sort of standoff together. Cara backed away. It didn't make a move. It only stared at the Sluagh. She imagined a tumbleweed billowing by as a trumpet blared the duel tunes from every old western she had ever seen.

"I need to get out of the O.K. Corral before the shooting starts," she whispered to herself.

The beast readied to attack. Cara dove out of the way just in time to miss the clash. The two spirits bit and clawed at each other. She watched from the ground as the pair battered each other like fighters in the ring. Somewhere deep in her mind, she rooted for the Sluagh. This was the beast's domain, which meant it had more control down here. If it won the battle, Cara would be at its mercy. Maybe if the Sluagh killed the Beast, she'd be able to escape its clutches.

There was a loud screech as the beast tore a hole in the Sluagh's left wing. It retaliated by clamping down on the beast's arm, tearing it free. The pair was locked in their struggle. Biting and clawing each other endlessly. Cara took the opportunity to search around for some way out of this place. She didn't know what to expect. She doubted there would just be a door standing at the edge, waiting to be opened.

She looked around at the vast empty space. There was nothing but the abyss for as far as she could see. No details of any sort jumped out at her. There was nothing to distinguish. No features or shapes to speak of. Everything was one large shadow.

The beast was thrust to the ground only inches from her feet. Cara scurried backward. The Sluagh cut through the air and landed on top of the wounded beast. It lashed out with its remaining arm, but the Sluagh pinned it down tight. The beast snarled up at the Sluagh and bit the air like a wild dog. Cara could only watch in horror as the Sluagh ripped the beast's other arm from its body, tossing them aside like used utensils. It let out a guttural scream as a brown sludge-like substance oozed from its wounds. It was the same brown liquid which had poured down the walls back in the house.

The Sluagh bent over, gripped the beats neck in its mighty jaws, and twisted. Cara heard a crunch and the beast stopped moving. The Sluagh stood still for a moment, staring at its prey before letting out a screech that sounded somewhere between a hawk and a lion's roar.

It turned to face her. Cara backed up, terrified this would be the end. She had its full attention now. At least it would be over quick. Jeffrey had told her how much torture living in this place with a beast would be. If she had to choose between fates, this was the better option.

"Well, what are you waiting for?" she cried out. "Get it over with you fucking bird!"

But the Sluagh did not attack. It turned from her and looked down at the bleeding body of the beast. One clawed hand reached out and picked up a handful of the brown ooze. Cara watched as the winged creature smeared the goop on its chest. Seconds later, the Sluagh began to pass through the floor and disappear.

Cara wasted no time running to the beast's body. Could that be the key to escape this place? Something in the blood, or whatever the brown syrup was, gave the beast the ability to enter this place. If the Sluagh could use it to leave, then hopefully she could too. Her trembling hand reached out and touched the goo. It was warm and awful. Cara pushed any squeamish thoughts aside and wiped it across her chest. Panic overtook her as nothing happened and she began to scoop handfuls of the slime and coat her body, being sure to cover as much as possible. The fear of part of her spirit being left behind filled her with dread.

At first, she felt nothing. Then something changed. It was a difficult feeling to explain. She could feel her surroundings. Not physically. Deep inside, she could sense the invisible cage around her. Even better, she could feel the exit now. Like the Sluagh had done, Cara started to pass through the floor.

Chapter 25

Fighting Dominic would be a challenge. Jeffrey couldn't harm the man's body. Even if he could, Dominic could heal his mortal being. There wasn't much Jeffrey could do to him. He needed Dominic's spirit outside of his body. The only way to accomplish this was with death. And since he couldn't kill Dominic, they were going in circles.

Jeffrey had decided to face Dominic head on. He let the man see him in full view. No tricks. No hiding. He managed to land several hits on Dominic and even toss him about the room several times, but it all seemed like wasted energy. Each time, Dominic stood back up with a smile on his face.

"You may have taken that creature away from me. But I didn't need him anymore," Dominic said, catching his breath.

Jeffrey stopped to listen. He didn't know where this sudden conversation would take him, but it was better than wasting his time fighting something he couldn't kill.

"Funny, you don't seem powerful to me. I'm throwin' ya around like a sack of potatoes."

"But you can't kill me."

"Don't get too flattered. I can't kill the living. Not allowed."

"That isn't the only reason you can't kill me," Dominic sneered. Jeffrey rolled his eyes.

"I assume y'all want me to ask what ya mean by that. But here's the deal, I don't care. I was givin' a task. Stop you. And that's what I'm gonna do."

He had enough of the games. Jeffrey dropped from the physical world and back into the astral plane where Dominic could no longer see him. He moved to the right and stopped. Dominic's gaze had moved to meet him. Knowing it could have only been a coincidence, Jeffrey stepped again. Dominic's eyes followed once more.

"What the hell?" Jeffrey muttered.

"I told you," Dominic started. "I don't need that creature anymore."

"Oh shit," Jeffrey said as Dominic lunged towards him. He didn't have to dodge the strike. Dominic could see him but couldn't interact with him. Whatever ability allowed him to see into the astral plane didn't grant him the ability to interact with it. Dominic passed through Jeffrey with ease. This only seemed to anger the brute.

"Seein' ain't the same as bein'," Jeffrey said and laughed. Y'all might think you're powerful cause you can see into my world. But ya can't touch it."

"I wouldn't be so sure about that," Dominic said. His eyes flicked down to Jeffrey's holster.

"Whatever you're thinkin' about tryin', it ain't gonna work."

Dominic had an overconfident look in his eyes. Jeffrey could tell he was planning to do something unexpected. The man's lips curled up in the corners to produce a strange and satisfied looking grin. Something started to happen that looked strange at first. Jeffrey had to take a step back and adjust his vision. A second Dominic had started to appear. It pulled free of Dominic's body like a snake from its skin. It took longer for Jeffrey to realize what was happening than it should have. His spirit was pulling free from his body.

The spirit version of Dominic leered at Jeffrey, looking pleased with himself. He had saved this big reveal for the final moments of their battle. Which meant, the whole time Jeffrey had toyed with Dominic had been nothing but a big game for the man. He'd had this ace up his sleeve the whole time.

Jeffrey started to clap sarcastically.

"That's a mighty fine trick. Sorry to tell y'all that ya just made it possible for me to kill you, now."

Jeffrey reached down and pulled the knife from its holster. This he could finally work with. He looked back at Cara's body and grit his teeth. She had died for nothing. Their trap had been worthless. Now, she was enduring the worst torment imaginable with that beast and it was all Jeffrey's fault. He should never have let her near this house.

"I'm going to take that knife from you," Dominic said. "And I'm going to cut your head clean off with it."

Jeffrey tightened his grip.

"Go on now, try it."

Dominic lunged forward and reached out with his large paw-like hands. Jeffrey dodged the strike with ease and lashed out with an attack of his own but missed. It wouldn't take much. One well-placed stab was all it would take. He was used to fighting with wandering spirits. They were strong but didn't think ahead. Most of them were like feral dogs. This, though, would be different. Dominic had the ability to plan and strike accordingly. It would prove a difficult challenge.

Jeffrey lashed out with the knife. The tip grazed Dominic's arm and he cried out in pain. The man retaliated with a heavy kick to Jeffrey's midsection that sent him sailing across the room. He rolled across the floor like a tumbleweed. Jeffrey never loosened his grip on the knife.

Back on his feet, Jeffrey lunged forward and tackled Dominic to the ground. He brought the knife down in a large swooping arc over his head, aiming for Dominic's chest. Dominic crossed his arms and braced against Jeffrey's, keeping the knife only inches from his chest. Jeffrey placed his left palm on the hilt and pushed. But Dominic wasn't letting up easy. He pushed back with equal force. Then he shifted his body weight and rolled over, pinning Jeffrey to the ground.

The two of them wrestled for control of the knife. Dominic pushed with all his might to turn the blade around. His strength was amazing. For such a new spirit, he shouldn't have been as powerful. Jeffrey wondered if it were due to the Sluagh granting him abilities or because he still had a mortal shell. He was uncertain what had made him more powerful. As they struggled with the knife, Jeffrey noticed a thin stream of mist that lined from Dominic's spirit and back to his body. The man was still tethered to his mortal shell. He was using it to power his spirit like a battery. Which meant-

Jeffrey knocked one of Dominic's hand free from the knife and gained control. Without sparing a second, he plunged the knife deep into Dominic's chest. The man winced like it burned but nothing else happened.

"How?" Jeffrey asked as he twisted the knife, hoping to end this man.

"Looks like you can't kill me with that thing, either."

Jeffrey pulled the knife free and kicked Dominic off him. He leapt back. There was no way to kill the man. He had failed. The Sluagh had transferred too many spirits. Death wouldn't be pleased. Hell, Jeffrey wasn't pleased. He had never failed a single mission as long as he had been a hellhound. And what a hell of a hunt to fail. There was no telling what kind of damage Dominic could do in the spirit world now.

A noise across the room caught both men by surprise. They turned to look only to see the Sluagh rise from the ground next to Cara's body. Somehow, the creature had returned from the beast's lair. Which meant the beast was probably dead. It also meant Cara was probably gone too. He felt a pang of shame course through him. There was little comfort in the fact that she no longer suffered at the hands of that beast.

"Looks like you're outmatched here," Dominic said.

The man was right. Jeffrey couldn't reap the Sluagh unless it feasted on something. He couldn't reap Dominic's spirit either. There was nothing left for him here. He had to retreat. Death would be unhappy, but what else could he do? He would have to call for her and explain everything. Maybe she would know what to do next. But he had to be alive to do it.

He readied himself to run when something else rose from the floor behind the Sluagh. The creature's gaze was so transfixed on Jeffrey, that it didn't notice Cara standing behind it. Jeffrey nearly fell to his knees. Somehow, against all odds, she had come back. There was a great story there, he was sure of it. And he would hear it out once they escaped.

"Why is that woman still alive? *How* is she still alive?" Dominic called out. The Sluagh turned to spot Cara behind him and growled.

"Ah, shit," Jeffrey said.

The Sluagh wasted no time lunging towards Cara. Her eyes grew wide with fear as the creature barreled into her like a semi-truck. Jeffrey had no time to reach the pair. The Sluagh had pinned her to the ground. Its beak opened and its head reared back, ready to strike. Jeffrey rushed forward, but he knew he wouldn't make it in time. The Sluagh would reap Cara right in front of him.

It stopped when something else entered the room. Like Cara and the Sluagh, the beast rose from the floor. Something was different about it now. There were gaping wounds in its chest that oozed a thick brown liquid. Its head was spun completely around and both arms appeared to be missing. Jeffrey stared at the front of the beast's body, but the back of its head. It was a disturbing sight. The beast growled and hissed as its head began to turn back towards the front of its body in an unnatural way. The sound of cracking bones echoed through the room. The Sluagh stepped away from Cara and towards the beast, poised to attack.

"T-that's impossible," Cara stammered as she climbed to her feet. "I saw the bird thing rip its damn arms off and break its neck. How can it still be alive?"

"If it didn't reap the beast, it ain't dead, sweetheart," Jeffrey cried out, readying himself for another fight.

Dominic took a step back. He didn't know much about the spirit world, but Jeffrey guessed he could recognize trouble when he saw it. Dominic stared at the creature like he was stuck in a trance. Jeffrey saw a perfect opportunity to strike. It would do no good but distracting Dominic would be his best chance of keeping him from interfering with the beast and Sluagh.

The beast wasted no time attacking its target. It and the Sluagh clashed in the center of the room. A whirlwind of long appendages and wings. Cara remained on the floor until the fight came her way. Jeffrey watched in the corner of his eye as she rolled to safety. She was still thinking like one of the living and not using her spirit body to its full potential.

Jeffrey sped across the room towards his distracted target. Dominic didn't see it coming until the last second. But that was all Dominic needed. He dodged the strike and countered a blow to Jeffrey's midsection. If Jeffrey had a pair of working lungs, the wind would have been knocked from them.

He slashed again with his knife but missed his mark. Not that it mattered. Behind him, the two creatures were still locked in their death battle. Only one would be walking away from the fight. Jeffrey could only hope it would be the Sluagh. It would be the easier target while it fed.

When Cara stood, she had to dive out of the way. The flailing claws of both creatures almost tore her spirit to shreds. She raced across the room towards Jeffrey but stopped to look down at her body for a moment. Jeffrey spotted her but had no time to offer any words of advice. He was too busy with Dominic who had now grabbed Jeffrey's wrist and attempted to wrestle the knife free.

"Y'all be disappointed if ya take this knife from me," Jeffrey said as he struggled to free himself from the man's grip.

"I don't need to hold the knife to kill you with it," Dominic said as he forced the blade back towards Jeffrey.

"Cara," He called out. "Y'all like to help?"

Cara shook her head like a trance had been broken. Her eyes fixed on Dominic and the knife as it slowly made its way toward Jeffrey. She raced across the room and attacked Dominic with all her might. But the man hardly moved. She tried to hit him in vital places, but he didn't budge.

"Can't...fight...like...livin'," Jeffrey said as he struggled to hold back Dominic. The man was strong. Nothing Jeffrey had ever fought had been able to overpower him like this before.

Cara planted her hands on Jeffrey's and pushed back against Dominic. The stalemate continued as the fight roared behind them. The Sluagh had opened another gash across the beast's chest. More brown goo oozed from it. There was a loud *thud* as the Sluagh pinned the beast to the floor.

The beast let out a final cry as the Sluagh's beak pierced its skull. Brown liquid gushed from the wound and the beast's body went limp. After a few seconds, a brown vapor began to rise from the corpse. Jeffrey looked over his shoulder to see the Sluagh feeding on the essence.

"This is it," he said to Cara, motioning with his head towards the feeding Sluagh.

She took a step back and closed her eyes. Jeffrey was certain the knife would be plunged into his chest at any moment. But Cara opened her eyes and flung a wild fist through the air. Her punch connected with both Jeffrey and Dominic's hands, right at the hilt of the knife. The shock of the punch sent the blade sailing across the room, free from both of their grips. Jeffrey went for the knife while Cara pounced on Dominic.

Jeffrey could hear the pair struggling behind him, but his gaze was fixed on the blade. It was the only thing that mattered now. They could finally be rid of the Sluagh if he hurried. His hand wrapped around the hilt. He felt the familiar heat and buzz. He turned to face the Sluagh. It was still feeding. Jeffrey smiled.

"Finally," Jeffrey said as he set his sights on the creature.

Dominic broke free from Cara's attack and lunged towards Jeffrey. She tried to grab hold of Dominic and keep him in place, but it was no use. He slipped by and tackled Jeffrey back to the ground. Jeffrey held the knife tight, not wanting to drop it. This was the final chance to reap the Sluagh. It would never come again.

The Sluagh was inhaling the last bit of brown essence from the beast. There were only precious seconds left to reap the creature. He tried to push Dominic off, but it was no use. Dominic had him pinned. For such an inexperienced spirit, he was powerful. That scared Jeffrey.

The last remaining shred of essence was gulped up by the Sluagh. This was it. The final chance. Jeffrey struggled to free himself again to no avail. But before he could accept his failure, Dominic's eyes grew wide and he pulled back from Jeffrey. His spirit snapped across the room and back into his body. Jeffrey watched the man drop to his knees and clutch his throat.

There was no time to wonder what had happened. His sights were set on the Sluagh. Jeffrey leaped across the room and drove the knife deep into the creature's back. It let out a loud shriek that rattled the windows. Any humans nearby would have heard it for sure.

At first, Jeffrey thought he had been too late. Then, the creature's wings flapped wildly. It shot straight up towards the ceiling and exploded into a cloud of mist. The mist swirled around the blade like a tornado before absorbing. The force of the whirling wind ripped the knife free from Jeffrey's grip and it clattered to the floor. He scooped it up and spun around to face Dominic, but the man had already fled.

There was a splatter of blood on the floor where Dominic had stood. A single shoeprint smudged the center of the pooling crimson liquid. Jeffrey looked at it and wondered what had happened. Cara stood there, staring down at her hand like she was struggling to comprehend something.

"You alright?" Jeffrey asked, walking to her side.

She looked down at the small piece of glass on the floor and Jeffrey understood what she had done. He was impressed. It wasn't easy for a new spirit to interact with the physical world like she had done. Though, he doubted she would have cared to hear that now.

"How did I..." she trailed off.

"There's something special about ya, that's for sure," Jeffrey said. "Not many spirits can break a window on their first ride, believe it or not."

"I can't believe," she stopped talking and looked at her hands. "How can I be dead?"

"Hey, at least ya know there's life after, right? Shouldn't bother ya too much."

Cara kept talking like she had not heard Jeffrey speak at all. He assumed she was mostly talking to herself to ease her mind. It wasn't an easy thing to realize you were dead. Or at least, he assumed it wasn't.

"I wasn't ready to die. I know no one is ever ready, but there was so much I hadn't done. It can't end like this. This just can't be it."

Cara walked over to her body and dropped to her knees. She looked down at her own face. Jeffrey could only imagine the strange feelings rushing through her spirit. He thought about placing a comforting hand on her shoulder but wasn't sure it would help. Instead, he opted to let her grieve in peace.

"I don't understand how I ended up in the house. You left and I was sitting in the car. I must have dozed off because I had a strange dream about my childhood. When I woke up, I was here. Somehow that beast lured me inside without me knowing. Like I was sleep walking."

"You are more in tune with the spirit realm than any other living person I have seen before," a familiar voice said from across the room. Cara and Jeffrey both turned to see Death standing against the farthest wall. "I am uncertain of why that is. But you have a strong connection with it," she explained further.

"But why me? Why would I have a connection? I'm nothing special. I'm a bodyguard, for fuck's sake. My whole profession I've done my best to blend in. Not be noticed. Now you're telling me I'm the god damned ghost whisperer?"

"I cannot explain what it is, but you have a connection with Jeffrey," Death continued.

"Woah, hold on. Like destiny or some shit?" Jeffrey said.

Death turned to face Jeffrey. She stared at him with that familiar cold look. He wished he could read her thoughts. That was if Death had any. She certainly knew more than she was letting on. Of that, he was sure. It seemed unlikely she could gather her connection to the spirit realm without understanding it. After all, this was her domain. Jeffrey might not have understood the cosmos, but he knew Death never gave up all the secrets.

"No, not destiny. But intertwined."

"What the hell does it matter anymore? I'm dead. What intertwined destiny bullshit could that be? What the hell is my purpose? If I'm so connected with the afterlife, then why am I in it? Why can't I woosh back into my body like that oversized asshole?"

He could tell she was upset. And with good reason. Dying was scary for most people. Even when they crossed over and realized there was life after death, they were still scared. It was probably the not knowing that scared them the most. If spirits were real, then so too must be heaven and hell. And wondering where you would spend your eternity was a nagging question. Jeffrey supposed he may have been lucky not to remember feeling this way.

"Look closer, Cara. There is something you are not seeing," Death said and pointed to her body.

Cara and Jeffrey both looked down. He couldn't speak for Cara, but he saw nothing special there. Just a lifeless body. He had seen countless of them. Death stepped closer and reached down to the open space between Cara and her body. Both Cara and Jeffrey gasped.

Chapter 26

The glass shard Cara had sliced Dominic's throat with had cut deep. Even while in his spirit form, Dominic had felt the pain. Blood had spurted from his neck in a rhythmic beat that matched his heart. He had snapped back to his body so fast, he barely had time to watch the Sluagh die. Jeffrey had reaped it with his knife, that he knew. Dominic could sense the presence of the Sluagh was gone. He was finally free of the creature. Its hold over him was no more.

Something still nagged at him, however. He wasn't as powerful as he could be. Jeffrey's knife had been unable to reap him, but there would be other ways. Somehow, he knew this. His spirit was not yet immortal. Since his mortal body could be hurt while his spirit was ejected, Dominic feared he could be stuck in the spirit world forever if his body died. If that were the case, he worried his spirit could then be reaped by Jeffrey's knife. Only with both forms together was he all powerful. Not until he consumed more spirits could he truly leave his body behind.

He needed more spirits. With the Sluagh's help, he would have become all powerful. No one would have been able to kill him or reap his spirit. He was happy to be out from under its control but couldn't help but wish they had progressed a little further.

Jeffrey's knife seemed to be the only thing that could harm another spirit. If he could somehow get his hands on it, he could continue what he had started. He assumed the knife only worked in Jeffrey's hands, but there had to be ways around that. If there were, Dominic would find them. Nothing was going to stand in his way.

Dominic pulled his hand away from his sliced throat. Blood still trickled from the wound, but it was healing. Not too much longer now. While he healed, Dominic drove down the road. He wanted to put as much distance between him and Jeffrey for now. The next time they met, he wanted to have no reason to eject his spirit. Jeffrey wouldn't stand a chance. Cara would be the last spirit he needed to fully power up his own. Then he would kill Jeffrey and this whole nightmare would be over. He would finally have peace of mind, knowing that there would never be an end for him.

He could feel Jeffrey's presence now. He didn't know when it had happened. If he concentrated hard enough, he could almost sense Jeffrey's location. When Dominic was fully healed, he would find Jeffrey and kill him with the knife.

A smile crept across his face. At least she was no longer among the living. Sure, she could wander the Earth as a spirit now, but her life was gone. He took relish in that thought. Though, he did not envy her. The thought of wandering the planet as a spirit terrified him still. The spirit world was too unknown and dangerous. He had already come across three separate entities that could kill his spirit form. Nothing was permanent, it seemed. And the thought of no longer existing still sent shivers up his spine.

On a long, dark stretch of road, Dominic pulled over. He wiped his hand over his neck to wipe away the last bit of blood. Finally, his wound had healed. The slit in his neck had shut. There was no more pain. Dominic pulled down the visor and popped open the mirror. The cut had left nothing behind. Not even a scar. Only a rust-colored stain on his shirt. He smiled to himself and pushed the visor back up.

Jeffrey would die tonight.

Chapter 27

She couldn't believe what she was seeing. There was a thin line of vapor-like material leading from her spirit back to her body. Cara had no idea what this meant. She had not noticed it before now. She didn't know if it had been difficult to see or if everything had been so chaotic, she wasn't able to get a good look. Jeffrey hadn't noticed it either. He stared at it next to her with his mouth open.

"Will somebody tell me what this means?" Cara asked.

Jeffrey looked over at Death like he sought her permission.

"It means, y'all ain't dead."

"What? Dominic murdered me. I felt it. He choked me to death. What do you mean I'm not dead?"

Jeffrey shrugged.

"No, that's not good enough. Death, you have to explain this to me." She had turned to face the slender woman who stared in her direction.

"It is fascinating. You are the first mortal I have ever encountered with this ability naturally."

"Dominic was able to do it, too," Jeffrey said.

"Yes, he was. But he has reaped many spirits and was granted these abilities through the Sluagh. Unknowingly to it, of course. But this woman possesses this power naturally. I have never seen this before."

"Alright, that's great. What does it mean?" Cara snapped.

"It means you can get back in your body and keep on livin'."

Cara shook her head. There was no way she could get back in her body. They were lying to her, or this was some sort of demented dream. Maybe the beast wasn't dead and this was all a part of its torture. It was preying on her fears.

"I can't get back in my body. I don't know how."

"Sorry, Cara. Y'all gonna have to figure that one out."

Cara turned her gaze to Death once again. It was easy to forget she wasn't mortal herself. Her beauty was so stunning. Not something she ever would have expected from something that folklore had described as a skeleton in a hood.

"You are tethered to your body. You are able to return at any time."

"Not helpful at all but thank you."

She stared at her body for several minutes. Her mind was focused on nothing but returning to it. It seemed almost impossible. Not knowing what to do, she closed her eyes tight and thought about returning. All her thoughts were focused on this one action. If she thought hard enough, she hoped to return. When she opened her eyes, she was still standing over her pale corpse on the floor.

"It's no use. I can't do it," Cara said.

"Death, ya got any advice for the lady?" Jeffrey asked. Cara was surprised to hear genuine care in his voice. He was actually worried about her.

"Do not do it. Let it happen," Death said.

Cara crossed one arm over her chest and gripped the bridge of her nose with the other. That advice did not seem helpful at all. She was trying to let it happen, but nothing was happening. All her energy was focused on making it happen. Nothing. Her spirit would not reenter her body. She wondered if Death was wrong. Maybe she had died and Death was merely being hopeful. Though, hopeful was not something she thought Death could feel.

"Alright," Cara whispered. "Let it happen. Let it happen."

This time, Cara did not think about anything. She didn't try hard to clear her mind, nor did she think about her body or spirit. She let go of the entire situation and let her spirit take over. It felt like an involuntary action. Like a muscle spasm. Something pulled at her from behind like a rope. Then she was falling through the air. An instant later, a burst of air burned through her lungs. She gasped for air. Her eyes shot open and stared at the ceiling. Jeffrey and Death were standing over her. Death's stare was blank and uncaring. But Jeffrey looked concerned. Once he saw she was moving, he changed his look back to stoic. But he had given himself away. Jeffrey cared about her now. For all his talk about not caring about the living, here he was caring for one all the same.

"Jesus Christ," Cara said. "That felt odd." She coughed and sputtered as her lungs started to work again. She could almost feel her heart starting back up and her blood beginning to pump again. It was the strangest sensation.

"Welcome back, ma'am," Jeffrey said, proffering his hand. Cara took it and pulled herself to her feet. Gravity and her own human mass pulled her back down to the ground. She felt heavy and sluggish again. Something she had freed herself of when she was a spirit.

"Alright, we gotta talk about the elephant here," Jeffrey said, turning towards Death. "Dominic. How do we stop him now?"

"His mortal form cannot be harmed as long as his spirit is in his body."

"Yeah, and his spirit couldn't be reaped by my knife, either."

"I was able to cut his throat when he was out of his body. Looked like it hurt him bad enough to run away. Guess he doesn't heal as fast when he's tethering."

"Look at y'all, coming up with phrases for your newfound ability."

Cara let out a short laugh. It felt good to again. After everything that had happened, she thought she would never laugh again.

"We need to find a way to get him out of his body so you can reap his spirit."

"Cept, I already said that's gonna do us no good. I stabbed him with the knife and nothing happened. Besides, it ain't like he's gonna just let us reap him. He's gonna stay in that body as long as he can. Death, got any insight here?"

She turned towards Jeffrey with her pale face and red lips. A thought fluttered through Cara's mind that reminded her of the goth kids from back in her high school days. If they only knew they were emulating Death herself.

"As for the Shard not reaping his spirit, his mortal body is keeping it powered. One must die for the other to be destroyed. As for how to remove his spirit from his body unwillingly, that is not something I am capable of doing."

"Would ya if ya could?" Jeffrey asked.

Death ignored his question.

"However, I can tell you this. He is powerful now and he can track you. Much like your knife, he can locate your presence."

"Shit, that's just great. He's gonna come around looking for us and we ain't got a damned plan."

Cara looked down at the floor. It felt like the room was wobbling around her. An exhaustion was setting in unlike anything she had ever felt before. She thought she would pass out right where she stood. Cara tried to shake her head to clear the feeling, but it wouldn't go away.

"You need to rest," Death said, looking at her. "Tonight's events have drained your mortal shell. You will collapse from exhaustion if you do not."

"We don't have time to rest," Cara said. "If he can track us wherever we are, we don't have the luxury. I'll be fine." But she wasn't fine. Her legs wobbled under her as she spoke and she almost dropped to her knees.

"I can cloak you from this man temporarily," Death said. Jeffrey turned to her with his eyes wide and mouth hung open.

"That sounds like y'all are breaking the rules of balance. Isn't that impossible?"

"Darlin', nothing's impossible," Death said.

Jeffrey began to laugh. Cara did not understand what was so funny. There wasn't time to ask, either. Death was right. She needed rest. If she collapsed from exhaustion, she would be nothing more than dead weight for Jeffrey.

Her eye lids fluttered. They were becoming harder to keep open. Her breathing became labored like she had climbed up the side of a mountain. Sleep was coming for her fast. She watched from her half-conscious state as Death reached out her hand and Jeffrey placed the knife in it. Cara was no longer listening to their words. The sound of blood pumping through them was too loud. A few moments later, her world began to go dark.

In a half dream state, Cara took in her surroundings. It seemed time had jumped without her being aware of it. She was now in a car, sunk down in the passenger seat. Her vision was blurry. She had never been so exhausted in her life.

Jeffrey was driving them somewhere. When she realized they were not in her car, she began to wonder what was going on. Words would not escape her mouth, however. She did not have the energy to speak. Cara tried to make a mental note to ask Jeffrey about it later but feared she would forget.

She drifted off again. When consciousness came back, they were sitting in a parking lot somewhere. Jeffrey had killed the engine and was now looking over at her as if he had just asked her a question. One she did not remember hearing.

"I said, can ya move?"

Cara nodded. Though, she wasn't sure her answer was true. She reached out a hand and pulled at the door handle. It took several tries to grasp it and pull. When the door was open, she nearly fell out of the vehicle. The world seemed to spin faster now. If she stood up, she feared she would topple over. Jeffrey noticed her hesitation and came to her aid. He held out his hand for her. Cara reached out and grabbed it, letting Jeffrey pull her to her feet.

The world spun faster, but she managed to keep herself upright. Up ahead, she spotted the red glowing sign that spelled out the words *Motel Grande*. Jeffrey aimed her towards one of the doors. The car door slammed on its own behind them, almost making Cara jump.

"Will...this...pass?" Cara managed to choke out.

"Yes. You need rest."

"What...about...Dominic?"

"Death gave us some time. Enough for ya to get the rest ya need."

"Good."

They arrived at the motel door and Cara watched Jeffrey reach inside and unlock the room. A handy trick she would have to remember for the future. For now, her world was getting harder to stay aware of. Sleep was threatening to overtake her entire body. The moment they were inside the room, she flung herself to the bed. Jeffrey closed the motel room door, slamming it harder than he should have, and walked past the bed. Cara didn't see much else. Sleep had finally come for her.

Chapter 28

Jeffrey watched Cara sleep for a few minutes. All sorts of questions buzzed in his head. Death had dropped a huge bomb on them before sending them on their merry way. Cara had a strange connection with the spirit world. She could do things like Dominic without having to kill for it. Something like this should not have been possible. He wanted to know why. And how.

It would have to wait for later. There were more pressing matters at hand. Dominic was on the verge of becoming too powerful. Though his conduit had been reaped, Jeffrey wasn't certain that would stop him. Dominic seemed hell bent on getting his hands on Jeffrey's knife. Even though only Jeffrey could use it, he was afraid the man would figure out a way to break those rules. He had broken rules that Jeffrey would have thought unbreakable. With Cara's newfound abilities, he was beginning to believe none of the rules mattered.

There was no telling how long Cara would be unconscious. Jeffrey almost wished he could sleep, too. Spirits could fall into a type of hibernation, but not truly sleep. They became dormant in an area and remained that way until something disturbed them. Jeffrey refrained going dormant. As a hellhound, he always needed to be ready. Besides, why resist moving on if you were just going to sleep?

As he tried to pass the time in the room, he heard a strange noise coming from next door. It sounded like a radio frequency. A constant static sound. It was unusual for the sounds of the living to break through the veil. It piqued his curiosity.

Jeffrey stepped through the wall and into the next room over. A woman stood in the center of the room with her back to Jeffrey. He concentrated on her to gain focus. She held a strange box in her hand which emitted the sound.

"Are there any spirits here?" she asked.

Jeffrey contemplated answering. Instead, he let the silence linger.

"Can you say something to let me know you're here?" she continued.

He laughed at the device. He had seen people use things like it before to hunt for his kind. Little did they know, it wasn't truly needed to hear a spirit. Any spirit in tune enough with the world of the living, like Jeffrey, could talk to any person they wished. It took some effort, but it was possible.

"What happened to you? How did you die?" the woman said.

Jeffrey felt compelled to say something now. Not because he wanted to speak with this strange, blonde-haired woman trying to speak with ghosts in this grungy motel. But because there were so many unanswered questions lately. He knew nothing about where he came from. The mysterious connection between him and Cara gnawed at him. Now more than ever, he wanted to know about his past.

"I don't know," he said out loud. By the look on the woman's face, he knew she had heard him.

"Did you say you don't know what happened to you?" the woman asked.

Jeffrey only said yes. He stared at this woman as he thought about everything. Death knew more than she was telling him, that much he was certain. But when it came to Cara, he believed Death knew no more than he did. They had discovered something strange. Something unusual. Cara didn't know it yet, but her world was going to change forever.

"Can you tell me your name?" the woman's voice cut through again.

He was done talking to this woman and he wanted the static noise to end. He smiled as he devised a plan.

"Jeffrey," he said.

The blonde-haired woman dropped to the bed with an astonished look on her face. Jeffrey had given her a taste of the world beyond her own. But now it was time to scare her away from it for good.

"W-what is it you want, Jeffrey?" she stammered.

He leaned as close as he dared and grit his teeth.

"Death."

He watched in amusement as the woman tripped on the end of the bed. The device in her hand sailed across the room and smashed against the door. The static ceased. Jeffrey laughed and stepped back in the room with Cara.

Messing with the living felt different, somehow. He didn't find it as amusing as he once had. Part of him believed it was because he had grown close to Cara. Though, he tried to ignore this nagging thought. There was something there that he could not define. Emotions were a human trait. He didn't know how they worked within spirits. Love was not something he had ever remembered feeling. But he cared for Cara all the same. When he thought she had died, an immense sadness had engulfed him. Even though he knew she would be alright in the spirit realm, he couldn't help but feel she had been cut off too early.

He looked down at her sleeping now and wondered what the future held for them both. The final conflict with Dominic could prove deadly for one or both of them. Jeffrey was not a martyr. He had no interest in giving his life for the cause. Even Jeffrey understood the risks. There had never been a threat like Dominic before. Not one he had been aware of.

There was no telling what new trick Dominic would have up his sleeve for their next encounter. They would need a plan to stop him. It wasn't going to be easy. He wasn't even sure it would be possible. But they had to stop Dominic somehow.

His mind was blank. Hunting spirits had always come easy to Jeffrey. Death pointed him in the right direction, and he hunted. They were easy. They had rules. This behemoth of a man had no rules. He was unpredictable. The one thing all the spirits Jeffrey had ever hunted weren't.

Death's cloaking would wear off late the next day. Cara would have enough time to sleep off the events of the past day and clear her head. Once she was awake, Jeffrey would see if she had any clever ideas. It pained him to ask the living for help with his task, but there was no choice. She had the luxury of thinking like the living, much like Dominic. Maybe she could think farther outside the box than Jeffrey. Jeffrey sat at the edge of the bed and waited for Cara to rest. It was going to be a long, boring few hours.

Chapter 29

Ever since their last encounter, Dominic had been able to sense Jeffrey. Something inside him pointed like a compass towards the spirit. But over the last few hours, the feeling had faded. He didn't know why. But he guessed Jeffrey had found a way to cloak himself temporarily. He couldn't explain how he knew this, only that it made sense. Soon, he would be able to pick up Jeffrey's trail again. And when he did, Dominic would be ready.

Now, Dominic headed back to the motel where he had first experimented with his own spirit. There was someone nearby he wanted to visit with. Someone, or something, that would turn the tide of his war with Jeffrey. That damned southern prick was the last thing standing in the way of true immortality. He wasn't about to let it be ripped away from him.

Dominic looked out at the parking lot and realized it was less vacant than he previously thought. There were spirits walking about. It seemed his awareness of what lay beyond the veil had increased. This comforted him. He felt vulnerable when using his spirit. In his mortal body, nothing could harm him.

Other spirits walked into rooms and walked the border of the motel. Some traveled down sidewalks like they were out for a stroll. None of them paid Dominic any attention. It was as if they could not see him at all.

He headed off towards the overpass like he had done earlier that night. It seemed like weeks ago, now. Across the field, he found the sidewalk that dipped down below a small bridge. He knew what he would find down there. There was no lying to himself. Dominic was nervous. There was no telling how this encounter would go. His heart galloped in his chest as he descended.

It looked just as it had before. The graffiti, the darkness, the tarp in the corner. It was all still there. He hadn't expected anything to change, but it was strange being back. This time he knew exactly what he would find behind the tarp. He would be ready this time. His ticket to beating Jeffrey was there.

Dominic reached out and pulled back the tarp. The shadowy creature huddled in the corner like it had been trying to sleep. Now disturbed, it turned towards Dominic and snarled. He stood face to face with a monster that looked similar to the spirit back in the house. It thought he was one of the living it could prey on. Dominic nearly smiled at how wrong the creature was. The spirit took a step forward. Dominic did not move.

The spirit continued to stalk towards Dominic. It snarled and snapped, ready to pounce at any moment. Though his heart raced, Dominic remained stoic. He continued to let the spirit advance, thinking it had the upper hand. When it was finally close enough, Dominic reached out a hand.

His hand came within inches of the shadowy spirit and a mist like form extended from his palm. Part of his spirit trailed out of his body like a small rope. As the spirit stepped closer, Dominic pressed his hand against it. The small, rope-like fragment of Dominic's spirit wormed its way into the shadow being. Dominic could not explain how he knew to do this. Only that it was something that he could do. The power he had gained from the Sluagh was incredible.

The little bit of spirit now inside the shadow creature acted as a sort of parasite. He watched the spirit convulse back and forth like it was having a seizure. It growled and hissed at the concrete above their heads before finally settling down and looking at Dominic with a look of submission. Now, it wanted whatever Dominic wanted. It would do whatever Dominic wanted it to do.

"I could really get used to this," Dominic said, looking at his hands.

He had never been someone with power, status, or money. Just some nobody with the fear of dying. *Just look at me now,* he thought. Fear of death was a thing of the past. Now, he was becoming a master of death.

"How is he hiding from me?" Dominic asked himself.

This spirit would offer up no answer. He knew that. But he hadn't come to this place for answers. He had come to build an army. This was only stop one. He would have several more spirits under his control before Jeffrey showed his face again. Still, the question of how Jeffrey was hiding plagued him. It was a useful trick he wanted to learn for himself.

"Once I kill Jeffrey and take his knife, nothing will be able to stop me," he said to his audience of one. "I won't need to hide from anyone because no one will be able to harm me. I'll be immortal."

He laughed while the spirit under his control stayed motionless. It would only react when Dominic gave it something to do. The idea was fascinating.

A few days ago, he was the servant of this horrible creature that forced him to do its bidding. Now, he was the one in control. Finally, he was no longer a servant but a master.

"Go now," he said to his puppet. "Find others like you. Make them my puppets."

The spirit nodded and went off from its hiding place under the bridge. Dominic heard a few spirits out from an early morning stroll scream as it barreled past them. Dominic grinned. His next meeting with Jeffrey would be his last.

Making his way out from under the bridge, Dominic admired the beauty of the sunrise. It cast its light on a brand-new day. A brand-new era for him. Soon, he would live without fear of death. The sun felt warm against his skin. A gentle peace flowed through his body. Anxiety was replaced with calm. Things were finally starting to look up for him.

Chapter 30

He was getting impatient now. Cara was still sleeping. Jeffrey knew humans needed their sleep to recharge but this seemed out of hand. The threat of Dominic was still out there and there was no telling what kind of ungodly powers he had formulated since their last meeting. If he could reap spirits on his own, they were doomed. He tried to hold on to hope that it would never be possible but there was no telling how much the rules had changed. The way Dominic had eyed his knife during their scuffle told him he still did not possess such power.

The sun had risen above the horizon hours ago and still Cara slept on the grungy motel room bed. She slept on her left side with her arm sprawled out underneath, cheek resting on top. A thin layer of drool hung from her lip. Jeffrey smirked.

She truly was a force of a woman. She fought better than most of the living he had encountered. He believed she was tough as nails. And her ability to control her spirit made her the most unique person on the planet. Still, seeing her drool into the sheets like a child made him laugh.

Death's cloaking would wear off soon. If they didn't have a plan by then, they would be in big trouble. Jeffrey had spent the night brainstorming but came up short. Any plan to bind him would end in failure. Cara might have been a hell of a scrapper, but he was stronger than her. Dominic would have no trouble overpowering her if it came down to a struggle and there was only so much Jeffrey could do.

He had hoped to bounce ideas off Cara. At this rate, they would be down to the wire when she woke up. They would be forced to wing it. Which Jeffrey was alright with. Most of his hunts weren't planned but improvised. This seemed more important, though. This was something that would benefit from a well-thought-out plan.

Cara began to stir. Jeffrey jumped up from his chair and stood over her. He was anxious to see her wake up from her hibernation. Not being a flesh and blood human but a spectral presence in the room, Jeffrey had no conscious thought how awkward it must have been for him to watch her while she slept.

Like some sort of undead monster, Cara began to rise. She stretched her hands out towards the ceiling and yawned with a wide-open mouth. Her hand wiped away a bit of drool from her chin. With glassy eyes that had yet to focus on the world around her, Cara took in her surroundings. Jeffrey could tell she wasn't quite awake just yet.

"Mornin'. You slept longer than I expected."

"How long was I out?" she asked through a yawn.

"Not sure. Not like I keep a watch or somethin'," Jeffrey laughed.

Cara shook her head like she was trying to shake some unseen thing from inside her mind. The concept of sleep had been foreign to Jeffrey for so long that he could not remember what it felt like to wake up. He looked at Cara and suppressed the urge to make a joke. Her hair was matted to the side of her face in a tangled mess.

"Now that y'all are awake, we need to discuss how to take on Dominic. Any ideas?"

"I'm a little groggy. Do we have any coffee?" she laughed.

"Death's little trick ain't gonna last long. We need to figure somethin' out quick."

There was a serious tone in Jeffrey's voice. One that even surprised himself. He couldn't remember the last time he had been this serious about anything. There was a lot on the line. Dominic could not be allowed to roam free.

"Okay, yeah. I get it," Cara said. "Sorry."

"No need to be sorry. Do you have any ideas? I've been at a loss."

"If you're stumped, I don't know how much help I can be."

"Maybe this is a problem that requires a livin' solution?"

"I'm not sure what you mean."

Jeffrey wasn't sure what he meant either. This whole issue was out of his area of expertise. It was certainly well beyond any living person's comprehension. Perhaps there was still something she could offer. Something he had not thought about yet. If Cara was meant to be here, then there had to be a reason for it. At least, he hoped.

No case in his memory had ever made Jeffrey worry. He was scared they would fail. Not entirely sure what failure meant to this case scared him ever more. If Dominic won, the balance would be thrown off forever. That he understood. Just his mere existence upset the natural order of life and death. Other than Dominic having the ability to never be reaped again, what other consequences would there be? Would the universe crack in half? Would the afterlife cease to exist? One thing he was sure would happen, Dominic would become more powerful than Death. A being that wielded that much power could not be safe for anyone. Death had rules and restrictions. From where they came from, Jeffrey did not know. But they hardly mattered. She could not break those rules even if she wanted to. The occasional bend, perhaps, such as cloaking them from Dominic but nothing more. Dominic's existence was a broken rule in itself. And Jeffrey understood he had to fix it.

The living were complicated and emotional creatures. Jeffrey understood this well. Even as a spirit, he had his range of emotions. It seemed something that transcended life. Death, whatever she was, had no inherent emotions. None that Jeffrey had ever witnessed. Even in the face of this imminent threat, she did not act the least bit worried. He liked to think it was because of her faith in Jeffrey, but he knew better.

Jeffrey paced now. He could see Cara's eyes following him in his peripheral vision. There was a look of concern and concentration splattered on her face.

"There are no bad ideas here," Jeffrey stated.

"Can his spirit still be reaped?" Cara asked.

"I ain't sure. I think so, but don't know how. Our last meetin' didn't go so well. My knife didn't do a damn thing. But I have an idea about that thanks to you."

"Me?"

"That's right. My knife didn't hurt him when I stabbed him but that little trick with the broken glass sure did. I think his body keeps his spirit alive and the spirit keeps the body alive. Follow me?"

"So, we hurt one and we can hurt the other?"

"Yeah, well, that's the idea. Of course, none of this matters if he found a way to absorb more spirits."

"Without that thing with him, he can't do that, right?"

Jeffrey shrugged.

"We need a way to keep his body down, right? Like an anchor," Cara asked.

"Ya got any ideas? That's where I'm stuck."

There was a long silence before Cara let out a sharp gasp.

"We need to lock him in something. Something that he can't get out of."

"Like what?"

"I don't know. Like a safe or a freezer."

"And how are we supposed to get him inside? He ain't gonna fall for a trap again."

"Then we don't set a trap. You said yourself that he's going to come looking for us after whatever it is Death did to hide us. We use that to our advantage. Find the perfect place and let him come to us. Then we lock him up, he ejects, I stab the body, and you reap him. Problem solved."

It was a loose plan, but it made sense. Jeffrey wasn't sure if he liked the idea yet. Too many things could go wrong. Though, it was exactly how he excelled. Off the cuff. A loose plan was a plan that couldn't fail. At least in his experience. And since he had no other plans of his own, it would have to do for now. Unless he saw something better arising.

"Alright, let's say we do this. How ya gonna overpower him? I know you can handle yourself, but this is different. *He's* different."

"Maybe I don't need to overpower him. Maybe I just need to trap him."

"I already said he ain't gonna fall for a trap again. He's smarter than that."

Cara sat on the edge of the motel bed and looked down at the floor. Jeffrey could tell she was in deep thought. This wasn't going to be easy. He wished there was a simple solution but there wasn't. And if they failed today, then it was all for nothing. Their failure could bring about the end of everything.

"Let me just think this through. We need to incapacitate his body, right?" Cara said.

"Yes."

"You don't need to answer."

"But y'all asked a que- "

"Shh, I'm trying to think."

Jeffrey shook his head.

"Alright, so we need to trap his body or knock him out so he pushes his spirit from his body. I hurt the body and you can reap him. How do we trap his body in something that he's forced to do that?"

"That's the question, isn't it?"

"Maybe we can trap him in something that could double as a way to hurt him."

"Ah, I think I see what y'all are sayin'."

"We just need to figure out what we could use. Like a giant furnace or a trash compactor or something."

"Cara, this could work."

He watched a smile light up her face as she jumped to her feet. She held up her hands in a victory pose. Of course, the small detail of where to trap him had yet to be figured out. But at least they had part of a plan now. The cage should be the easier part. But Jeffrey had no clue where to go. The mortal realm was Cara's expertise. He wouldn't be able to come up with a place on his own.

There were ways to trap spirits. Like in his car. If he could get a spirit there, he could surely hold them for as long as needed. He had done it before on several hunts. Especially when after the type of spirit the living called a woman in white. They were really Augurs, but they didn't know that. Many of them preyed on victims on long stretches of dark roads, pretending to hitchhike. Then, they would kill their prey and consume the spirit. Jeffrey had a particularly fun case with a woman in white a while back. He had picked her up in his car, fooling her into believing he was about to be another victim. But when she readied herself for the kill, she found Jeffrey calmer than any living person would be. Once he revealed who he was, the fear struck her instead. Desperate to escape, she tried to leave his car but found it impossible. His ghost car could be used as a temporary cage for spirits. On Dominic, however, it would be useless. The power needed to provide a living person a ride, let alone trap them, would be more than Jeffrey could conjure up.

"I've got it!" Cara yelled.

Jeffrey was pulled from his daze. Turning to face her, he saw the bright smile on her face. It was full of pride and excitement. He couldn't wait to hear what she had come up with. Knowing her, it was probably the perfect plan.

"I know exactly what we need to do."

Chapter 31

"Are you sure this is going to work?" Jeffrey asked as they pulled in front of the towering building.

Jeffrey's car growled like a lion. He was happy to be back with her. After learning about Cara's special ability, he knew she would be able to ride in his car like any other spirit. He was happy to be right. It had been too long since he had taken Mia out for a spin.

"This is going to work. I know it."

Her assurance gave him confidence. Besides, it was a solid plan. He had a few questions when she had first laid it out, but now he had a good feeling it would work. And if things went south, they would improvise. His area of expertise anyway. He knew they would pull this off.

"Death's little spell should be wearing off soon."

He pointed towards the sun. It was sinking closer to the horizon. When they were cast in darkness, her cloaking would wear off. Of that he was also certain. They needed the cloaking to wear off if they were to lure Dominic to his demise.

He killed the engine. The pair sat in silence for a moment. Both knew what was at stake and their next steps. Cara was smart. She knew what they were up against.

"Let's get up there and do this thing," Cara said with an obvious shake in her voice.

"Ya don't have to hide the fear from me, Cara."

"Who said I'm afraid?"

"Well, shit, if ya ain't you're either willin' to join this side of the veil or you're the bravest person I've ever met."

"What if the plan doesn't work? What happens if we fail?"

"That ain't gonna happen. Our plan is solid. There's no way it can fail. Go wrong, sure. Fail outright? Nah."

"You're making me feel *loads* better," she said, sarcastically.

Jeffrey let out a short laugh. He was surprised to find himself nervous. Something he had not felt on a hunt since, well, ever. He could not remember a single time being this nervous. It wasn't everyday a hellhound found himself face to face with the fate of existence.

"Ready when you are," Jeffrey said.

The pair climbed out of the antique Corvette. Cara shut her door, but Jeffrey didn't need to. Once they were outside, the vehicle disappeared. Jeffrey expected Cara to question the disappearance or offer up a look of astonishment. Her lack of interest meant she was finally accepting this world for what it was. He liked that. She was diving headfirst into the hellhound life with him. The perfect companion to have at his side. When her time finally did come, she would make one hell of a hellhound.

As they approached the sky-high hotel, Jeffrey spotted a few other spirits milling about. They were oblivious to the fact that this building would soon become a battleground. He thought about warning them but decided against it. They needed everything to appear normal for Dominic.

The spirits crisscrossed the parking lot and several headed into the hotel, probably looking for a place to loiter. It was funny. Jeffrey had been a spirit for decades and even he didn't understand what they did for fun. He never partook in such things. Hunting was his life. When there wasn't a target, Jeffrey liked to wander. He tried never to stay in the same place long.

A lot of other spirits, like the ones at this hotel, loved to stay near places. Whether it was because they had died there or had a significant memory from their life. Whatever it was, Jeffrey did not share that same sentiment. The detachment made him better at his duty.

One spirit spotted Jeffrey and gave him a polite wave. Then he spotted the knife on Jeffrey's belt and realized what he was. hellhounds had a reputation for bringing unwanted attention to the regular spirits just trying to live their after lives.

"Are there always this many spirits around?" Cara said, looking astonished.

"Wait," Jeffrey said, stopping. "You can see them now?"

Cara nodded.

"I don't know what it is, but I can see them. Not clear as day. But I can see them. It's like they're behind a thin curtain or something. What's going on?"

"Must be the connection Death told ya about. Now that y'all are opened up to it, you'll probably notice more and more."

For Cara, this was a good and bad time to develop this awareness. Once Dominic left his body it would help her keep track of him or even fight him. It could also serve as a distraction. Any other spirits around might draw her attention from the task at hand. But Jeffrey trusted her to stay on target. It was something she was used to, after all. The life of a professional bodyguard must have been somewhat similar.

"Remember the plan?" Jeffrey asked, trying to keep her mind focused.

Cara turned away from the other spirits wandering around and kept up with Jeffrey as they marched towards the front door.

"Remember it? I came up with it. How could I forget?"

"Just making sure y'all are staying focused."

"Do you honestly think this is going to distract me?"

"Might."

Once inside, they walked past the reception desk. Jeffrey didn't notice, but the concierge gave Cara a funny look. Like she couldn't understand how someone could sail past her desk without stopping to check in or ask for directions. Cara didn't pay her any attention either. The pair headed straight for the main elevator, ready for their task at hand.

The metal doors swung open and the two of them stepped inside. Cara mashed the close door button several times until the doors slid shut. They needed to be alone in the elevator so they could converse. Trying to keep her cover while talking with Jeffrey would be a difficult task and one they couldn't afford right now.

Cara pressed the sixth-floor button. About halfway up the building. It seemed as good a place as any. It didn't matter which floor they chose. They just needed to be above the ground floor. As the elevator began to rise, Jeffrey tapped his foot.

"These things are slow, ya know? Don't know how y'all live with them."

"Well, we sort of have no other choice. Some of us can't phase through floors and walls."

Jeffrey laughed. "Fair enough."

He took in his surroundings. It was a dingy, poorly lit elevator. The wood paneling that lined the walls looked cheap and overdue for a cleaning. The buttons on the circuit board were grimy from years of nasty human fingers prodding at them. How any living person could step foot in one of these disgusting boxes was beyond him. Not to mention the shear panic of being in a small box overhanging a large fall. One cable snap and goodbye life. It would all be over.

The elevator came to an abrupt halt on floor six. A loud *ding* cut through the air before the doors slid open. Before them stood a beige hallway with blue carpet covered in a white triangle pattern. Not the sort of place Jeffrey had imagined their final epic showdown for the fate of the balance between life and death. He had pictured maybe the middle of a cemetery at midnight. Seemed more fitting.

"We've got about an hour before sundown," Cara said. "We should hold up in one of these rooms to wait it out. Timing will be everything."

Jeffrey agreed and the pair headed down the hallway towards a vacant room. He stuck his head into several doors to find an unoccupied room. The first room he saw two living people tangled in the bedsheets, thrusting and moaning. The room next door housed a man listening to the couple with his ear firmly pressed against the wall. In the third room, he found a man eating a whole pizza by himself and watching some strange television show. Finally, on the fourth try, he found an empty room.

He phased through the door and unlocked it from the inside. Pulling the door open, he let Cara in.

"Welcome to my room," he said with a smile.

"Thank you, sir."

"Hey, ya wanna pass the time by scaring the guy next door?" Jeffrey laughed.

"Is that really how you like to have fun? Scaring the shit out of people?"

"Why not?"

Cara rolled her eyes, but Jeffrey spotted the slight smile there. She found the idea amusing. Even with her disapproving tone, she thought it would be funny. But probably not enough to follow through with it.

"Fine, we ain't gonna mess with him. But it's fun. Trust me."

"I'll take your word for it. We have a lot we need to go over before we get ready for Dominic. Once Death's cloaking wears off, do we know how much time we'll have."

"As soon as it wears off, I'll be able to sense his presence through my Shard," he said, tapping his knife. "He's still my target."

"Shard, huh?"

"That's what we hellhounds call our knives. It's a shard of Death's scythe."

"Oh, wow. Look at you. Embracing the hellhound title."

"Well, ya know, it's growing on me."

Cara sat down on the couch just below the window. She stared at the disappointing view outside. Jeffrey knew she was searching for a distraction. The poor woman had a lot going on. So much of her life had changed overnight. Taking it all in wouldn't be a fast process.

Jeffrey approached the couch and took a seat next to her. Emotions weren't his strongest attribute. A hellhound bogged down with emotions was one who would fail. Plenty of spirits were in tune with their emotions. Especially the ones who stuck around the meaningful places from their lives. He just was not one of them.

But he understood it some now. Something about Cara made him feel something he could not remember feeling in a long time. He was still uncertain of what it was. Burying the thought, Jeffrey reached out a hand and placed it on her shoulder. Her eyes met his gaze. The two stared at each other for a moment, not speaking. Then, Jeffrey noticed the single tear rolling down her cheek.

"Jeffrey, what the hell is all this?" she asked. "What has happened to my life? Yesterday, it was business as usual. I had clients. I had a normal life. And now, I'm in a hotel with a ghost, waiting to spring a trap on a psychopath that wants me dead. A psychopath that can't die. I mean, it's just- "

"Crazy?"

"Yeah, exactly. But that wasn't enough for me. I had to also find out that I've got this odd connection to you or the spirit world or whatever. Oh, and I haven't even mentioned that fact that I've met the Grim Reaper herself. I mean, come on. What has happened? What's going to happen from here?"

"What do ya mean?" He tried to force his voice to sound compassionate but couldn't tell if it was working.

"I mean, what happens after you reap Dominic? What then? I go back to my old life? I'm supposed to just carry on like none of this happened? Just running around seeing ghosts everywhere I turn. How the hell am I going to get used to that? Let's not even talk about what *I* can do with my own spirit."

There was nothing Jeffrey could say to make any of this make sense. He knew the living went about their lives not knowing about the spirit world. Some believed in ghosts, of course. Some believed in a life after death or even heaven and hell. But for the most part, the living was completely oblivious to the reality of this world under their nose. Death had always proclaimed the living needed to be oblivious. Knowing such things would upset the balance. And Jeffrey could see now what she meant. Not to mention the religious zealots who might commit suicide to get to those hoped for pearly gates faster.

"Look, I get how ya feel. Trust me, I do. We have a lot in common. Y'all can see my world, see us. I can see the livin'. Most spirits can't or don't. But I do. When a wandering spirit harms one of the livin', I see it all. I get to watch the person die, then become one of us. And sometimes, I see that spirit get killed as well. I've seen more death in my time than I could count. I think it's why I've disconnected myself from y'all's world so much. I can't stand thinking about it. So, sure, y'all might have to suffer with that sight from now on. Ya might see what I see. But know this, y'all won't ever be alone. I'll always be by your side."

He gripped her shoulder tighter. It was a strange feeling. Her physical body touched his hand, but he could feel her spirit beneath. Something he had never experienced before.

"Thanks, Jeffrey. I think I just needed to vent. I'm feeling a bit overwhelmed by everything. But knowing that I'm not alone helps. I just hope that I'm not crazy and all of this isn't in my head or something."

She laughed. Jeffrey could hear the slight shake in her voice.

"I can feel his presence," Jeffrey said. "Death's spell wore off. He's coming for us and he's close."

"Well then. Let's get to work."

"Y'all sure you got this? It's gonna be a hell of a run up those stairs once this starts."

"I can handle a little cardio upstairs. Just be ready to do your part."

"Don't ya worry. I got this."

Cara smiled and the two parted ways. Jeffrey remained in the corridor while Cara headed off towards the stairwell. This was it. The final chance to end Dominic once and for all. He just hoped they could pull it off. He just hoped that Cara's plan worked.

Chapter 32

Running down the stairs, Cara panted as she descended each flight. Every step threatened to toss her down the steps like a rag doll. She moved faster with each passing second. At the bottom of the flight, Cara burst through the doors harder than anyone in the lobby expected. Several people gasped and turned their heads towards her. The concierge let out a shrill scream of surprise.

"Are you okay, ma'am?" the concierge asked.

"Sorry, took the stairs all the way down. Too much momentum." Cara laughed and headed out of the lobby.

She left behind a stunned and confused audience. Soon after she left, the lobby went back to normal. A few spirits who had been walking through the lobby at the time were completely oblivious to the entire scene. They were deep in a conversation with each other, heading towards the back of the hotel.

Unseen to Cara, something else had entered the lobby behind the two spirits. As she made her way towards her goal, it crept up behind the two talking spirits. After a few seconds of ignorant bliss, the spirits did not notice the monster behind them. Until it let out a quiet growl. Both turned in unison to see a shadowy spirit standing before them. They instantly recognized the beast. All spirits were aware of the wandering ones. Whether it was instinct or a run in with one, they knew them by site.

Both spirits cried out in terror. The beast sunk its sharp claws into the chest of the spirit on the right, burying its arm to the elbow. The other spirit did not wait to see what would happen next. It ran towards the wall, hoping to leap through it to safety. But the beast was too quick. It bolted down the hallway, dragging its captured prey from its hand like a ventriloquist running with his dummy. The beast caught the fleeing spirit by the back of the head and yanked down. In a pool of brown sludge, the trio disappeared.

None of the living people in the hotel lobby saw this event unfold. They didn't see the beast return from its dark world either. If the beast wished, it could show itself to the living and even attempt to take a couple of them with him. It refrained. Instead, it seemed focused on the task at hand.

Back upstairs, Jeffrey gripped his knife in his dominant hand. Dominic was here. Right outside, in fact. For some reason, the man had yet to enter the lobby. Jeffrey could only wonder if the man was being cautious. Had he figured out it was a trap? No doubt, he already suspected it. But his newfound powers would make him cocky. He would take them on headfirst all the same. At least, that was what Jeffrey and Cara had counted on. They had no clue what ace he would have up his sleeve, but they expected something.

Up from the floor rose a dark figure. It took Jeffrey a moment to realize what he was looking at. Before him stood the dark silhouette of a beast. It stared at Jeffrey with blood lust in its eyes. The long, spindly arms at its side flexed, ready to pull Jeffrey down into that deep, dark abyss.

"What the hell?" Jeffrey asked, knowing he would get no response. "Dominic has pets now?"

Jeffrey laughed. The beast snarled. It was a wrench in the plan, no doubt. But he had taken on beasts before. He would come out on top again. His confidence began to fade when he heard something crack behind him. Another darkened shape rose from the floor. Another beast stared at him, ready to strike. It was then Jeffrey realized what was happening.

"Shit," he said. "This might be harder than we thought."

The two spirits stared at Jeffrey, ready to pounce. He tried to formulate a plan in his mind before the charged, but it was too late. Both beasts began to move. The one in front charged forward while the one behind lunged through the air. Jeffrey decided leaving was the best option and phased through the floor to the level below.

The beasts were only momentarily confused before they followed through the floor. Jeffrey slashed through the air with his knife, hoping to catch one by surprise. He miscalculated where they would appear and missed on both swings. One caught him by the wrist, the other slashed at him with its razor-sharp claws. Jeffrey managed to dodge the brunt force of the strike, but the fine tips still grazed his body.

"Sonofabitch," he yelled.

Wrestling his hand free, Jeffrey lunged backward and away from the two snarling beasts. If Dominic had found a way to control wandering spirits, they were bound to be in trouble. Cara would certainly be in trouble. He could handle these two. It would take a little caution, but Jeffrey had faith in himself. But Cara was downstairs alone with the possibility of more of these things. Or worse, Dominic. The plan would have to wait. He needed to get to her.

"Alright ya ugly bastards," Jeffrey said, waving the knife in the air as a taunt. "Let's make this quick."

The two spirits rushed at Jeffrey simultaneously. Their weakness was the lack of cognitive abilities. Beasts behaved like wild animals most of the time. Running on nothing more than instinct and hunger. Jeffrey pushed one aside. It sailed past Jeffrey, the momentum carrying it into a random room. The other flailed both hands out in an attempt to plunge its claws deep into Jeffrey's midsection. Jeffrey's arm stretched out as his body leapt backward. His knife sliced through the beast's throat. There was a gurgling sound for a moment as it gripped at its throat. Mist poured from the wound like blood until the whole being disappeared in a cloud of vapor. The essence swirled around the knife and disappeared.

"That's one," Jeffrey said.

Before he could turn to face the direction he had thrown the other, he was tackled to the ground. A white-hot pain erupted in his right arm. He looked down to see one clawed hand buried deep in his arm. The creature was starting to pull downwards.

A powerful kick from Jeffrey's right leg sent the creature up into the air and off Jeffrey. He wasted no time passing through the floor once again. A few of the living walked down the hallway and passed through Jeffrey. He hardly noticed them. His attention was focused on the ceiling above, waiting for the beast to follow. Too much time passed without nothing happening.

"Damnit."

Jeffrey floated in the air and phased through the ceiling, finding himself back in the hallway above. A yell came from one of the rooms. Some unlucky person had a run in with Jeffrey's friend. Wasting no time, Jeffrey bolted towards the source of the sound and passed straight through the door.

The beast stood in the corner of the room, nothing more than a shadowy blur to the living person residing in the room. It scared them all the same. They slowly backed away towards the front door, never taking their eyes off the figure. Jeffrey thought about revealing himself to scare the person out of the room faster but thought better of it.

"Hey, hey. Eyes here buddy," Jeffrey said to the beast. "Y'all don't want them. Ya want me."

The instinct to hunt prey had taken over. Whatever temporary hold Dominic had over this creature had been severed for a moment. Which told Jeffrey he wasn't yet at his strongest. There was a chance of success tonight. If only he could make sure Cara was safe.

Behind Jeffrey, the door creaked open and slammed shut. The living person who had been staying in this room was gone. Now, it was only Jeffrey and the beast. It glared at Jeffrey with its ugly maw gaping open. He could see the sharp, rotting teeth in its mouth. Beasts were truly disgusting spirits. Corrupted by decades of anger and hate. He wished Dominic had brought a group of augurs instead. Most of them resembled beautiful women. At least his final showdown would be easy on the eyes.

The beast rushed forward. Jeffrey wasted no time ducking under its rapid strikes and rolling to the floor. Before the beast could spin around and go for second attack, Jeffrey stabbed the creature in the back. He made sure to plunge the knife as deep as it would go. Mist poured from the wound before the beast exploded into a cloud of vapor. Like before, the knife gobbled up the essence like a late-night snack.

"And that's two." Jeffrey said, amusing himself. "Now, to find Cara and see if she needs help."

He stepped out into the hallway and stopped dead in his tracks. There were two more beasts staring at him on either end of the hallway. Both snarled and snapped their animal-like jaws. Drool fell from the beast's mouth to his right. The one to his left, guarding the elevator, brandished its claws.

"Fine, two more of y'all. Less I gotta hunt later." Jeffrey held his knife up and readied himself for battle.

• • • •

DOWNSTAIRS, CARA HAD found a good hiding place that allowed her to watch the lobby doors. She needed to wait for Dominic to arrive before moving forward with her plan.

Lucky for her, Dominic could sense Jeffrey because of the power his knife emitted. He could not sense Cara. When Dominic arrived, he would head upstairs. Then she would put her plan into action. As she went over what she and Jeffrey had discussed, Cara spotted the ogre of a man stepping over the threshold. The sliding doors opened wide and he lumbered inside. His head swiveled numerous times as he surveyed the area. Cara ducked down low to avoid being spotted.

Dominic carried on past the concierge desk. The woman called out towards the man, asking if he needed help, but he ignored her. The woman sighed in defeat as Cara slunk back towards her goal. When she turned around to face the maintenance closet she had located earlier, she was met with an unexpected sight.

Standing before her was a dark figure, like a shadow. Only, this shadow had features like a person. They were exaggerated features, more in common with an animal than a person. Its eyes bulged out of sunken sockets. Nostrils flared like a gorilla. Long, shaggy hair framed the face on either side. Its mouth hung open, revealing rows of razor-sharp teeth that resembled a great white shark. Two muscular arms hung from the torso and stretched farther towards the floor than seemed possible. It glared at Cara with a hungry look on its face. It looked similar to the beast that had nearly killed her the day before.

"This can't be good," Cara said, her voice cracking with a hint of fear.

Her eyes darted to the closet and back to the spirit before her. The spirit never took its gaze from her. She took a small step away, but the spirit remained still. There was no fighting this thing. At least not Cara. Her only hope was to lead it to Jeffrey so he could reap it. But not before she finished her task.

She looked over her shoulder and spotted Dominic entering the elevator. Time was not on her side.

"Alright, I'm just going to have to get around you. Uh, somehow."

There was still a lack of confidence in her voice, but the fear was starting to subside. The spirit wouldn't pick up on it. It only wanted one thing. Without much warning, Cara rushed at the spirit. It brandished its razor-sharp claws and swiped at her. She managed to dodge its strike, though the tip of one nail clipped her shirt. Cara juked left and right before diving forward, rolling between the beast's legs. As she rolled back up to her feet, she sprinted towards the closet. As one hand gripped the knob, her right leg was pulled out from under her. Her left hand swung up in an attempt to grip the knob but missed. Her leg was pulled back and up. Now, Cara was looking down at the knob as the lower half of her body headed towards the ceiling. Her right hand shot out and wrapped around the knob in a death grip as she tried desperately not to be pulled up and to her death. She could see small blobs of brown goo falling around her. The beast was trying to drag her back into the abyss.

Her forearm burned as she pulled with all her strength. She only needed a few inches in order to reach the knob with her left hand. If she could get both hands firmly on the door, she would be able to pull herself free from the spirit's grip.

The two played tug of war with her body for a few seconds before Cara finally got her left hand on the knob. She pulled with all her might. The spirit's grip was tight and its strength tremendous. She let out a scream when the sharp claws dug into the skin on her ankles. But she did not let go.

From behind her desk, the concierge perked up. Cara's scream had echoed through the lobby. From her position, she couldn't see what was going on. She walked around her desk and stood in the center of the lobby. The picture before her was one straight out of a horror movie.

Cara's body floated up towards the ceiling, her toes practically touching it. Two hands were gripped around the knob for dear life. An invisible force yanked at her as she struggled to keep her hands held firm.

The concierge let out a scream of terror and turned towards her desk, most likely running for her phone. Cara fell from the ceiling, her hands slipping free, and hit the floor hard. She attempted to cry out for the woman to run, but her voice would not come. The exertion of fighting with the spirit mixed with the hard hit had rendered her breathless.

The spirit had switched targets. It stormed off through the lobby towards the panicked woman behind the counter. Cara looked up at the door and back at the spirit. She had precious seconds to get her task done. There was no time to take on the spirit and save the woman, but she couldn't just let her die.

She ran into the maintenance closet and shut the door behind her. In the back of the little room stood the panel she had spotted earlier. Her eyes scanned the breakers and found the one labeled main. Without a second wasted, Cara flipped the switch, casting the hotel into total darkness. The familiar sound of power loss echoed through the halls.

It would be too dark to see the spirit or the concierge. The maintenance closet was cast in a total darkness. Even the door, which was only a few feet away, was impossible to see. She shut her eyes and concentrated. There was one way to take on the spirit.

• • • •

BACK UPSTAIRS, JEFFREY stood in the hallway on the sixth floor. The two new beasts had proven difficult, but manageable in the end. They both had been reaped. Now, the power went out and darkness covered everything. He knew it meant Cara had done her part. Now, he hoped it meant Dominic was right where they wanted him.

A major upside to being a spirit, the darkness of the living world did not render Jeffrey blind. He could still see. There was an awareness to the darkness, but no effect on his eyes. Dominic being human would be unable to see. At least until he ejected from his body.

A bellow came from the elevator shaft that could have only come from an enraged Dominic. Cara's plan had worked as she hoped. Cutting the power to the hotel had caused the emergency break to engage in the elevator. He was trapped in the shaft somewhere between the floors. Now was the time to lure him out.

Jeffrey raced forward and poked his head through the sliding doors. He could see the elevator below him. Even if Dominic pried open the doors, he would be stuck staring at only about a foot of open space into the hallway on the sixth floor. His large frame would never allow him to squeeze through.

"Bein' an ogre of a man has its challenges, huh?" Jeffrey taunted from above.

Dominic pounded a large fist against the elevator door and the sound echoed through the shaft. Jeffrey sneered. This was exactly what they wanted. Get Dominic angry. Get him out of his body.

"Hey, what happens to y'all if I cut this cable and the breaks give out? I know ya heal and whatever, but can ya heal if the body is torn to ribbons?"

"I'd walk away from it without a scratch."

"Are ya sure about that? Cause we can test out that theory right now."

Jeffrey reached out and vibrated the cable. He knew Dominic would hear the sound. It would help to increase his panic.

"If you touch that cable, I will tear your soul apart piece by piece," Dominic growled.

"And how are ya gonna do that from in your little cage? Sounds to me like you're afraid. Afraid that I'll cut this cord. Afraid to stop me."

"I don't fear anything anymore!" Dominic bellowed.

"Nah, I think ya fear me. And that's fine. You have every right to be afraid."

Another fist slammed against the elevator door.

"Come on, now. That ain't how they open. Tell ya what. I will open the doors for you if you admit you're afraid of me."

"Come in here and face me. I'll show you fear!"

"Let's just take a look at these breaks, huh?" Jeffrey laughed.

He had finally struck a nerve in Dominic. There was a commotion inside the elevator. Then a short silence before Dominic's spirit came flying out and tackling Jeffrey in the hallway. Jeffrey could feel the immense power in Dominic's spirit. He had only grown stronger since their last encounter.

"I'm going to pry that knife from you and carve up your annoying little spirit," Dominic said through clenched teeth.

"Well, come on then," Jeffrey taunted.

• • • •

DOWNSTAIRS, CARA HAD ejected her spirit from her body. She wasn't as confident or as powerful as Dominic. Her spirit walked from the closet like a newborn deer. She stumbled over her own feet as she learned to walk and move around without the weight of her physical body.

"This would be a useful trick on a job," she quipped.

Up ahead, she spotted the beast approaching the concierge. The woman looked around in the darkness like she could sense something was approaching. It would only be a matter of seconds before the beast pounced and dragged her away.

Cara sped up, trying not to trip over her own feet. When she was close enough, she dove at the monster, tackling it to the ground. The woman behind the counter screamed at the unexpected noise but didn't run.

"Lady, get the hell out of here," Cara yelled.

Cara could see the woman's frightened face. The darkness did not obscure anything for her. Instead, there was a thin layer of smoke-like fog. Almost like a curtain separating the two planes of existence. Finally, the woman got the hint and took off screaming. Her hands were outstretched in front of her to keep her face from smashing into anything in the darkness.

Cara wrestled with the beast before she was thrown off and sent flying across the room. It was a powerful being. There was no use trying to overpower it. She needed to lure it to Jeffrey so he could reap it. He was probably busy with Dominic at the moment, but it didn't matter. This thing was going to kill her if she did nothing.

She headed for the stairs but stopped in her tracks.

"I don't need to use those, right?" she asked nobody.

She raised her head and looked at the ceiling above her. A few seconds later, her feet lifted off the ground and she headed for the ceiling. As she passed through, the beast leapt into the air and followed.

Jeffrey and Dominic were still fighting in the hallway when Cara appeared from the floor. The sight of her spirit threw Jeffrey for a loop. This had not been part of the plan.

"Incoming," she announced before something tackled Jeffrey to the floor.

His knife sailed from his hands and down the hallway into darkness. Both Dominic and Cara craned their necks to see where it landed. Both rushed towards it at the same time. Dominic was faster. Cara was right on his heels. Her disadvantage was the lack of experience being outside of her body. Dominic had more time to practice his abilities.

A large hand gripped the handle of the knife and a beaming smile crept across his face. He turned to face Cara and stared daggers at her. The knife twirled in his hand. Behind Cara, Jeffrey struggled to fend off the beast. Without his knife, there wasn't much he could do.

Jeffrey spotted Dominic holding his knife. A fear surged through his body. But he was surprised to realize it wasn't fear for himself that he felt. Instead, he was afraid for Cara. She was standing before the brute in her most vulnerable form. He wasn't certain he would be able to reap her spirit but didn't want to find out the hard way.

As Dominic pulled an arm back to strike Cara, time seemed to slow down for Jeffrey. Cara dropped to her knees and put her hands above her head in a useless effort to defend herself. Jeffrey rammed a shoulder into the beast, knocking it sideways. Dominic's arm was arching up over his head now. Jeffrey dodged around the beast, grabbing its left arm. A well-placed kick to the back of the beast's knee sent it off balance. Jeffrey used the momentum the yank the spirit by the arm and up over his shoulder. The spirit somersaulted through the air towards Dominic. Just as the blade was about to come down on Cara, it pierced the beast instead, exploding into a fine mist.

Before Dominic could realize what had happened, Jeffrey rushed the man. He made sure to grasp the knife firmly so Dominic could not stab him with it. The two men struggled over the knife as they bounced from wall to wall. Jeffrey landed punches that had no effect on the man.

Cara stood and watched the spectacle before turning her gaze towards the elevator. There was only one way she could help Jeffrey now. She saw the thin layer of his spirit stretched down the hall like a tether. It led directly through the elevator doors.

All at once, Cara snapped back to her body. The process knocked the wind from her lungs and rocked her body backwards. She tumbled down into the back of the maintenance closet.

Jeffrey dared a look behind him and saw that Cara was no longer there. He was relieved to see her out of danger, but the relief didn't last long. Dominic delivered a powerful kick to Jeffrey that sent him sailing down the hallway and through the wall. Jeffrey phased through, knocking a picture off the wall as he did. A few of the living residents in the room yelled in surprise. Jeffrey ignored them and dove back through the wall to face Dominic.

"You put up a good fight," Dominic said. "I'm just too powerful now. You can't stop me. And it looks like I can use your little knife. I no longer need that creature to reap spirits. The power is all mine."

"Y'all know what they say about absolute power," Jeffrey said as he dared to inch closer.

"I would never expect you to understand. It's never been about the power. It's the control. Life and death are now under my control. There's nothing left for me to fear. I can never die."

"It's funny how y'all livin' fear death, even when you see there's something after."

"You forget, I can see into your world." He spun a finger in the air in the shape of a circle. "Eternity here is not guaranteed."

"I guess ya have a point." Jeffrey took another step forward.

"But I can have that guarantee. And I can give that to everyone here. With the help of your knife, I can reap whatever creatures dare cross me and no one can stop me. I can be the savior of the afterlife."

"Sounds to me like tryin' to play God."

"Why not?" He flipped the knife in his hand. "If God's dead, someone should take over."

"Sorry to burst your bubble, but God's not dead. It's just not what you're expecting." Jeffrey slid even closer now.

Dominic let out a guttural groan.

"Yeah, I've heard that sentiment before. He's not some man in a beard sitting on a cloud. It doesn't matter what God is. He made the universe and all its rules. But rules are made to be broken."

"I suppose ya haven't met Death yet. Her whole thing is balance. If ya tip the scales too far one way, everythin' else falls. You see something broken. But I see somethin' unbalanced. And Death really loves her balance."

While Dominic prepared to retort, Jeffrey took a chance at rushing him. Dominic was completely blindsided. Jeffrey rammed his whole body into Dominic and made a grab for the knife. He was unable to pry it free from Dominic's hands. His attempt to overpower Dominic ended with him in a tug-of-war for the knife.

The two spirits yanked back and forth, trying to overpower the other. Jeffrey knew he wouldn't be able to wrestle long. He needed a miracle. He needed Cara to finish their plan. Jeffrey twisted the knife and wrapped his arm around Dominic's wrist. The leverage allowed him to hold the knife firm for a few seconds while he tried to wrestle it free. But Dominic gripped him by the back of the neck and pulled him back.

Dominic used all his force to heave Jeffrey to the floor. The pair toppled over, but Dominic held the knife firm. From his place on the floor, he swung it at Jeffrey. Quick thinking was all that stood between Jeffrey and eternal darkness. He flung himself up and away from Dominic's swing.

Now Jeffrey stood between the elevator and Dominic. He took a large step backward, trying to keep as much space from Dominic as possible. With Jeffrey's knife, he was the most dangerous spirit alive. The wandering spirits that Jeffrey hunted could not use his knife. Only Death could grant the ability to use a shard and yet somehow this mortal man was wielding it. Jeffrey didn't understand. But it didn't matter now. All that mattered was killing Dominic.

"I don't want to kill you, Jeffrey."

"Good one. Almost bought it."

"I'm serious. I understand what the fear oof not existing can cause. It pains me to cause that in others."

"Sure, right. Like all the other poor souls you let the Sluagh take."

"I had no choice. It made me take those lives. It ate those spirits. I was prisoner to it. Now I'm free. And I don't have to kill you. You have the choice to join me. You work for Death, right? Well, I am the new Death. So, work for me instead!"

Jeffrey shook his head.

"Sorry, not how it works. You ain't Death. And ya ain't gonna be Death. But you will be dead. But I'll tell ya what, if you give up the knife, I'll give you the chance to summon Death and let her reap ya. Y'all get to move on and find out what's on the other side. Maybe ya have to pay for ya sins, maybe not. But it's damn sure better than me reaping ya."

Dominic let out a bellow of a laugh. He twirled the knife in his hand. A smirk crept across his face and his eyebrows rose in what Jeffrey could only assume was an expression of victory.

"Goodbye, Jeffrey."

The ogre of a man lunged forward, swinging at Jeffrey. Mere inches separated him from a certain death. Dominic swung again and again, and with each swipe of the blade, Jeffrey feared for his mortal spirit. Keeping focused on the shard, Jeffrey spun away, but Dominic reached out and caught him by the throat. With a large hand, Dominic pressed Jeffrey against the wall. Any attempt to phase through the wall by Jeffrey was met with failure. Somehow, the man's spirit was keeping him in place much like Jeffrey's car.

Dominic's arm came arcing down towards Jeffrey's face. Jeffrey stopped fighting and used all his might to block the incoming strike. The pair found themselves in a stalemate. Jeffrey's hands were gripped around Dominic's wrist, pushing back as hard as he could. Dominic pressed down with equal strength. One of them would give out before too long. Jeffrey feared it would be him. Dominic's power was too great.

• • • •

CARA'S LEGS BURNED as her mortal body climbed up the stairs. It felt like a heavy weight doing nothing but holding her back now. With the piece of glass in her hand, she had no other choice. She had to travel the old-fashioned way. Relief came when she pushed open the seventh-floor access door.

Cara was oblivious to the fight going on one floor below her as she turned to face the elevator doors. With all the strength she could muster, Cara pried open the metal doors. There was just enough room for her to slip through. Half her body remained in the hall and the top half bent down to spot the elevator. The stopped elevator looked to be about one floor down. In the darkness, it was hard to see.

Cara held her breath as she took a leap of faith. Her body dropped like a stone towards the car below. As she landed, she bent her knees to soften the blow. Still, she tumbled over sideways and fell to her side. The shard of glass slipped from her grasp and slid to the edge of the elevator, threatening to fall. Ignoring the pain in her side, Cara leapt forward and grasped her shard before it slipped into the darkness of the elevator shaft.

In her haste to pick up the piece of glass, Cara gripped it too tight and sliced open her hand. Blood poured from the wound, making it difficult to keep a firm grasp. Despite the pain, she tightened her grip. Pulling herself to her feet, she let out a cry. Her hand shot to her side and cradled her hurt ribs.

She winced in pain as she reached down and grabbed the handle of the elevator hatch. On the other side of the elevator doors, and one floor below, Jeffrey let out a bellow of pain. The sound lit a fire in her step. Cara gripped the handle and flung the hatch open. Without hesitation, she dropped inside the elevator.

Pain in her side caused her to scream and fall to the floor. As she picked herself up, she spotted Dominic standing inside the elevator like a statue. His eyes were closed and the thin line of spirit stretched away and through the metal sliding doors.

"Please still be alive, Jeffrey," she said. "Don't let me be too late."

Swinging her arm as hard as she could, Cara sliced the shard of glass through Dominic's throat much like she had back in the house. A stream of blood spurted from the wound, launching through the darkness. Cara heard the sickening *Sploosh* of his blood landing on the floor behind her. Another spurt erupted from his neck. An artery had been severed.

• • • •

IN THE HALLWAY, JEFFREY knew something had happened. The expression on Dominic's face had gone from anger to fear in a split second. The tip of the knife was stuck in Jeffrey's chest. Dominic only needed to push a little farther to complete the reaping. But something had stopped him in his tracks.

His grip loosened on the knife. Jeffrey wasted no time prying it from the man and taking a swing, but Dominic's spirit did not stay still. It shot back towards the elevator at lightning speed. If he made it back into his body, there would be no second chances. He wouldn't eject again.

Jeffrey turned to face the retreating spirit. For the second time that night, time seemed to slow down. He could see the fearful expression on Dominic's face as his spirit flew backwards towards the elevator, the tether reeling him in like a fisherman's line. Jeffrey spun the knife in his hand so the blade was pointing straight up at the ceiling. Pulling his arm back over his head, Jeffrey flung the knife forward with all his might.

It sailed through the air, end over end. Dominic's spirit had almost reached the safety of the elevator doors as the knife sailed closer. Dominic let out a wild yell of terror as his eyes watched the knife gain on him. Finally, the blade sliced through his spirit and embedded itself in the metal doors with a loud sound of metal grinding together.

For a moment, Jeffrey wasn't sure what had happened. He could not tell if the knife had hit its mark or not. Before he could fear the worst, a cloud of black mist appeared in the hallway and circled around the knife. The mist of reaped souls had never appeared black before. It rushed around the knife like a tornado. Jeffrey thought he heard the cries of terror in Dominic's voice coming from the mist as it was inhaled by the hilt and disappeared.

Dropping to his knees, Jeffrey sighed in relief. It was finally over. Dominic was gone. His spirit reaped. He almost couldn't believe it was finished. When Dominic had him pinned against the wall, he had thought it was all over. The knife was close to reaping his spirit forever.

"Cara," he yelled, heading off towards the elevator.

Whatever she had done saved his life. Yet, he nearly forgot about her in all the commotion. She must have been in the elevator where Dominic's body was sure to still be. A fear welled up inside Jeffrey that he would pass through the doors and find Dominic alive and well; Cara's body sprawled out on the floor.

To his relief, he found the body of Dominic in a pool of his own blood. Cara was sitting on the floor, wrapping her hand in a piece of cloth from her shirt. She looked up and saw Jeffrey peering at her.

"Sliced my hand open. Couldn't climb back out with just the one hand. Is it over?"

Jeffrey gave her a smile. Despite the pain she was in, she still managed to worry about winning. She was tough. For one of the living, anyway.

"He's gone," Jeffrey said, flashing her the knife.

"Good, cause my ribs fucking hurt. You'd be on your own," she laughed and winced.

"Y'all are the reason we won. Couldn't do it without ya."

Jeffrey reached out a hand to help her up. The pain would subside soon enough and whatever had broken would mend. For her sake, they needed to leave before someone got the power back on and found the body. She was still human, after all. They might try to track her down and accuse her of murder. Though, technically not incorrect. They would never believe the truth. The living didn't want to know about the other side, as much as they fooled themselves into searching for answers. They were happy being ignorant.

Much like Dominic, he had known of the afterlife. He knew that death wasn't the end. And yet, he had still feared death in the end. All natural things died and needed to die. It wasn't the end but another step in the journey of mortal beings. But many mortal beings still held to a firm fear of the unknown and would do whatever it took to stave it off. Had Dominic embraced the unknown, his spirit would have moved on from this realm and to another. Instead, he had chosen obsession and fear which consumed him in the end.

Cara reached up and took Jeffrey's hand. Even though she was in her mortal body, interacting with her took no effort on Jeffrey's part. Death had been right. They shared some sort of connection. He wished he understood it better. Something bound their spirits together. Death must have known the answer. Of course, she never spilled her secrets.

"Let's get out before the fuzz shows up and takes ya away."

"The fuzz?" Cara asked with a laugh. "How old are you?"

Jeffrey stifled a laugh. Mostly because he did not know that term was out of date. Not to mention he did not know where that term came from. He was happy letting Cara have her fun. Her smiling face beamed up at him from inside the elevator. Jeffrey loved her. The sort of love one has for their child. He could not explain why or what it meant.

"Can you climb back up there?" Jeffrey pointed straight up through the hatch.

Cara nodded. Jeffrey stayed by her side the entire journey out of the elevator shaft and back through the hotel. Once they were out of the lobby and in the parking lot, he felt better. A few moments after they sat inside his car, the lights sprang to life inside the hotel.

"Our cue to leave, I think," Jeffrey said and started the engine.

They tore off down the road with the hotel in the rearview mirror. Jeffrey imagined the poor bastard who came upon the corpse sprawled out in the elevator. Normally, he would have found the idea funny. One of the living having the shock of their lives. Now, he could only think about how close they had come to failure. Cara could have been killed tonight. And he could have been reaped. But he shook the feeling off. It didn't matter anymore. They had won. If Death didn't already know, and he assumed she did, he would find a nice place to pull over and summon her.

"Glad to see you have completed your task," a voice called out from the back area of the Corvette.

"Jesus Christ!" Cara yelled, snapping her head back.

"Ya get used to it eventually," Jeffrey said, motioning towards Death.

"Thank you for dealing with Dominic, Jeffrey. With his spirit reaped, the balance has been restored."

"Y'all know me," Jeffrey sneered. "Actually, without her help we'd probably be worshipping that man as the new God or whatever."

Death turned her gaze upon Cara who was turned in her seat facing Death. The two women locked eyes for a moment and Cara looked away. Jeffrey knew what she was thinking. It was weird looking Death in the eyes, literally. Something that had taken him a long time to come to terms with.

"You have my eternal gratitude," Death said with no emotion evident in her tone.

"Uh, you're welcome?" Cara half asked, half stated. "Happy to help keep the balance."

Death gave Cara a nod that she could only assume was a form of acceptance at Cara's new abilities and duties to help Jeffrey.

"Ya know, you look kinda funny back there since there ain't no seats an' all. It's like-" Jeffrey looked into the rearview mirror and laughed. "Never mind, she's gone. That's Death for ya. Straight to the point. No frills."

"I still can't believe I've met Death. Doesn't make sense to say out loud. So, uh, what now?"

"I'm taking ya home. We'll figure it out from there."

The pair drove along in silence as they headed down the road. Their journey had finally come to an end. Their task completed. The sound of the engine roared under the hood. Both Jeffrey and Cara sat in comfortable silence. There was nothing left to say. They had won.

Epilogue

He was back in the familiar setting of Cara's luxury apartment overlooking the ocean. It felt like a lifetime ago they had first taken on Dominic here together. Everything had been cleaned up and put back the way it had been before the man's attack.

Jeffrey paced through the living room, thinking about the offer Cara had made him. It was a nice offer. But a spirit could go wherever it wanted. Live wherever it wanted. Why be trapped in one place?

"Do ghosts- "

"Spirits."

"Right, spirits. Do spirits even live somewhere? Like, do you have a place you call home?"

"Some do. Well, sort of. Some stay in the homes of the loved ones they left behind. But they ain't the best bunch to hang out with. Bad company, if ya understand. A lot of them end up becoming the things that I hunt. Unfinished business," Jeffrey said with air quotes, "Will turn ya angry over time."

"Well, come on. This won't be like that and you know it. You aren't one of them. And besides, we're pretty much like family. You can stay here. Come and go as you please, I guess. But you're always welcome here. Might be kind of cool to have a ghost, I mean spirit, roommate."

Jeffrey laughed.

"Alright, I'll stick around for a while. But only cause I like ya and ya saved my life."

"Great, look forward to having you around. Like having a puppy," she teased. "I'm going to go take a shower. Make yourself comfortable."

Cara made her way into the bedroom. Jeffrey looked around his new home. It was strange to have a place to stay. Spirits didn't quite live in places. But it felt nice having a place to frequent. Before he could get too comfortable, Death appeared in the living room before him. Her familiar tight black dress and pale skin was comforting.

"Hello, Jeffrey."

"Hey, Death. How's it going. Y'all got a good case for me to work? I'm in. What we got?"

"I am not here with a hunt. I am here to tell you something."

This piqued his interest. Death never swung by for a chat. She must have had something important to say.

"Come with me," she said, proffering her hand. Jeffrey reluctantly took it, worried where she was taking him.

A second later, they were somewhere dark and dingy. Grey stone walls surrounded them like a prison. It was a place Jeffrey had never been before and did not understand what they were doing here.

"This is a place the living call Houska Castle." Death said. "They have many myths and legends regarding it."

"Alright, and?" Jeffrey was confused.

"Most are false, as their kind often is about such things, however there is a hint of truth to their stories."

"This ain't like you. What's going on?"

"The creature that accompanied Dominic."

"The Sluagh?"

"Correct. It came from here."

Jeffrey motioned around at the strange medieval room. He did not understand the significance.

"The living believes this castle to be built over the gates of hell. This is not true. However, the castle did serve as a gateway to keep certain things at bay."

"Ya mean this Sluagh thing was locked down there."

Death nodded.

"Alright, so who let it out?"

"That is why I am showing you this, Jeffrey. Long ago, when I split my scythe into seven pieces, I used them to lock away certain evils that threatened humanity. Evils such as the Sluagh. Each shard became a key."

Jeffrey looked down at his knife in wonder. Not only was it a special weapon he could wield, but it unlocked secrets in the Earth. It was truly fascinating.

"So, ya broke your scythe and handed keys out to all your hellhounds? One of 'em go rogue?"

"No. None of my hunters may use the shard as a key. You do not possess such power."

"Well, someone does," Jeffrey said with a snort.

"That is exactly why I brought you here, Jeffrey. There is only one other being that could access the shards and locations. It was the reason I broke my scythe in the first place. To keep it locked away."

"To keep what locked away?" Jeffrey was nervous now. For the first time, he noticed fear in Death's eyes.

"An ancient evil older than anything you know. If it unlocks all seven crypts, the world as we know it shall cease to exist."

Jeffrey didn't respond. He remained deep in thought. If this ancient being was enough to scare Death, then he was terrified. He looked around at the strange paintings on the walls. One with the body of an animal and the torso of a human caught his eye. It smiled a strange smile and wielded a bow. He wondered at its meaning.

"Alright," Jeffrey started. "Where do I come in?"

"Keep your shard close, Jeffrey. When the time comes, I may need your help to defeat this being."

With that, Jeffrey found himself back in Cara's living room. She emerged from the bedroom wrapped in a robe and towel draped over her wet hair. He stood in a stunned silence for several moments while she went about drying her hair. She had not noticed his absence.

"You're unusually quiet, Jeffrey," she said as she stepped back into the bedroom to change.

"Ya know," Jeffrey said. "Just decompressing." He let out a nervous laugh and thought about what may happen the day Death came knocking and requesting his help.

Acknowledgments

First and foremost, allow me to thank *you,* the reader, for picking up this book and reading through to its conclusion. With the number of books to choose from, I'm beyond thrilled you've decided to read mine. Without readers like you, I would simply be a crazy person sitting in front of his computer screen, talking to his imaginary characters.

If you could do me one small but powerful favor. Please consider leaving a review for this book on whichever platform you choose. A simple review can go a long way for us authors and it doesn't have to be a long-winded and captivating tale of the emotional journey you took while reading the book. Something simple as "I liked it" or "Meh, it was alright" will do! It helps more than you know, and it really makes an author's day!

This book has been a long time in the making. It started with a simple short story contest that bloomed into the very idea you finished today. In case you were wondering, I did not win that short story contest. But I think creating Jeffrey Raines and his universe was a fair trade-off.

First, I need to thank my friend Kristin for helping me name the character. The last name of Raines was her idea and I loved it so much, I promised her a signed copy when it was published. This was a few years ago, now. She may not remember. But don't worry, Kristin. I remember.

I wouldn't be anywhere without the help from my friend, and talented author, Wofford Lee Jones. His notes on this story helped push it to the next level and craft it into a stronger tale that I hope you thoroughly enjoyed. I appreciate all of the feedback he gave. Please consider checking out his books by heading to his site www.WoffordLeeJones.com[1]. If you love paranormal horror stories, he's got a few you're going to love. Soul Dreams and Hell Night in Hopewell are particularly spine-chilling.

Next up, my wonderful patrons. Eileen, Nicole, Roxie, Mark M., and Mark C. Their support has been most appreciated whether it be voting on polls to help me name characters such as Cara and Dominic or allowing me to insert them into my story. I did a promotion a couple years ago called Dedicate or Die where patrons could decide to either have a death scene craft-

1. http://www.WoffordLeeJones.com

ed in this book using their name OR get mentioned in the dedication section. Hopefully now the "To the survivors" dedication makes sense to you. Go back and look for those death scenes. You'll find one for Eileen, Nicole, and Mark M. I hope they all loved their death scenes!

And of course, I have to thank the wonderfully talented Seraphyne. That cover art is just spectacular. Her art just blows me away. From the moment I commissioned her to create an image of Jeffrey Raines, I knew I wanted her to create my book cover. You can show her some love by heading over to her Instagram Seraphyne_studio and checking out her art and even commission her for your own work. She's got amazing talent!

Last, but certainly not least, I have to thank my wife for putting up with my constant writing and jabbering about plot lines and character arcs. I'm sure she has had enough of hearing about Jeffrey Raines over the past couple of years and will be excited to know the book is finally finished. And now, she gets to hear all about book two! She is so supportive of my work, and it means the world to me. I love you, Melissa. And our two boys, Desmond and Logan!

Again, thank you for reading this book. I hope you enjoyed it. And if you've read through all of this, a special thank you to you, too. See you in the next book!

Don't miss out!

Visit the website below and you can sign up to receive emails whenever Evan Bond publishes a new book. There's no charge and no obligation.

https://books2read.com/r/B-A-ZJVF-DYMAC

Also by Evan Bond

Ethan McCormick Series
To the Wolves
Sins of the Mother

The After Death Series
After Death

Standalone
Death Can Wait
Getaway
Echoes of the Past
Charred Remains

Watch for more at https://www.evanbondauthor.com/.

About the Author

Evan Bond is a thriller/suspense author who loves blending his love of the outdoors with his writings. He is the author of the best selling psychological thriller *Echoes of the Past* and his intense action-packed survival account *Death Can Wait.* He has always had a passion for telling suspenseful stories. Even at a young age, he was crafting horror stories to share with his family and friends. Evan Bond lives in Tampa, Florida with his wife, Melissa, their two boys, Desmond and Logan, and their cat and dog, Whiskey and Loki. When he's not writing, he can be found adventuring in the outdoors with his family and calling it "research" for his next novel.

Read more at https://www.evanbondauthor.com/.

www.ingramcontent.com/pod-product-compliance
Ingram Content Group UK Ltd.
Pitfield, Milton Keynes, MK11 3LW, UK
UKHW022024190726
13853UKWH00005B/2101